THE STONE MANOR

THE STONE MANOR

TERRI HALE

Enchanted Window Press

This book is a work of fiction. The names, characters, places, and incidents are products of the writer's imagination or have been used fictitiously and are not to be construed as real. Any resemblance to persons, living or dead, actual events, locales or organizations is entirely coincidental.

Author photograph © Rachel Archer Photography

Cover photograph © James Hale

Cover Art © 2013 Kelli Ann Morgan / Inspire Creative Services

Interior book design by Bob Houston eBook Formatting

Published by Enchanted Window Press

Library of Congress Control Number: 2013950164

ISBN: 978-0-9899380-0-6

For my parents,
Who have loved and encouraged me.
I followed my dreams and they brought me here.

"...weary with wintriness, she travelled towards the southern regions of her globe, to meet the spring on its slow way northwards; and how, after many sad adventures, many disappointed hopes, and many tears, bitter and fruitless, she found at last, one stormy afternoon, in a leafless forest, a single snowdrop growing betwixt the borders of the winter and spring. She lay down beside it and died. I almost believe that a child, pale and peaceful as a snowdrop, was born in the Earth within a fixed season from that stormy afternoon."
George MacDonald, *Phantastes*

Prologue

Winter – 1746 Isle of Skye

As the moon ascended the northern sky, the mist froze and the first flakes of snow fell. Mairi MacDonald stood on the hill overlooking the glen. Below, the ceremony had just ended. The sound of a fiddle echoed from the hillsides and floated toward her. She watched the bride and groom enter the circle near the fire and join hands for their first dance. Hours passed, and she remained, bound to the hilltop by a lover's promise not kept. An ancient poem rose in her soul, transformed into song, and escaped through her lips. As the fiddler rested, the melancholy melody drifted down the hillside, carried along by the icy mist until it reached the fire below.

Alexander MacDonald turned as the faint sound of a fairy song reached his ears. Suddenly the fiddler set in motion a highland reel. The bride took his hand; the spell was broken, and the next dance began. The snow moved across the glen, falling harder and harder. The wedding celebration ended, and both clans, the MacDonalds and the MacLeods, took shelter in the stone manor.

Mairi fell to her knees, brushing tears away before they froze on her pale skin. Her body shook as the snow covered her hair like a crystal veil. The faint light from the peat fires inside the Manor of Glen Rowan faded, and she removed the malachite necklace from around her neck as the winter night stole her last hope...and deep in the hillside beyond Druid Wood, Rhan, Lady Fate, remained in her sanctuary, honoring her promise.

The snow gone and the spring rains in full force, Mairi boarded a ship for the Americas to meet her two brothers, who had fled Skye after Prince Charles's defeat at Culloden. She was but nineteen. In a small bag were a change of clothes, a leather bound journal her grandmother had given her, and a small wooden box. As she waited on deck, she looked toward the standing stone on the hillside and caught sight of her grandmother. Mairi memorized her commanding figure, even as the mist moved in to swallow her whole.

1

Distant Shores

A broken heart is not the end of all things. It can, if mixed with a hint of magic and a large amount of fate, lead to a life beyond ordinary dreams.

Rhan, Lady Fate

The sun reflected off the side of the huge cruise liner, partially blinding the passengers attempting to board. And the air, usually heavy with the smell of salt, seemed lightened by the laughter of young children and the excited voices of adults as they walked up the giant ramp. Seagulls squawked overhead, and the whispered sound of luggage being pulled along the red carpet completed the illusion. The perfect family holiday.

Kathryn Trent watched from the dock at the Port of Galveston in her rolled-up jeans and black tank top. She took a deep breath and walked away toward the street. Kathryn had never felt more alone. She was meeting her sister, Beth, for lunch at a nearby restaurant, Willy G's. With each step, the sunshine challenged her dark thoughts. But to no avail; they refused to lighten.

When they were young, she and her husband, John, used to love to travel around the world. Then, the boys came along, and it became more difficult. About that time airplanes began crashing, and the new age of terrorism invaded the world of flying. It was then that Kathryn found it more and more difficult to step onto an airplane. She worried that if something happened to her and John, who would take care of the boys? Then there was the whole terrifying thought of actually crashing.

Just as Kathryn arrived at the restaurant, her cell phone rang. It was Beth.

"Hey, Kathryn. I'm ten minutes away. Sorry, I got carried away on my beach walk this morning. I found lots of sea glass for the shop, though."

"It's okay. I'll get a table on the patio and order a cup of coffee."

"Try to get one in the sun," Beth said. "It's such a glorious day."

Kathryn loved Beth. She loved the way her sister brightened everyone's day, whether the sun was out or not. She loved that they were best friends, in spite of their twelve-year age difference. Her dark thoughts took flight.

"I promise to get a sunny spot if one's available," Kathryn said. "See you shortly."

The hostess seated Kathryn at a table in full sun right by the waterfront. She ordered a cup of coffee with cream and sugar and pulled a folder out of her green leather bag, ancestral charts. Kathryn noticed an older woman and her daughters seated at a table nearby. She missed her mother.

Looking down at the pages of long dead relatives, she wondered what it would be like to have lunch with her mom. Kathryn looked toward the restaurant's interior and saw her mother's reflection looking back at her from the large glass window. Even with her dark wavy hair that usually hung far below her shoulders but was now tied up in a messy knot on top of her head, the resemblance was strong. Fate had played a terrible joke on her family when her mother, after years of hypochondria, truly died an untimely death when the neighborhood ice cream truck swerved to miss a squirrel and drove up into their yard, hitting her while she was planting pansies.

Kathryn buried her mother and graduated from high school in the same month. She was eighteen; Beth was only six. Their father would never be quite the same. Kathryn wore the paisley cotton dress her mother had made especially for her graduation to the funeral and to her commencement. She tried to wear it again to a summer dance but had a panic attack when she put it on. She was never fond of paisley after that. Paisley, pansies, and popsicles, these were a few of her least favorite things.

On Kathryn's eighteenth birthday, the stone manor first entered her dreams. In it, the sun was covering the countryside with light and warmth as she felt herself driving along a one-lane track. As the road curved sharply left, an expansive stone manor came into view. It sat just off to the right, overlooking a beautiful valley. In the beginning, only the manor existed.

Then one night the dream changed, and Kathryn distinctly heard a young woman's voice. She spoke with a Scottish accent. *Your true happiness awaits you here. Love once lost, forever found within these walls.* Kathryn woke up with a smile on her face and a feeling of utter contentment. All she had to do was find the stone manor, and her life would be complete. What she failed to notice were the three little words nestled amid the promise of eternal happiness—*love once lost.*

Kathryn spent the summer after her junior year of college in Edinburgh, Scotland, on a study abroad program. While the other students congregated in pubs and drank away the doldrums of the classroom, she scoured the countryside in a rented Land Rover, searching for her manor. She returned to Texas to complete her final year at the university, and although frustrated at having never found the manor, she held tightly to her dream.

Convinced her love and happiness rested in the stone manor

alone, Kathryn eventually completed college and traveled back to Scotland for a graduate degree in British literature. Every moment not spent in class or studying, Kathryn searched for the elusive manor.

At the end of her studies, Kathryn gave up on her dream and flew east, far, far away from Scotland to Indonesia to escape the dream and frustration. She took a job teaching English, but the dream followed her to Java. It would not release her. It was there she met her husband John, who told her that he, in fact, had a stone manor in England, as well as a condominium in Houston. Of all the things that attracted Kathryn to John, and there were many, the stone manor stood out most. It seemed both romantic and ironic that he lived in Houston, her hometown, and at the same time possessed what might have turned out to be her dream manor. Kathryn married John. His stone manor was, in fact, a brownstone in London. The wrong manor but not a bad trade after all. The dream stopped.

For a moment, with the smell of the sea filling the air, Kathryn allowed her mind to wander to another time, an older time, and a place wholly unfamiliar. Always she heard the voice, always she saw the stone manor, and always *he* was there—waiting.

A seagull squawked, and the mist disappeared in the bright Texas sunshine. Kathryn took a sip of her coffee. Only two people in the world knew about her dream, John and Beth. In John's mind, the dream was fulfilled with their marriage. Consequently, it was never a topic of conversation between them.

Kathryn saw Beth glide through the restaurant doorway onto the terrace wearing a turquoise sundress. Her blonde hair was braided and glowed against her tanned skin. Her blue eyes sparkled as she smiled, and everyone on the terrace took notice of her. Yet, she was totally unaware of the attention she attracted.

"Hey," Beth said. "You looked like you were deep in thought." Beth pulled her chair out and sat down. "Sorry I'm late."

Kathryn held up her half-full cup of coffee. "I've been consoling myself with a nice cup of java."

Beth set a bag full of sea glass on the vacant seat next to hers and waved to the young waiter. He smiled and hurried to their table.

"What would you like to drink?"

Beth flipped through the menu to the beverage page and pointed. "I'll have a Shiner Bock, please. And, I'm absolutely starving. Can we go ahead and order our food?" She glanced at Kathryn. "Do you know what you want?"

"Yes, I've had plenty of time to think about it." Kathryn smiled. "I assume you're having your usual?"

"Always," Beth said.

"What would you like?" the waiter asked.

"I'll have the shrimp poor boy," Beth said.

The waiter turned to Kathryn, "And for you?"

"Fish and chips, please."

"So that's one Shiner Bock, a poor boy, and an order of fish and chips. Any appetizers?"

Beth and Kathryn both said no in unison.

"I'll get this turned in and be right out with your beer."

"Thanks," Beth said. As he walked away she leaned toward Kathryn and said, "Okay, so he's really cute, a bit young, though. What do you think?"

Kathryn shook her head and laughed. "You're hopeless."

"No, see that's just it, Kathryn. I'm always hopeful. Always looking for possibilities."

"I'm thinking *looking* is all you need to do with this one." Kathryn took another sip of coffee.

Beth glanced around the patio for the waiter and sighed. "I guess you're right. Again."

The waiter returned with Beth's beer, and Kathryn commended her for only *looking*. The next ten minutes were filled with talk of sea glass and Beth's next buying trip to Guatemala. Suddenly a loud horn sounded, and everyone turned toward the harbor as the cruise ship sailed by.

"Oh, Kathryn," Beth said clapping, "we need to take a cruise. Who knows, you might meet someone."

"A bit soon, I think," Kathryn said. "The divorce hearing is in five days."

"Kathryn, how can you not want to take a Caribbean cruise? Lots of sunshine, sea air, exotic ports to be explored. What's not to love about that? And, in five days the hearing will be over and the divorce papers signed. John did leave nine months ago. A cruise would be a great way to test the waters—no pun intended."

Kathryn smiled.

"Not yet," she said. "Can we change the subject?"

"Sorry. Yes," Beth said and took a long drink of her beer. And the waiter returned with their food. She noticed the charts on the table. "What are those?"

"Ancestral charts," Kathryn said, straightening the pile.

"So, seriously—genealogy? This is what you're going to do with your newfound freedom?"

"It's not as bad as it seems, Beth. In fact, I think even you will find this interesting." She took a bite of hot fish and smiled. "Mmm."

"Okay, so I'm interested. Go on."

"Do you remember the dream I had when we were young, the one I used to tell you as a bedtime story? The stone manor dream?" Kathryn dabbed her lips with her napkin and folded it neatly in her lap.

"You're talking about the one that took you to Scotland to study? Away from me? That dream?" Beth took a bite of her sandwich. "Go on then."

"It's returned. Since John left, I mean. And, standing near the manor is a man, all shrouded in mist and shadow. I can't really make out what he looks like."

Beth was just about to take a drink but quickly put down her glass. "Oh, Kathryn. How mysterious."

"I know, I know. So anyway, Grandmother used to talk about having ancestors from Scotland. She didn't know any details, but she was proud of it." Kathryn picked up the top ancestral chart and handed it to Beth. "I know the stone manor is somewhere in Scotland, and I'm willing to bet you when I find our Scottish ancestors, I'll find the manor." Kathryn took her last sip of coffee.

Beth looked at the chart. "So, where did you find this information?"

"An ancestry website." She picked up the small stack of papers. "This is as far as I've gotten. So, what do you think?"

Beth handed the papers to Kathryn and looked toward the bay.

"What are you thinking, Beth?"

Beth turned back to Kathryn and set both elbows on the table, placing her chin on top of her clasped hands. "Well—my first thought was hang on to that mysterious dream of yours, but genealogy research? Really?"

"Hey, do you have any idea how much information there is on the Internet about this? It's amazing."

Beth feigned a cough. "Amazing?"

Kathryn salted her French fries. "You travel, you love history. How can you not think this is interesting?"

"You know you're in danger of becoming a librarian."

Kathryn took another bite of fish and set the fork on the edge of the plate. "A librarian." She stared at her plate, loose strands of her dark hair blowing across her face.

"Hello, earth to Kathryn." Beth tapped the glass tabletop with her neon melon nails.

"Sorry, but I was just thinking of all the books. Rooms and rooms of books. The smell of paper and old glue. You know, if you really concentrate you can smell the ink on the pages of a new release."

Beth stretched out both arms. "And there it is, ladies and gentlemen, planets are colliding, our universe is expanding, and the smell of ink and paper is in the air. Really, Kathryn, don't you know that every post-menopausal woman is either researching her ancestors or publishing her first novel? Don't rush it, you'll be there soon enough."

"You laugh now, but someday you'll grow up and find I am not a freak show, little sister."

"I am grown up, Kathryn, and it's still funny. You know, if you didn't look so much like Mom and I didn't look so much like Dad, I'd have questions about our being related." Beth took a large bite of her sandwich.

"Well, sorry you're saddled with me for a big sister."

Beth chewed and swallowed quickly. "Hey, I'm sorry. I can't imagine a more amazing big sister. We both know I'd never have made it without you after Mom died." Beth reached across the table and took Kathryn's hand. "Really and truly."

"Pity?" Kathryn asked.

"Love," Beth said. "Truce then?"

"As always."

Beth squeezed Kathryn's hand. "I said those were my first thoughts. But, after further reflection…"

Kathryn took her hand away to cut another bite of fish and interrupted. "You've been reading Jane Austen again."

"Always, thanks for noticing. Anyway, I do love history, and I really do think this could lead to something fun, at least a trip to Scotland. So, I'm revising my earlier idea about the cruise. I think you should go to Scotland and look for this mystery man. Oh, and of course, the stone manor."

Kathryn laughed. "Slow down now. I'm not quite ready for a trip abroad."

"Is it the fear of flying thing?" Beth took her last bite of sandwich.

"No,"—Kathryn shifted in her chair—"there is that, but I need to trace our ancestors back to Scotland first. In fact, it's on my schedule for tomorrow. While you're hunting for more sea glass, I'll be on the Internet."

"Our last day at the beach and you're spending it on the Internet?" Beth asked.

"It will be worth it when I find them. I know they're there." Kathryn waved for the waiter and asked for the check. "Look, it's still early afternoon. Let's go back to the beach house and get some sun."

"Now, you're talking my language." Beth raised her glass. "Cheers."

Kathryn paid the bill, and they drove the fifteen miles along the coast to their beach house. At one point Beth, in her red Mini Cooper, pulled up next to Kathryn on the four-lane highway and revved her engine. Kathryn laughed and drove on at the speed posted, hoping to signal a big "no" to Beth. Her silver Lexus SUV was not the racing type. Or maybe she wasn't the racing type. Either way there would be no contest of speed that afternoon.

Eventually, they arrived at their beach house. It sat on stilts and had two stories with a balcony wrapping around all sides. It was just behind the low natural sea wall, only a few steps from the sandy beach and an unobstructed view of the Gulf of Mexico. Their father had bought it when they were young, and even though it had been rebuilt several times due to hurricane damage, it was still a wonderful place to get away from the busyness of the city.

After arriving and changing into their swimsuits, they made their way to the almost empty beach. It was private, and even during the high season there were never many people there. Beth quickly lay out her towel and stretched out on it to tan. Kathryn walked to the water's edge and let the waves lap at her feet. The gulf was unusually calm. She took this as a good omen but couldn't help but wonder what the view would be like from the shores of Scotland. Of course, her problem was not knowing which shores she should be standing on. Kathryn hoped to discover this the following day with the help of the Internet.

The afternoon passed with no interruptions, only the sun, the sand, and the sea. They ate a light supper on the balcony and spent the remainder of the evening listening to the sounds of the sea gulls and the waves along the shore. The wind had picked up, and the waves grew larger, filling the air with the smell of salt and kelp. Kathryn stood and walked to the wooden railing along the balcony and leaned against it. She closed her eyes, took in a deep breath, and tried to still her mind. The stone manor appeared, and she smiled. Perhaps this would be her new home. Maybe tomorrow she would have answers.

2

In Search of the Ancestors

The next morning, Kathryn took a walk along the beach at sunrise, avoiding the turquoise man-of-war washed up on the sand. She found it difficult to enjoy what had always been a relaxing stroll. Her "prove up" hearing was in four days, and the thought of standing before a judge and giving her reasons for requesting the divorce unnerved her. Her lawyer had assured her it was basically a formality and there was nothing to be concerned about. John had moved to London with Courtney, his young intern, so at least he wouldn't be there, something allowed in the state of Texas. All she wanted was to hear the two magic words: "Divorce granted," and be done with it.

"Kathryn," Beth called from the balcony. "Coffee's ready."

"Be right there," Kathryn said and waved.

She walked to the stairs and dusted the sand off both feet, then hurried up to the balcony and her waiting cup of coffee. Beth handed her the piping hot mug, and they sat down in the wicker chairs.

"So, how was your walk?" Beth asked.

"It was fine. Lots of man-of-war washed up on the sand."

"Aww, I hate that. I mean, I don't want them in the water stinging me, but they're just so beautiful. Seems like a harsh way to die," Beth said and took a drink of her hot tea.

Kathryn sat quietly sipping her coffee and staring out across the gulf. There was a light breeze, and the sunshine was already warming the May morning air. Ian, her eldest son, would be graduating from college in less than three weeks. She'd have to see John then. She wondered if he'd bring Courtney. Kathryn knew it was inevitable, that uncomfortable first time meeting of all of them together in one place. She knew there would be tension, lots of it, and she hated it for Ian's sake.

"Hey," Beth said. "You're unusually quiet. What are you thinking about?"

Kathryn slid down in her chair and propped her feet on the ledge of the balcony. "Lots of things."

"Anything you want to talk about? That's why I'm here."

Kathryn looked over at Beth and smiled. "I know. Thanks for that." She let out a deep sigh.

"I've been thinking about the hearing on Thursday. What I'll say and all. And I've been thinking about Ian graduating in a few weeks and Courtney being there, too." Kathryn raised her arms up and rested them on top of her head. "I just want his graduation to be perfect. I want it to be a big celebration."

"It will be," Beth said. "You'll see. Once the hearing is over you'll have a few weeks to get ready for graduation. I'm not saying it'll be easy, it won't. But you'll have made it through the worst of it. We'll go shopping, and you'll be a knock-out."

"Shopping." Kathryn sighed. "I won't be able to afford such things soon enough. My part-time job at your store won't pay my bills for long, I'm afraid." Kathryn leaned over and gave her sister a big hug. "But, thanks for trying to cheer me up. Oh, and thanks for the job. I don't mean to sound ungrateful. I love you."

"I love you, too." Beth stood up and stretched. "And, you can always come on full-time. I could make you a partner."

Kathryn laughed. "Now, we're talking charity. It'll all work out."

Beth stood up and stretched her arms over her head. "Hey, if you're okay, I'm going for a run on the beach."

"I'm better now that we've talked. I just needed to say it out loud and get it out of my head."

"Okay, so I'll see you in a bit." Beth walked to the stairs and stopped. "I think you need to go in and find our long-lost Scottish ancestors."

"Yes, ma'am," Kathryn said. "I'll get right on it."

Beth ran down the stairs and onto the beach, as Kathryn picked up their cups and walked into the house. After rinsing and loading them into the dishwasher, she walked to the table where her laptop sat open, waiting. She pulled the ancestral charts from her bag, laid them out next to the computer, and opened up the ancestry website. Kathryn typed in the information she had on the earliest ancestral name listed on her charts.

First and Middle Name(s): Andrew Jackson Last Name: Little
Name a place your ancestor might have lived: Texas
Estimated birth year: 1847

She hit the search button and waited. The next page that appeared had a listing with a number of entries for Andrew Little. Kathryn found the one that matched her information and clicked on it to see the family tree. She discovered spouse and children's names, then, parents. She continued farther and farther back, generation by generation, until she hit the jackpot. What she'd been dreaming of. What she'd hoped to find. A MacDonald ancestor. *Can't get more Scottish than that, Grandmother.*

Kathryn let out a quick shrill scream and began clapping. She quickly filled in the blank ancestral chart sitting by her laptop.

Husband: James Little Born: 1778 Place: VA

Father: unknown Little
Wife: Nancy MacDonald Born: 1788 Place: GA
Father: James MacDonald Born: 1755 Place: NC

Kathryn was so excited; she laughed out loud and with a shaky hand, hit the back button one more time to the final entry on the ancestral tree.

Husband: James MacDonald Born: 1755 Place: NC
Father: Ranald MacDonald Born: about 1720 Place: Isle of Skye, Scotland

She pushed away from the table and jumped up, laughing. "Oh, my God. MacDonalds from the Isle of Skye. I've got to tell Beth. She won't believe it."

Kathryn ran out of the house and down the stairs, running into Beth as she stepped onto the bottom step.

"Whoa, whoa," Beth said, grabbing Kathryn to keep from falling backward. "What's wrong?"

Kathryn gave her sister a big hug and kissed her on both checks. "I'm guessing that's how our ancestors greeted each other in the 1700s, on the Isle of Skye, in Scotland."

"What? You found them? Are you kidding me?"

"Yes. I mean, no. I'm not kidding you. And, yes. I found them, and they're beautiful," Kathryn said.

"Wait a minute. I love history, and I've seen pictures of Scots in the 1700s. Beautiful? Really?" Beth laughed and slipped her arm through Kathryn's. "Show me."

They hurried up the stairs and into the house. They rushed to the table, and sat down in the same chair. Kathryn pointed to the screen. "Look, Beth. Our Scottish ancestors, right there in black and white. No pictures, just words. But, aren't they beautiful words?"

Beth looked at the screen and laughed. She pointed to the name on the screen. “Is that our ancestor? Ranald MacDonald?”

“Yes, and we’re proud of that name aren’t we, Beth?”

“Well, of course we are. Who wouldn’t be. I was just hoping the first name would be something strong and romantic like…Alexander or Angus.” Beth smiled.

“Who’s to say our Ranald wasn’t some mighty Highland warrior? I can picture him right now. All kilted up and carrying a huge sword.” Kathryn raised her eyebrows.

“What does that mean? All kilted up?” Beth asked.

They both laughed until tears rolled down their cheeks.

Beth brushed the tears away and stared at Kathryn. “I’ve never seen you like this. It’s like you’re sixteen and just kissed your first boy.”

Kathryn grabbed a tissue and dabbed her eyes. She crossed her arms and looked at Beth. “Sixteen?”

“I’m just sayin’.”

Kathryn turned back to the screen. “I’m not going to be able to sleep for days.”

“You’d better sleep some. You don’t want to look like crap for your hearing.” Beth threw her hand to her mouth. “Sorry, I shouldn’t have brought that up right now. Forget I said it.”

“It’s okay. Right now, in this moment, not even a divorce hearing can take away what I’m feeling.” Kathryn put her arm around Beth. “But, when it does settle in and I recover from the excitement, I’ll need you to be there.”

“Hey, big sister,” Beth said, “I’m not going anywhere. And this is perfect.”

“What do you mean?”

“I’ve got a surprise for you back at the store. I knew you should have it when I found it. This just proves it.” Beth stood up, walked to the refrigerator, and grabbed a bottle of water. “Wow, I need a shower.”

"Wait a minute. What surprise? What is it?" Kathryn asked.

"It's a surprise, duh. Not telling." Beth walked toward her room. "I'll clean up, and we can spend the rest of the day on the beach working on a tan and talking about Scotland and where that stone manor of yours might be. Okay?"

"Sounds perfect. But sit down for a minute. I decided to wait till you came up to go back any farther on this website. Who knows what we might find." Kathryn patted the chair beside her.

Beth sat down and leaned in close to the laptop. Kathryn clicked on the name James MacDonald. Nothing there.

"Okay what does that mean?" Beth asked.

"I guess that's all the person who researched discovered," Kathryn said. "I'll have to keep looking. But hey, this is enough for now. Let's head to the beach."

Kathryn quickly put on her swimsuit and sat back down at her computer looking up websites on the Isle of Skye. It looked magical, wonderful. When Beth appeared ready for the beach, Kathryn showed her the pictures she'd found and they decided at that moment, a trip to Scotland was in their future. The remainder of the day was spent making up stories about who their ancestors were, and why they came to America, and the possibility of one of them having had a stone manor. In the evening, they spent hours researching all they could find on the Isle of Skye.

Not one word was spoken about the upcoming hearing. Not one thought was given to the uncertain future Kathryn faced. They were wrapped up in an adventure of their own making, one that would fill their dreams that night with hope.

After a long night's sleep, Kathryn and Beth took a final morning walk together on the beach. They returned to the house, packed, cleaned, and loaded the cars for the forty-five minute drive back in to Houston. Beth had offered to buy lunch at her favorite restaurant near the shop and said that afterward, they could stop and pick up Kathryn's surprise. She promised not to speed, even though she was famished. Kathryn thought it was a great plan, and they were off to Houston.

Halfway through their fajitas for two at Nacho Mamas, conversation turned from plans for summer and the new Barnes and Noble opening to more intimate topics.

"So, Beth, don't you ever get lonely?"

Beth looked up from stuffing her tortilla with chicken and cheese. "Lonely? Why are you asking?"

"I don't know. I was just wondering. It's been five years since…" Kathryn paused staring into her Coke Zero as if it were a looking-glass.

"Since Ben left—yeah, I do get lonely. But I love my life. I love my shop and Mrs. Podhorzki and"—Beth took a bite of her fajita and thought for a moment—"I love the warm sunshine and my apartment above the shop filled with all my favorite things. And I love you and the boys, and Mr. Nightly—"

Kathryn interrupted. "But what about being alone? Do you love being alone?"

"I don't think about it much, I guess. I meet a lot of interesting people when I travel, buying things for the shop. I have friends all over the world. How lonely can that be?"

"But when you come home at night, you're still alone."

"Not really, I have Mr. Nightly." Beth smiled and took a sip of her margarita.

"Cats don't count."

"But I like my men hairy."

"Come on, Beth, I'm being serious."

"I can see that. I know you're really lonely right now. I promise it will get better."

Kathryn sighed and shook her head. "I'm sure you're right. I just can't get there right now."

Beth held up her glass as if to toast. "Good news is you don't have to. There's no time limit on grieving, and that's what is happening." Beth took another drink. "Good Lord, I sound like a therapist. I don't mean to."

Kathryn reached over and squeezed Beth's hand. "It's okay. I need someone to help me through all this, and I'm glad it's you." She picked up the last of her fajita and said, "Enough about being lonely. Let's talk about my surprise."

Beth pointed her finger at Kathryn and shook it slowly. "Hey now, there you go again. Patience, patience. Two more bites, and I'll be done. Then we can go to the shop."

They finished the last of the fajitas and the chips and hot sauce and asked for the check. After paying the bill, they drove to the Compass Rose, Beth's shop near the city center district. When they arrived, they parked in the lot behind the building.

The shop was in a hundred-year-old three-story building. It was on the ground floor next to the Organic Bouquet and Chocolate Haven. Kathryn and Beth walked arm in arm around the side of the building where a blooming bougainvillea climbed up the wall like a vast purple flame reaching for the sky. They rounded the corner onto the sidewalk and stopped outside the storefront next to a large rock container, filled with red geraniums and yellow marigolds. Displayed in the large window was a collection of textiles and carved wood, purchased on Beth's latest trip to Pakistan and India.

"You've changed the window display without me," Kathryn said. "It looks great."

"Thank you. I didn't realize how much I missed doing it myself. It's not as good as when you set it up, but it was fun all the same. I think this is the first time in the last nine months I've arranged it on my own."

"I did kind of take that over when I started working here. Sorry about that," Kathryn said.

Beth walked to the door and held it open for Kathryn. "I'm not complaining. I love your window displays."

"Why thank you, ma'am." Kathryn pretended to hold out skirt tails and curtsy before walking into the shop.

As they entered, Mrs. Podhorzki greeted them with a smile. "Welcome home, my dears. How was your trip?"

"It was wonderful as always," Beth said. "How've things been around here?"

"Fine, fine. Lots of interesting customers, as always." Mrs. Podhorzki turned toward a German couple nearby who were looking at the collection of Texas pottery on display. "Excuse me, won't you."

The aroma of sandalwood filled the air. Beth danced her way to the back of the small shop as sounds of a mandolin from a gypsy serenade hung in the air. Antique wooden shelves lined the walls, filled with pottery and glass from around the world. Kathryn loved Beth's shop. Large batiks covered the ceiling, as if it were the tent of an Arab prince in *Arabian Nights*.

Kathryn walked to her favorite area, the book section, just left of the front counter. Travel books, award-winning children's books, Texas authors, and folklore from around the world lined the shelves. She breathed in the sweet, soothing aroma of the dried lavender that filled the willow baskets hanging from a wooden dowel across the front window.

Kathryn started working at Beth's shop a week after John moved out. Before that, she had volunteered at a community center teaching English as a second language off and on for years. Beth had suggested she come work at the shop two or three days a week, mostly as a distraction from the impending divorce. Kathryn loved working there. She loved being with Beth and Mrs. Podhorzki.

Kathryn returned the Easter Island travel guide to the shelf, and noticed her sister emerging from behind the beaded curtain in the back of the store. Beth glided to the front of the shop, balancing a wrapped package on top of her head, as if it was a fruit-filled basket and she was on her way to a market in Brazil.

Beth handed her the gift and smiled. "Go ahead, open it."

Kathryn took it and smiled. "This is really exciting. My birthday's not even till October."

She set down the book and began unwrapping the package. The paper was forest green with gold-embossed elephants. Inside was a small wooden box, carved with Celtic symbols and three animals in the center. She opened the box and found a note inside. As she read it, tears formed; she quickly wiped them away.

> This came in a container from the East Coast.
> I think it might be an antique box, maybe handmade from Scotland or Ireland. As I looked at it, I thought of you.
> I think you were meant to have it, though I don't know why. I just know it should be yours. Who knows, maybe it came from a stone manor somewhere far, far away.
>
> All my love,
> Beth
>
> P.S. Mrs. Podhorzki said she sensed it should belong to you as well, and we know she claims to have the second sight, passed down from her Latvian grandmother. XOXO

"Oh, Beth. I love it." Kathryn said.

She ran her fingers over the interlacing oval loops, which formed a beautiful pattern of unending knotwork that bordered the box. Three animals were carved in the center. There were two birds and a small animal of some sort. There was also a small white stone inlaid into the front of the box. It looked like a small piece of marble. She flipped the box over and noticed something etched in the wood. It looked odd. Lines and dots. She ran her fingers over the etchings. As she did, a chill ran through her body, and for a moment, she thought she heard a Highland reel being played on a fiddle. She quickly set the box on a shelf and rubbed her arms.

She looked up at Beth. "How odd. I'm suddenly cold."

Beth grabbed her hands and rubbed them. "Your hands are like ice. Are you okay?"

"Yeah. I don't suppose you heard a Celtic fiddle playing a moment ago?"

"It's not Celtic, it's Romanian. Mrs. P's playing it through the shop speakers."

"No, not that. Another fiddler. So, you didn't hear it then?"

Beth picked up the box and examined it. "No. But maybe it's a magic box. Hey, if I rub this white stone on the front of the box, maybe a leprechaun will appear. Maybe I should keep it." She looked up at Kathryn and winked.

Kathryn took the box from Beth and held it close. "No way. I love it. Thanks, Beth."

"You're welcome. I occasionally buy containers from an antique dealer out of North Carolina. I do it because it's like treasure hunting. You pay a set amount based on the size and weight of the container. The dealer auctions them off, and I usually bid on the smaller containers. My bid won on the one this box was in." Beth reached over and touched the box. "I knew the minute I saw it you should have it.

The German couple left with a set of four salt-glazed mugs and smiles on their faces.

Mrs. Podhorzki saw Kathryn holding the box and said, "Oh, Kathryn, dear. You've got the box, I see. I told Beth there was something special about that box, and she said it reminded her of you. Now, what do you think about that?" All this was said without taking a single breath.

Mrs. Podhorzki was a second-generation immigrant from Latvia. She had a rather large, round figure and a full head of white hair. Beth had told Kathryn she thought she must be related to Mrs. Claus, perhaps a second cousin once removed. She was always very pleasant and full of stories and remedies from the Old Country. She had walked into the shop two years ago, and as soon as she opened her mouth to speak, Beth knew they would be forever friends.

Mrs. Podhorzki's husband had died ten years earlier, and she had been living with one of her six children. One day she decided to take a walk and ended up in Beth's shop. After a very long conversation over a cup of excellent British tea, Beth offered her a job and she accepted. It was perfect, since Beth often traveled on buying trips. She felt very confident leaving the shop in Mrs. Podhorzki's hands.

"You know, Kathryn—your sister—she worries for you."

"Shocker."

Beth raised her hands as if in defeat. "You see, Mrs. Podhorzki. This is what I put up with from my big sister."

"You joke, I think, but I'm serious," Mrs. Podhorzki said.

"Well, she needn't worry," Kathryn said. "I'll be fine, really."

"I know you will, dear. I think we all need a good cup of tea." And she disappeared into the back of the shop.

Kathryn walked to the jewelry counter and picked up a string of Ohrid pearls from the Republic of Macedonia, displayed alongside a lapis necklace from Chile. She envied her sister's adventure-filled life and thought how silly her question had been during lunch. How could anyone be lonely with all of this?

"Oh, do you like the pearls? I bought them on a recent trip to Eastern Europe. Macedonia is a beautiful country, quite a well-kept secret."

"They're lovely." Kathryn placed them back on the counter and put her arm around Beth's shoulder.

Soon Mrs. Podhorzki walked out with a tray, and seeing the sisters arm in arm, she smiled. "Tea time, ladies."

The three sat down behind the counter and enjoyed their afternoon tea. Mrs. Podhorzki explained the nuances of a delicious black tea. The front door opened, and several women walked in together. Beth stood and welcomed them in. She asked if they were looking for anything in particular, and they said they were just looking. They agreed to let her know if they had any questions, and she sat back down behind the counter.

Kathryn pulled her wooden box from her leather bag. No strange sounds or sensations. She was anxious to get home and do a little research about what the animals were on the box and what they might represent.

Beth noticed her staring at the box and turned to Mrs. Podhorzki. "Did you know, that's a musical box?"

"Why, no dear. In what way?"

"It seems Kathryn heard a Celtic fiddler when she held the box the first time."

"Did you now, Kathryn? You know, I think this is a sign. Did you see or feel anything as well?" Mrs. Podhorzki leaned closer to the box.

Kathryn held the box out to her. "Here, feel free to look it over yourself. Beth evidently thinks I'm crazy."

Beth protested. "That's so not true. I'm actually wishing I had a magic box myself."

"Well, anyway I did hear something, but only for a minute, and faintly. I also felt very cold when I held it. But I'd like to know what you think. What are these three animals?"

Mrs. Podhorzki took the box and put on her reading glasses to get a better look. She studied them for a moment and then handed the box back to Kathryn.

"Perhaps—well, to be sure—these animals were chosen for very specific reasons. In my country, certain properties are attached to different types of animals. Cuckoos are considered to be foretellers of human fate. Horses, stags, and swans are all protectors and have a life-bringing force about them. I could tell you such lovely stories, but that's not helping us here, is it now? Let me see"—and she pointed to the carvings—"there are two birds and something that looks like maybe a marten, or an otter, possibly. One of the birds is larger than the other and seems to be a bird of prey, of some sort." Mrs. Podhorzki leaned back and removed her glasses, letting them fall to her chest, where they hung on a gold chain around her neck. "Well, dear, as I said before, I think you were meant to have this box, but beyond that, I can not say more."

Kathryn placed the box back in her bag like it was made of glass. She smiled at Beth and stood. "I've got work to do and discoveries to make. I think I'll head home."

"You're welcome to spend the night. Unless you're tired of me." Beth set the cups on the tray and stood.

"I'm never tired of hanging out with you. But I have a doctor's appointment tomorrow afternoon, and I only have beach clothes with me." Kathryn walked to the door. Beth followed her.

"A doctor's appointment? What kind?" Beth asked.

"Just my annual checkup. Nothing to worry about."

"Okay. Well, if you're sure you don't want to stay, call me tomorrow after you're finished at the doctor."

"I will. I love you."

Kathryn gave Beth a kiss on the cheek and a big hug. She waved to Mrs. Podhorzki, who had walked over to the customers looking at the jewelry display. She patted her purse, thanked Beth for the wonderful surprise, and was out the door. The late afternoon air was warm and muggy. A typical spring day in Houston.

Kathryn heard the sound of traffic on the nearby freeway as she walked to her car. The drive back home would be slow this time of day, lots of time to think. She was determined to steady her thoughts on the mysterious box, her new treasure. When she arrived at her car, she unlocked the door and slid in. She left the door open for a moment to release the hot air. While she waited, she closed her eyes and imagined the box sitting on an old table somewhere in the stone manor. So many unanswered questions. So many possibilities. She opened her eyes, closed the door, and started the engine. For the first time in months, Kathryn felt something resembling hope about her future, even excitement. She turned on the radio, and as Lady Fate would have it U2 was singing, "It's a Beautiful Day." As Kathryn pulled out of the driveway onto the street, she turned up the radio and sang long and loud. It had been a beautiful day, indeed.

3

The Spinning of Tales
Summer – 1741 Isle of Skye

Mairi sat spinning wool with her grandmother, Margaret, while the logs in the hearth popped with a summer fire. A thin layer of blue smoke hung under the reed-thatched roof and filled the room with the sweet smells of peat and porridge.

Margaret was a storyteller, not by trade, but by nature. When she spun the tale of her narrow escape from the massacre at Glencoe or the miraculous birth of her daughter, Anne, in the Fairy Glen, her listeners found themselves caught up in the story, like threads woven into a tapestry.

Mairi loved her grandmother. She was the calm that held their family together when the winds blew, threatening to unravel their faith and fortune. Mairi's mother had died shortly after Mairi was born. She, too, would have died if not for their neighbor, who was just weaning her own child. The woman's name was Sara, and she took Mairi in and became her wet nurse.

For the next nine months Mairi lived with her cousins in the neighboring croft. Margaret would go every morning, after preparing breakfast for Mairi's father and brothers, and rock her, singing soft melodies and whispering stories about her mother. After several hours, she'd return home. Then, each evening after supper, whether rain or snow, Margaret would walk the rugged mile back to the croft. While Sara tended her eight children and readied them for bed, Margaret took Mairi in her arms and rocked her to sleep and put her to bed. In this way, she said, Mairi would know to whom she belonged.

Sara was a good mother, but they were of meager means. It was often said, the Isle and the sea fought together to free the land of its human inhabitants. But crofters were worthy adversaries and clung tightly to the moors, raising sheep and cattle and scant family gardens. Margaret's family was of no great means either, but they had enough to share with those around them. Each day, Margaret brought freshly baked bread and porridge to Sara. Every two weeks, she would bring dried mutton so the family would have meat for their stew. It was a small price to pay for saving Mairi's life.

Mairi looked at her grandmother and wondered if her mother had favored her. When Margaret spoke, the sound was tender and strong. *Would my mother's voice sound the same? Would she tell me stories? Stories? You have to live to have stories to tell.*

"Grandma, how is it you can sit here day after day and spin?" Mairi laid her wool thread on the flagstone and looked at her grandmother's weathered face. "You lost your husband, your home, and your two wee babes at Glencoe."

"Aye." Margaret continued her spinning without raising her eyes.

"Didn't you ever want to leave this isle, go back to the mainland, and fight back?"

"Fight? No child. Fightin's brought nothin' but pain and sadness," Margaret said. She continued to spin as the firelight cast shadows across her face. "I've seen enough death in my time. I've been very happy here."

"Grandma, why is it the menfolk go off to battle and travel across the sea on . . . well, I can only imagine what kind of adventures? And look at us, we have to sit home and spin and tend babies . . . and sheep."

Margaret smiled and laid the spindle down. "Child, can you imagine your good father or your brothers havin' the patience to spin wool and tend to the wee ones?"

Mairi exhaled, sat back hard against the primitive rowan chair, and asked, "But why can't I be happy just tendin' and carin'? Why do I feel like—like—I don't know, like I can't breathe?"

Margaret shook her head and laughed. "You are your mother's daughter indeed, child. Aye, you are indeed. She was as restless as you at thirteen." Margaret leaned close, cupping Mairi's thin face in her weathered hands. "You have her spirited eyes, full of fire and wonder. You'll find your own path, Mairi. Just keep your eyes open. Watch for it."

A cool breeze blew through the small open window and tossed Mairi's hair across her face. She turned and gazed across the glen.

"The sky is clearin'. I'll take the sheep out to graze." Mairi grabbed her bow and quiver of arrows hanging above the mantel, and ran out the door. It was a common sight for women and girls of the isles to pass their time spinning wool by hand on the hillsides and moors while their herds of sheep grazed. In spite of the whispers and disapproving glances of the village women, Mairi preferred the bow and arrow to the spindle and thread.

Margaret's sturdy frame filled the doorway as she watched her granddaughter hurry off to herd the sheep to the Fairy Glen. Mairi was tied to that glen heart and soul, just as her mother, Anne Fay, had been. Margaret knew it was Anne who called her to the glen, a whisper riding on the wind.

The Fairy Glen was a place of mystery and magic, from the wee hills to the wee lochs. Mairi had been warned by her grandmother to stay away from the portal to the otherworld found at the entrance to the rock castle atop the hillside, and to respect every blade of grass and every heather bloom in the glen. It was believed that the fairies shared the glen with people who honored it, but woe to the man, woman, or child who took even one stone from the brook that tripped its way into the loch.

Seated next to the brook, caressing a day-old lamb, Mairi watched a large rabbit emerge from its burrow and dash across the glen. It paused to graze on the heather, then darted off again. Mairi smiled and sighed. This was her own private domain, where the sheep grazed in safety while she practiced with her bow and dreamed of other worlds—both here in the Fairy Glen and beyond the great sea.

The villagers spoke of a New World to the west, wild and wonderful. Several ships had anchored in Uig Bay a fortnight past, and Mairi had watched from the high stone overlooking the sea as a host of families boarded with what few personal possessions they were allowed. She had even seen a girl who looked to be her age, though the distance from the hilltop to the ship put Mairi at a disadvantage to a clear view.

In the following weeks, Mairi had driven her family to distraction with questions of the New World. At night her dreams were filled with dark forests and great rivers full of every manner of fish and animal. Then there were the dark ones she had heard tales about, with hair and eyes as black as the cave of Glen Conon.

But then, people had begun disappearing from the island, especially young people. Many a young girl had been taken and shipped off to the Americas, sold as a slave or a wife, oftentimes both. Her father warned her not to leave the cottage alone, unless accompanied by bow and arrows. Mairi knew the kidnappers would never come into the Fairy Glen. They feared it.

As the rabbit emerged from a bush, an eagle screamed overhead. Mairi remembered her grandmother's story about the massacre in Glencoe. She closed her eyes and imagined that fateful night…

Donald MacIain woke his wife and their two young sons. Screams and the clash of steel against steel filled the air. He could smell smoke and hear a crackling fire overhead. The thatched roof of their stone cottage was ablaze, and pieces of fiery reeds were raining down like dragon's breath.

"Run, Margaret, take the boys and run to the hills!" Donald shouted. Before she could protest, he grabbed his sword and was gone. Margaret snatched their two sons from the bed, and dressed only in their nightclothes and bare feet, they climbed through the lone window facing the mountains, hoping to escape unseen. Margaret ran, dragging the two boys, Robert, aged three and Andrew, two, along beside her. They hid behind a formation of rocks on the side of the mountain. Holding her two young sons, one under each arm, Margaret closed her eyes and prayed.

Eventually, the screaming and the whirling and clanging of metal blades stopped. Light from the blazing village and the lingering smell of smoke signaled the devastation that lay below. Paralyzed by fear, Margaret remained behind the rocks until a heavy snow began to fall.

Donald had not come for them. It could only mean one thing; he had been killed. She knew if they tarried they would either freeze or be found out. They could wait no longer. Placing Robert on her back and carrying Andrew in her arms, she began the climb up the mountain and beyond to safety.

Soon she came upon a small group of women from her village, some too old to be on the run, other mothers with young children, all hurrying to escape. They traveled together as the snow fell harder and harder.

As the long night turned into days, with no sign of food nor shelter, Margaret watched as one by one, women and children fell dead to the ground. Of her own two sons, Andrew was the first to succumb to the elements and hunger. She carried his lifeless body in her arms, unable to let him go. Hours later Robert sank to the ground and joined his brother in the long sleep. Margaret lay Andrew's cold, still body next to Robert's and wept. The ground was frozen solid.

Unable to bury them in the crystallized earth, she let the Highland snow provide their final covering. As tears froze on her cheeks, she looked at the two tiny mounds of snow at her feet.

A sound—the wail of the deepest of suffering—forced its way from the inner sanctuary that held Margaret's soul and shattered the silence of that dark, frozen night. Her unborn child moved. Awakened from despair, Margaret trudged forward. The remainder of her passage to Skye was shrouded in mystery and fog. Highlanders helped her along the journey, but how she knew the way was another matter all together. An invisible hand led her to the Fairy Glen.

With a start, Mairi jumped up just in time to see the eagle swoop down with talons extended and lift the rabbit from the glen floor. She tightened her grip on the lamb. The peace and quiet of the Fairy Glen had been crushed. With her bow and quiver strapped to her back, Mairi herded the sheep back toward home, tears falling on the soft coat of the lamb in her arms.

4

Manor of All Dreams

Kathryn lay shivering uncontrollably on the table, staring at the ceiling, avoiding eye contact. She noticed a small black spot on the fluorescent light. It began to move.

"So, you say you haven't had any problems?" Dr. Romano asked. He looked like he was from Florence, but he wasn't. He was from Pittsburgh.

"No, none," Kathryn said.

"And when was your last period?"

"Colorado."

Dr. Romano looked up. "No, not where, when?"

Kathryn smiled. Her lips quivered. She wasn't sure if it was from the sub-zero temperature in the examining room or her nerves.

"Sorry," she said. "I meant, I was *in* Colorado last August. That's when I had my last period."

The doctor stood and washed up. "In August," he said, drying his hands on a paper towel. "It's now May . . . so let's see . . . nine months." He reached for his chart on the counter next to the sink, ran his fingers through his jet-black hair, and pulled a black pen from the pocket of his white lab coat. He scribbled something down. "So, you've had no problems. Nothing unusual. Don't appear to be ready to deliver a baby at any moment." He smiled.

"No," Kathryn said, beginning to feel a bit tense.

"Go ahead and sit up for me. No hot flashes?"

"No."

"No mood swings?"

Her mood was beginning to swing, but she wasn't telling him. "No," she said, attempting to smile.

"No night sweats?"

"If you mean unsolicited night sweats, no."

He looked up from the chart. "What?"

"No," Kathryn said. "No night sweats, no day sweats. You know, I really never sweat much at all."

"Okay," Dr. Romano said, tapping his pen on a particular spot on the chart. "I'd like to do a simple test. I'll send in the nurse to draw blood. We'll have the results in about fifteen minutes."

He stood and walked out the door.

"Okay," Kathryn said, her voice trailing off. She closed her eyes and drew in a deep breath. I don't think I can handle anything else. Maybe this is just something small—unimportant. I'm sure whatever it is has to do with the stress I've been under these last few months. Now that I think about, it was that trip to Colorado where I found the texts from Courtney on John's phone.

A knock sounded on the examining room door. Kathryn opened her eyes and turned to see the nurse walking in with her tray of needle and tubes.

"Don't worry, honey," she said. "This will only take a minute, and then you can dress and head back to the waiting area."

The nurse tied an elastic band tightly around Kathryn's right arm, then grabbed it between her own large right hip and left arm. She poked around and found a good vein. Her lips curved into a vampire-like smile. "You'll only feel a slight stick."

Kathryn dressed when the nurse left and returned to the waiting room. During the next fifteen minutes, she attempted to read the cover story in last month's *Good Housekeeping*, "Lies My Mother Told Me: Myths About Sex and Marriage." She was unable to concentrate.

The nurse finally called Kathryn back to Dr. Romano's office and seated her in front of his mahogany desk. The door opened, and he walked in smiling. Kathryn felt momentary relief.

"Well, your ovaries are dead."

That can't be good.

His mouth continued to move, but she didn't hear a word because her ovaries were dead. She wondered if there might have been another way to say that.

Maybe, "You've successfully navigated your way through menopause," or "Your ovaries don't seem to be functioning anymore," or "You'll not be needing your ovaries anymore." But, "Your ovaries are dead." That seemed so final—so morbid.

"So, I think that's about it," the doctor said as he smiled and extended his hand. "You should make an appointment in a year. Everything looks great."

Kathryn shook his hand, and before she could say anything else, he flew out of the room, like a bat leaving its lair for the next victim. He left her no instructions. No directions for what to do with dead ovaries. She was hoping her body knew what to do with them. For now, she would just have to trust they'd be laid to rest in a proper manner.

After paying the bill, Kathryn walked to her car and climbed in. She was still not sure what to do with her news. She felt certain she was too young for this to be happening. She started the engine and turned up the A/C. *I'll call Beth.*

"Hello. You've reached the Compass Rose. This is Beth. How may I help you?"

"Beth, it's Kathryn. Are you busy?"

"Nope, customers just left the store. Is your doctor appointment over?"

"Yes, I'm still in the parking lot. Just about to head back to the house." Kathryn put the phone on speaker and set it on the dash. She drove out of the lot and turned toward home.

"So, how'd it go?" Beth asked. "Everything okay?"

"Well, I'm not sure."

"What do you mean? What happened?"

"Dr. Romano did some blood work. He said my ovaries are dead. I don't know whether to mourn or to throw a party."

Silence.

Beth cleared her throat. "I'm sorry. I can see how that would be weird. He said it just like that?" Beth asked.

"Yes, just like that. It *is* weird. It feels like another loss." Kathryn turned into the Starbucks drive-thru and waited in line.

"Are you planning on having anymore children?" Beth asked.

"What?"

"I said, are you planning on having anymore children?"

Kathryn laughed. "No."

"Then I say let's party. I'll be at your house in an hour."

"Don't you have to work?" Kathryn asked.

"Yes, but Mrs. Podhorzki's niece is here helping for the next couple of days. They'll be fine without me."

"That's crazy," Kathryn said.

"I'm serious," Beth said. "No dwelling on the negative. Drag out your party hat. Dust it off. I'm on my way."

"You know what, Beth? I really appreciate it, but I've got to work on what I'm saying tomorrow in court. I'm in the drive-thru at Starbucks, and I'll be home in another five minutes. So thanks, but I'm okay, really."

"Are you sure?" Kathryn could hear Beth tapping her nails on the counter.

"Yes, I'm sure."

"Well, drag out your party hat just the same and get it ready.

You and I are going to party in the very near future. I'll meet you at your house in the morning at eight. I'm driving."

"You don't have to go tomorrow, Beth."

"I'm going, and I'm sitting right beside you through the whole thing. No arguing about this one."

Kathryn pulled up to the drive-thru window. "Okay. Thanks. I'll see you in the morning at eight. Love you."

"Love you, too," Beth said.

Kathryn ordered a tall Frappuccino. After a short wait, she drove home sipping her favorite hot weather drink. She pulled into her driveway, put the car into park and turned off the ignition. The May sun poured through the window. She leaned back against the headrest and closed her eyes.

This had been a year of change. Sean and Ian made fewer trips home for visits. And on those rare occasions—after they left to return to school—she would leave their rooms just as they were when they walked out the door; beds unmade, dirty clothes on the floor, dresser drawers gaping open. Kathryn allowed her mind to pretend her boys still lived at home. She'd never gotten used to her nest being empty.

Her marriage had ended, and her sons were mostly grown and on their own. She hadn't planned on having more children at forty-eight, so she wasn't sure why the doctor's news was so troubling. She exhaled and opened her eyes. Too many things ending. Too many losses. Then Kathryn remembered Beth's words. "No dwelling on the negative."

Her cell phone rang, breaking through her thoughts. She picked it up and said, "Hello."

"Mom, what's up?" It was Ian, her oldest son.

"Oh, nothing much. I just got home from the doctor."

"Why? Are you sick?"

"No, it's just my annual checkup."

"Is everything okay?"

I love Ian. She could see his broad smile and his dark hair. He looked just like his father.

"Yes, Ian. Everything is fine." She smiled.

"Mom, Sean and I talked about it, and if you want us to, we can come tonight after Sean gets out of class." *Silence.* "That way you don't have to be alone."

"You guys are sweet, but no. You need to go to your classes. I know you have finals coming up, and you have graduation soon. Don't want to mess that up." Kathryn loved her boys. "Anyway, Aunt Beth is picking me up and going with me. So see. I won't be alone."

"Are you sure?" Ian asked.

"Yes, I'm sure. Are you still coming Friday?"

"Absolutely. Around lunch. We'll take you out to eat."

"It's a date, Ian. And hey"—Kathryn started her car—"thanks for calling. I love you."

"I love you too, Mom. Off to class. I'll call you tomorrow. Bye."

"Bye." Kathryn pulled the car into the garage. *Home.*

Kathryn grabbed the plaid hot pads and took the lemon pound cake out of the oven and set it on the granite counter; it was the boy's favorite, and they'd be home in two days. The sweet citrus smell filled the kitchen. With John gone, she rarely cooked anymore. She caught her reflection in the oven door; a loose strand of hair hung across her face. She reached back and removed the clip, and her long dark hair cascaded down, falling far below her shoulders. *John used to love it when I wore my hair down.* She stared at her dim reflection in the oven door. *Oh, don't be so pathetic, Kathryn.*

She walked back to her office, located in the fifth bedroom, and flopped down in her chair facing her laptop. Next to it lay ancestral charts, each one documented with names of parents and siblings, wife or husband and children. Exact dates and locations of births for the more recent entries, but the earlier ones, from the early 1700s, were more difficult to find.

Kathryn loved researching her past. What caused them to leave their homes on the East Coast and move west to a land wild and uncharted? I envy them really. What courage they must have had. What sense of adventure. To leave everything familiar, everything they worked so hard to possess, and just walk away into the uncertain future.

She reached for the wooden box Beth had given her and studied the designs on top. She wondered who had taken the time to create it. Was it a gift? Was it an artist who made it to sell? And why *those* animals? Kathryn opened the lid and raised the box to her nose. She took a deep breath and thought for a moment she smelled the sea. She remembered the strange, cold sensation she felt when she first held it. It frightened her then, but now—now the box felt comfortable in her hand like a favorite book. Only, she couldn't read this one. It held secrets, this box. Secrets she was determined to unlock.

She took her journal from the stack of books on her desk and began to write with her favorite black pen, the gel tip one that rolled out ink as smooth as chocolate icing on a cake.

> Secrets. I am the proud owner of a box of secrets. It smells like salty air. Hmm, maybe it traveled on a ship to get here. Or maybe it was made of driftwood that washed up on a rocky shore in Scotland. The carvings are beautiful, unending chains that weave in and out of each other, and three animals that were obviously carved because they held some special meaning. Beth thinks the box is magic, or possesses some kind of power. Silly Beth. She also lives with a cat, named Mr. Nightly. Mrs. P, who claims to have her

own powers isn't even sure what the animals are. I think one is surely an eagle or a hawk. But why? Why these three? Oh good. More research.

Kathryn set aside her journal, picked up the pages of her ancestral notes, and stared at the many names written on the lines that were labeled *Mother*. Often, only a first name appeared, their family names lost when they married. She realized she was in danger of becoming a first name only on a chart that someone would find in years to come.

She stared at the word "Mother" and thought of her own. Sitting atop a shelf next to her desk was an old family photograph. Three-year-old Kathryn sat in her father's lap, her hand holding Tommy's tiny arm as he sat cradled in their mother's arms. After his sudden death, her mother took every picture of him, put them in a box, and stored them in the attic. She never looked at the photographs again. It was as if those two years never existed. But they had, and though they were forbidden to talk about him—or even speak his name—Kathryn missed him. She had needed to talk about him.

When Beth came along seven years after his death, their mother smiled again. But only for a short time, and then she fell into a deep dark place, one that she could not find her way out of. Kathryn always resented her mother for that. She should have tried harder to be happy. She still had two daughters who loved her and needed her. Not until Kathryn had her own two sons did she have any idea what her mother might have possibly gone through. Even now, she could not imagine losing one of them. Kathryn reached over and touched her mother's face. *I miss you, Mom.*

Kathryn looked back at her cluttered desk. A stack of opened mail sat in the basket next to her laptop. She picked up the pile and started sifting through it—a letter from her lawyer explaining about the hearing, bills, bills, and more bills, the moving company estimate. Suddenly she felt afraid. Kathryn opened a desk drawer and pulled out a blank ancestral form. She wrote John Gilbert Trent on the top line titled Father. She sat up straight and wrote her name on the line underneath, titled Mother: Kathryn Ann Silverton Trent.

She would not be a first name only on a chart. Silverton was a good strong name, and tomorrow she would take it back for her very own. Tomorrow. Tomorrow, she would be brave.

5

The Magic Box
Spring 1742 - Isle of Skye

Mairi leaned against the standing stone overlooking Uig Bay and watched as a ship sailed away toward the Americas. It was her fourteenth birthday, and she felt like a prisoner, exiled on her misty isle. She imagined herself at the helm of the ship, fleeing pirates in the Caribbean, just like in the stories she heard from her uncle, who'd recently returned from Jamaica.

She loved telling stories of her own, a gift she had inherited from her grandmother. The family would gather round the fire at night, and Mairi's words would lead them into distant lands on adventures of brown-skinned people from the Americas, or the fairy folk from their very own isle. Her stories, full of intrigue and violence, troubled her father and caused some concern to her grandmother. But her brothers, well, they loved them and followed her to her bed each evening begging for more adventures. She promised to continue the following evening only if they agreed to spar with her, whether with sword or shank. It mattered not to her, just so she honed her skills as a warrior. She would not always be tending sheep and carding wool, she hoped.

"Mairi."

She turned and saw her father riding up from the village on their black mare. He waved and motioned for her to come ride. Mairi ran down the hillside, sliding on the damp heather, stopping just short of the mud track. Her father reached his hand for hers and pulled her up and onto the back of the mare. She wrapped her arms as far as she could around his large frame and held on tight. He gave the horse a swift kick and a whistle, and they took off at a full run.

Her father reigned in the mare just outside their house, where her grandmother was standing in the doorway, a shawl wrapped around her shoulders and head. "Mairi, where have you been, child? Birthday or no, I need your help with supper."

Mairi slid off the horse and apologized. "Sorry, Grandma. I was watching the ship sail away. Sarah MacArthur and her family are onboard, and the Grahams."

Her father tied the horse to the elder tree by the front door, and they walked inside. Now, many a cottage on the Isle had an elder tree guarding it. It was said to protect against malevolent spirits of every type, and—to be sure—the Isles were harbor to a hoard of spirits, good and ill. It was best to be rightly situated at home then—a Bible on the mantel and an elder at the door. Mairi's grandmother loved the white blossoms in the early summer and the fragrance that filled the air when the tree was in full bloom. Mairi, however, always felt it smelled of death, that overpowering sweetness that surrounded a body in a roomful of flowers, just before it was carried away to be laid to rest.

"Surprise!" A great shout came from inside the cottage, as Mairi walked in the front door. The room was filled with her brothers and kin from nearby.

Her grandmother had prepared a large pot of stew, and after everyone had their fill, her uncle Alastair, took up the fiddle and played a reel. Everyone spilled into the yard like ants from a mound.

A Beltane fire had been built, for it was the first of May, and for the next hour dancing and laughter filled the sea air, with her uncle on the fiddle and her father on the pipes. As storm clouds rolled in, everyone poured into the house again. The fiddle was placed back on the hearth, as everyone found a spot around the fire.

Mairi sat by her father as her grandmother told about the day she was born and the joy they all felt at the birth of a baby girl in a houseful of boys and men. Sara shared how Mairi grew her first months in their home, full of adopted sisters and brothers. Others shared memories of her and offered blessings for the future.

"Mairi," her brother, Ranald, said. "Do you have a story for us?" Everyone clapped. "Just one, please."

Mairi looked around the roomful of the people she loved and smiled. "Aye." She stood, so as to move around, for who could tell a tale while sitting still as a mouse?

"There was only the sound of gentle waves risin' and fallin' upon the beach like a giant's breath as he sleeps after a day of terrorizin' the local villagers." Mairi walked slowly around the fire. "The sun beat down and heated the sand. A young dragon lay near the openin' of a sea cave, warmin' himself in the mornin' sun.

"Morag sat up and rubbed her eyes tryin' to make sense of where she was." Mairi looked past all her eager listeners. "Another wave rolled in, and she tumbled forward onto the sand. A rope was tied around her waist, and she felt somethin' hard against her back. As she untied the rope, several small wooden planks fell around her. She looked up and down the beach—debris lay scattered here and there. She struggled to stand, reachin' for a plank to help steady her legs.

"Where am I?" Mairi held the back of her head and stumbled back and forth through those sitting nearest the fire. "Morag walked to what looked like a piece of heavy fabric and tried to lift it off the sand. It was heavy canvas—a sail!

"She kept repeatin', 'A sail,' louder and louder. 'The ship…where is the ship?' " Mairi moved slowly around the room, limping.

"She sat down and closed her eyes, the torn sail in her hands. The sounds of a fierce storm filled her thoughts—and she suddenly remembered everythin'.

"She had been on a ship in the middle of a storm. The deck quaked each time the heavens thundered. Bolts of lightnin' pierced the darkness. And then, the rain." Mairi closed her eyes and turned her face to the ceiling. "It pelted Morag's skin till she thought she might bleed.

"The captain yelled above the storm, 'All hands on deck, tether the sails, and prepare for the worst.' He looked at her and yelled, 'Boy,' for she had cut her hair and put on boy's clothin', 'get up here now.'

"She fought the wind and the rockin' of the ship and climbed the slippery steps to the sterncastle, where Captain Kidd stood grippin' the helm, tryin' with all his might to steady the ship into the wind." Mairi's brother Ranald yelled out, "Aye, Captain Kidd, a great Scottish pirate if there ever was one."

The crowd shushed him and Mairi continued. "As I was sayin', Captain Kidd grabbed Morag's skinny arm and called for the first mate to tie her to the planks that made up the wall of the deck.

'But, Captain, sir," Mairi yelled, as everyone in the room leaned in. "What have I done?

'You've done nothin' wrong, lad. But you're too small to hold your own against an angry sea. It'll sweep you up and swallow you whole. Sit tight now. I'll release you when it calms.'

"There she sat—afraid and humiliated.

'It's all right, lad,' yelled the first mate, half smilin'. 'We've all of us been lashed to the plank when we first sailed.'

"The sea worsened." Mairi picked up her fathers walking stick. "And then, Morag heard a mighty crack." She struck the flagstone floor with the stick. Everyone jumped and Margaret smiled.

"The central mast was cleft in two and fell across the deck of the giant ship and into the sea, takin' a half-dozen sailors with it to their watery graves. God rest their souls."

Everyone in the croft followed Mairi in crossing themselves as she continued.

"The ship, she tossed back and forth, back and forth. She swayed up and crashed down, she swayed up and crashed down. Another loud crack and the foremast fell across the helm, landin' right atop Captain Kidd, God rest his soul." More crossing. "He fell to the deck under the weight of the mast, and the helm spun out of control. The ship moaned and creaked from deep in her belly as she broke apart. Then, all went black and was quiet as a tomb."

Mairi closed her eyes and bowed her head. No one spoke, no one moved. The only sound heard in the room was the crackling of the fire. A moment later, she opened her eyes and looked around, holding her hand to her forehead as though to cover her eyes from the sun.

"Morag found herself shipwrecked on the beach. 'Am I the only one to survive? Am I here all alone?' Then, she looked up the beach and saw the dragon. She thought she had been dreamin' when she first saw him, but her heavy breathin' and rapid heartbeat told her it was no phantasm. It was real. She tried to make her way to the shelter of the evergreen woods that lined the shore. Just as she stepped into the trees, she heard a sound." Mairi crouched low and whispered. Everyone leaned ever closer to her. "A low, terrifyin' growl, like none she had ever heard before. Morag turned slowly and there, not two yards away, stood the dragon."

Mairi straightened up and said. "I think I'll stop here for now." Everyone sat up and, all talking at once, asked her to continue. She laughed and said, "It's my birthday. I've entertained you all enough for one night."

Everyone clapped and thanked her, assuring her grandmother they would all be back as soon as Mairi was ready to finish her tale. They all bid the family a good night and left for their own crofts.

"Well done, child. How do you do it?" Her father shook his head. "You have your grandmother's gift, I think."

"It started with a dream, Father," Mairi said.

Margaret slipped her hands under her apron so none could see how tightly she held them. "What do you mean, a dream?" she asked.

"Oh, you know, I have lots of dreams."

"But, I am thinkin' this one you've had more than once."

Mairi frowned. "Well, yes, I have. Is there somethin' wrong, Grandma?"

"How does this tale end? For you and the dragon?" asked Margaret.

"I can't tell you, that'd give away the story." Mairi smiled and looked around the room at her father and brothers. "And remember, her name is Morag, not Mairi."

"But in your dreams it is you, is it not, child?" Margaret asked, placing her hand on Mairi's head. "I'm sorry, Mairi. I'll say no more now, but we'll speak of this again."

Mairi's father went to his bed and pulled out a small package from under the straw mattress.

"Here, darlin'. This is for you."

"Open it quick, Mairi. You're goin' to love it," Ranald said.

"Ranald. Quiet now, all of you," William said, pointing his pipe at each of the boys.

Mairi took the package bound in leather and unwrapped it. The soft skin fell open revealing a box made of rowan wood. Carved symbols covered the lid, interlocking ovals for a border with three animals in the center. A white marble stone was set into the front of the wooden box. Mairi ran her fingers, first along the carvings on the top of the box, then over the cool, smooth surface of the stone.

"This is beautiful, Father. I've never seen anythin' like it. Where did it come from?"

William took the box and flipped it over, revealing a line slashed with strange markings and dots and the initials WM under them.

"Look, Mairi. This is your name in the old language. Not many can read it, and there, just under it, are my initials."

Mairi stared at the box. "Your initials. So, you made it then?"

"Aye, I did at that. From one of the rowan that fell in the last storm."

"And those lines and dots, how is that my name?"

William traced the lines with his finger. "The first hatch mark, here, is an M, the single dot is an A, the four dots represent an I. Next, the five hatches make an R, and finally, the last four dots another I. It's an ancient form of your name."

"It's like a secret code, Father, isn't it?" Mairi loved all things secret.

Her father took the box and pulled his dirk from his belt. He gently placed the blade under the edge of the stone and popped it out of its place. A small hidden drawer appeared. Mairi's eyes widened, and a broad smile broke across her face.

"There's more than one secret to this box. Look, a place for somethin' special." He handed Mairi the box.

"Oh, Father, I love it."

He brushed a wisp of hair from across her face and smiled. "You are fourteen now, I'll call you a child no more. Look at you, the image of your mother, may she rest in the Creator's hands forever."

Mairi's grandmother pulled a small piece of fabric folded over from her pocket and handed it to her. "Take this, my love."

Mairi carefully turned back the fabric and discovered a small dried flower. She looked up at her grandmother. "What is it?"

"It's a snowdrop. I picked it from the Fairy Glen at the exact place where your mother was born. I never gave it to her because she believed that it was bad luck to take anythin' from the glen. But it was so beautiful at the time, and it was as a remembrance. I've always suffered with guilt over her death. What if she was right? What if I brought bad luck her way and it ended in her death? A blessin' attend her departin' and travelin'." She kissed her thumb and pressed it to her forehead. "I want you to take it and return it to the glen for me. Maybe she'll be at peace then." Margaret wiped a tear from her cheek with the corner of her apron, and then turned and stirred the fire.

"Mother, you should know that you had nothin' to do with Anne's death. It was her time, and none of us could've done anythin' to change that." William wrapped a sturdy arm around her shoulder.

"Say what you will, I'd like the child to return the flower all the same. I'll not rest till she does."

Mairi placed the stone inside the rowan box. "I'll return it in the mornin', Grandma. I promise." Mairi turned to her father and held out the box. "So tell me what do these symbols mean?"

The peat fire popped, and the sweet aroma filled the cottage. William leaned close to Mairi and took the box. He held it so everyone in the room could see. "The pattern around the border is an oval love knot. This represents my unendin' love for you, Mairi, and the intricate squared patterns in the corners are shield knots. These are for protection and represent the four corners of the earth. So no matter where you go, dear one, if you carry this box it will banish everythin' evil from your path."

"We could all use a box like this, Father," Mairi's youngest brother, Hugh, said.

"Aye," the other three agreed.

"You've each got a sword and a dirk. That should do the job." William pointed to the three animals in the center of the box. "Now, these are very powerful symbols indeed. The larger bird is a hawk, the messenger between the Otherworld and this world. He is the bird of far-memory. If we are ever separated, he will bind us together in thought."

"I like the hawk, Father. I like him very much," Mairi said. "And this little one. What is the small bird?"

"Ah yes. She is a wren, a sacred bird. Sometimes a fairy in disguise. Sometimes a messenger from God."

"And that funny-lookin' creature with four short legs and a tail?" Ranald asked.

"This is an otter. They possess deep magic and are revealers of hidden treasure. He is a strong protector and a guide as well," William said. "The shores of our island are filled with otters. They are highly esteemed. It will remind you of home."

"Why is it, Father, that I feel I will be leavin'?" Mairi asked.

William laughed and patted her head. "Mairi, every father knows that one day his daughter will leave home. You will find a fine husband, and he will carry you away. But enough about leavin' home." He rubbed the white stone with his forefinger. "This is Skye marble and represents everythin' pure and good on our fair isle."

Mairi took the box from him and held it close. "Thank you, Father. I will keep it with me always. I promise. I have never had such a wonderful gift. I will sleep with it to be sure of sweet dreams tonight."

She stood and gave her father, grandmother, and brothers a kiss good night. She went into the room she shared with her grandmother, dressed for bed, and lay the box next to her pillow. She slid under the wool blanket and rested her hand on the box, running her finger over each carving. That night her dream of stormy seas and a dragon would surely be replaced with magical creatures of a different kind. All worthy companions on a journey yet to be taken.

6

Come What May

Kathryn sat at a small table on Beth's balcony writing in her notebook and breathing in the warm air filled with the sweet scent of honeysuckle. Beth burst through the open door singing "You are My Sunshine." Kathryn gently closed the notebook and laid down her pen.

"I see you're hard at work telling secrets," Beth said. She pulled a wicker chair across the stone-covered balcony and sat down at the table.

Kathryn frowned. "I'm just writing down a few thoughts after this morning. And why aren't you downstairs in the shop?"

"It's six o'clock. I just closed up and sent Mrs. P. home. I thought I'd come up and check on you. See how you're doing."

"Six o'clock, really, already? I guess I lost track of time." Kathryn attempted a smile.

"Hey, I've been thinking all afternoon about this morning." Beth said.

"Me, too," Kathryn said.

"But I've been thinking how amazing you were in there. You were calm and steady. You told your story from beginning to end without notes. You were flawless."

"Believe me, I've had a lot of time to practice." Kathryn said.

"Well, anyway. You were fantastic, and I think we should celebrate."

"Oh, Beth, please." Kathryn said. "I really don't feel like celebrating."

"I don't mean we're celebrating your divorce. I know you're still working through it, emotionally, I mean." Beth stood and pulled Kathryn to her feet. "I want to celebrate your new life. Because like it or not, it begins today."

Kathryn exhaled loudly and smiled. "Okay, okay. What do you have in mind?"

"I'm treating you to a lovely dinner out."

"I'm not dressed for a lovely dinner out. I've changed into my jeans."

"I know, I've already thought about that. We're going to make a side trip to the mall. And if we leave right now, we'll have plenty of time." Beth moved toward the doorway. "What do you say, Kathryn. Humor your little sister. I'm your best offer. I'm afraid."

"You're my only offer." Kathryn grabbed her notebook and followed Beth into the apartment. "Sure, why not. But there's no need to go to the mall. We can just stop by my house and I'll change."

"No, Kathryn. I've got something in mind already."

"Okay, okay. Just one request for our dinner out," Kathryn said.

"What's that?" Beth picked up her Guatemalan bag and pulled out a paperback book.

"Just not that upscale sushi place you love."

"You mean the Raw Deal?" Beth laughed.

"Yeah, that would be the one."

"Okay, your choice. We'll talk about it on the way to the mall. But first, I got something for you." She handed the book to Kathryn.

"What's this?" Kathryn looked at the cover. "*Collins Rambler's Guide—Isle of Skye*. What's this for?"

"How long has it been since you flew alone?" Beth asked.

"Let's see, maybe twenty-five years."

"What? You can't be serious?"

"I always traveled with the family, or just with John. Why? What are you thinking, Beth?"

"You can do this, Kathryn. You've just forgotten how to fly."

"I've forgotten how to fly?"

"Yes. But you'll remember how. I'm sure of it."

Kathryn waved at Beth as if pushing her comments aside.

"Look. You stayed with John through his first affair because you loved him and the boys. And you were determined to make it work. I watched you, Kathryn. I could never have done that."

Kathryn held up two fingers. "Technically, second 'indiscretion'."

"Second," Beth said a little too loudly. "So, Courtney is the third?"

Kathryn closed her eyes and nodded. "But the first one was a very long time ago. We were just figuring this whole married thing out."

"Kathryn, there's not a whole lot to figure out. It's the forsaking all others thing. Why didn't you bring that up today?"

"I wanted the judge to be empathetic toward my case, not pity me." Kathryn handed Beth the book and walked to the couch. She fell hard into the cushions and placed her hands over her face. "See, I'm not so strong."

Beth moved next to her on the couch and slid her arm through Kathryn's. "You are strong. Strong and brave. You are. It's time to fly away, Kate. I know just where to start."

The crowded mall echoed with noisy teenagers and hungry young children. They shopped their way through the first floor and rode the escalator up to the second level. Kathryn questioned her own sanity, going shopping on that day, of all days. She longed for the solace of her empty house and at the same time dreaded it—the solace and the empty house. Too many conflicting emotions to be shopping. She glanced up at Beth, who was carrying two Anthropologie bags and drinking a latte. Kathryn sighed. How different they were now. Beth loved being out in the middle of the action, whatever and wherever that might be. Kathryn preferred smaller, quieter venues, a boutique, for example, on a quiet side street. There had been a time when Kathryn led the way on adventures the two would take together. When had all that changed?

Deep in thought, she followed Beth into a department store and found herself standing at the cosmetics counter.

Beth looked at the clerk's nametag. "Hello, Chloe. My sister is here for a makeover."

Chloe smiled. "Awesome. Just have a seat here on the stool. What's your name?"

"My name's Beth, and this is Kathryn." Beth pointed to Kathryn and motioned for her to sit down.

Kathryn gave Beth a half-smile. She didn't think Chloe looked old enough to wear makeup, much less sell it, but before she had time to protest, she was seated in a chair facing the jewelry counter being madeover. Kathryn pulled her hair up in a ponytail and tried to relax. Maybe this was just what she needed, a new start from head to toe. At least Beth seemed to think so. Kathryn smiled.

"And why are you smiling?" Beth asked as she pulled up a stool and sat next to Kathryn.

"I feel kind of like an old house that is being updated. You know, replacing the avocado kitchen and the pink tile in the bathroom." Kathryn laughed. She was caught off guard by how good that laugh felt.

"Come on, Kathryn," Beth said. "You're not an old house.

Think of this as pampering yourself. You're just changing out the beautiful oak floors for some cool marble tiles."

Kathryn smiled and winked at Beth. "Good analogy, I like yours much better. Not as funny, but much better."

The makeover began with a demonstration of proper skin care. Then, Chloe applied foundation and blush to Kathryn's face. Next, she pulled out a tray of eye shadow samples and began to work on her eyelids. Chloe had just begun to apply eyeliner, when Kathryn noticed a young woman in her early twenties at the jewelry counter. She was tall and looked like she had just stepped off a runway in Milan. Her black knit halter barely contained her breasts. A short skirt covered very little of her long slender legs, which looked even longer in her four-inch Italian heels. The color of her short bobbed hair reminded Kathryn of raspberries. Kathryn smiled as the well-dressed man standing next to her, with graying temples, clasped a pearl necklace around her neck. How sweet. It must be her birthday. If we'd had a daughter, I wonder if John would be so attentive? Suddenly the man leaned over and gently kissed the nape of the young woman's neck.

"No!" Kathryn shouted.

Chloe jerked, and the eyeliner pencil skidded across the middle of Kathryn's eyelid, up through her eyebrow and across her forehead. The tray of eye shadow crashed to the floor, and Chloe and Beth looked stunned.

"Good Lord, Kathryn," Beth said. "What is it?"

Kathryn's mind raced to excuse her bizarre behavior. "I just remembered, I left the curling iron plugged in."

Beth grabbed the mirror and held it to Kathryn's face. "Kathryn, look at your hair. There's no way you used a curling iron."

Kathryn didn't notice her hair; all she saw was the black line separating her left eyelid and forehead. She lowered the mirror and looked across at the couple in front of the jewelry counter. The man was paying for the pearl necklace, and the young woman had her hand tucked into his back pocket. Kathryn suddenly felt nauseous.

"Here, let me remove that eyeliner. I'm almost finished." Chloe placed the eye shadow tray she'd just cleaned up from the floor on the counter and was dabbing make-up remover on a cotton ball.

"I'm so sorry," Kathryn said.

"Oh, it's no problem. Really, I always leave stuff plugged in at my apartment. It's like I'm calling my roommates every other day from work to unplug something."

Kathryn felt humiliated and shaken at the same time. Chloe finished quickly just as she'd said. She held the mirror to Kathryn again and smiled.

"What do you think?"

Kathryn was surprised and pleased. "It's looks—good. I look good, I think."

"You think?" Beth asked. "Kathryn, you're a knock-out, and John's a fool."

"Beth," Kathryn whispered.

"Just sayin'." Beth turned to Chloe. "She looks great. You did a super job."

"Thanks. You look beautiful, Kathryn. Would you like to purchase any of the makeup I used today?" Chloe asked.

"Yes, I'll take one of everything you used."

"Oh. Wonderful. I'll ring that up. I've got a cool promotional bag I'll put it all in." Chloe began gathering the products and totaling them up. When she finished, she handed the black-and-white polka-dotted bag to Kathryn.

Kathryn paid the bill and thanked Chloe, then followed Beth out of the store and back into the busy mall.

"Look, there's Pretzel Palace," Beth said. "I'm buying."

"Aren't we about to eat dinner?"

"Can we really come to the mall and not have a pretzel? Really, Kathryn. We're living it up."

Kathryn laughed. "Oh, I forgot."

Kathryn and Beth ordered pretzels with sea salt and sat on a nearby bench, eating them. An older couple walked by arm in arm, wearing walking shoes and talking in whispers. Kathryn wrote their life story in her head as she watched them pass. They had raised a large family and were enjoying their retirement years traveling and taking long walks in malls together. Their grandchildren and great-grandchildren loved to come to their spacious home in the Woodlands for long holidays. In fact, they had just celebrated their sixtieth wedding anniversary in London.

"Kathryn, come back." Beth said. "You're staring off into space."

"Sorry, did you see that cute little couple?"

"Not really. But I did notice the guy looking at the Tiffany window. He must work out. You know, he looks like he might be your age." Beth pointed her pretzel in the man's direction.

"Oh my God, Beth. You're killing me," Kathryn said, quickly pushing Beth's pretzel back down.

"I'm doing my best to cheer you up, but you've gotta help me out here," Beth said.

"Okay, let's walk," Kathryn said and stood.

They gathered their bags and began walking toward the escalator. Kathryn took a deep breath. "So, I've been thinking about what you said earlier, about learning to fly again."

"Yes?" Beth raised an eyebrow and waited.

"As you know John and I decided he would keep the brownstone in London, and I'd keep our house here in Houston."

"Okay," Beth said. "So?"

"So I don't think I can afford to keep the house. Anyway, I don't really have any desire to stay in it anymore. Too many memories." Kathryn stepped off the escalator.

Beth jumped onto the landing like a child and slid off onto the tile floor. "And?"

"I've decided to sell it and maybe take a trip." Kathryn stopped and looked at Beth. "To the Isle of Skye."

"What?" Beth's half-eaten pretzel fell to the floor. "Are you serious?"

"I know, I know. I'm crazy. I've been home alone too much and gone loony." Kathryn felt her face flush red.

"You know, Kathryn, this is just like in a movie. The heroine is abandoned by her—man. And she goes off on a great adventure. Always finding another, much better, man in the end." Beth kicked the pretzel under a nearby bench, and they began to walk. "Kathryn, I think this is the best idea you've ever had. It *is* crazy. Crazy awesome."

"Well, I won't be looking for another man anytime soon. But I do like that whole being crazy awesome thing."

They laughed and pushed through the crowd and into Banana Republic.

"So, when are you thinking about going?" Beth asked.

"Right after Ian's graduation." Kathryn stopped at a rack of sundresses and began looking through them. "John and I gave Ian a six-week back-packing trip to Europe for his graduation. He gets to take a friend, and he's taking Sean."

"Aw, how cute is that?" Beth smiled.

"Yeah, but don't say that out loud to the boys."

"Oh, Kathryn. This is so exciting." Beth headed straight to a rack of plaid skirts, grabbed a size eight, took a white blouse off the rack next to the skirts, and found a sheer green scarf to match the green in the plaid. She took Kathryn's hand and led her into the dressing area. "I think you should try this on, for the sake of the ancestors. We're Highland lassies, you know."

Kathryn laughed out loud. "I think the word is lasses. Lassie was a dog."

"Oh crap, you're right. Sorry."

Kathryn took the clothes and stepped into a dressing room. She slipped on the skirt and wondered if it was the right plaid for the MacDonalds. She managed to button the last button on the blouse and wrapped the scarf around her neck. Kathryn stepped back to take a long look at herself. At her feet lay the baggy jeans and black t-shirt she'd taken off. A mist reformed in Kathryn's mind, and she stood in the midst of it, alone, in her plaid skirt. *I've lost my way somehow. My life is mist and shadows.* She opened the dressing room door and walked out.

Beth smiled and pulled the rubber band from Kathryn's hair. She took the green scarf from around her neck and tied it like a headband. She stepped back and extended her arms. "Ah, now there's that Highland lass I once knew. Okay, *Braveheart*," Beth said, "if John ever gives you any more trouble, you can call on our clansmen and have him drawn and quartered. I've heard it's quite painful."

Beth put her arm around Kathryn's shoulder and whispered, "Isle of Skye?"

"I know."

Beth pulled the tags from the clothing. "You're wearing this out of the store. No more sad, baggy clothes for you, big sister."

Kathryn paid for her new outfit, and they headed to the parking garage. When they arrived at Beth's Mini, they threw the bags in the back seat and dropped the convertible top down. Beth insisted Kathryn try out her new skirt at the Stuffed Goose Bar and Grill. She agreed.

After more margaritas than any one woman should be allowed to drink, Kathryn had Beth drive her home. Beth took Kathryn's keys and helped her into the house. After a slow stroll to the master bedroom, Beth helped Kathryn first into her pajamas and then into bed. Kathryn slid under her feather comforter and closed her eyes. As Beth tiptoed out of the room, a whisper came from the bed.

"This is not how my life was supposed to be. What am I going to do?" The whisper turned into weeping.

Beth returned to the bed, slipped off her shoes, and crawled in next to Kathryn. "You're going to sleep, and tomorrow, when your head stops throbbing and the fog is gone, we'll look for tickets to Scotland. Remember, Isle of Skye? Ian and Sean are coming tomorrow, too. Everything will look different, you'll see." She smoothed Kathryn's hair from her face. "I'll stay here tonight; you'll be okay, Kathryn. We're just a couple of crazy awesome lasses."

"You got it right this time," Kathryn said.

"And you're going to get it right this time, too," Beth said.

The white noise sound of katydids in the backyard serenaded the sisters as they lay in bed. Their May melody grew louder and louder until it reached a crescendo, fell silent, then began again. Kathryn put her pillow over her head to quiet the noise. Tomorrow the boys would come for a visit, and then on to her father's the following day for his birthday. She wondered what he'd think of her idea about leaving. She could hear Beth's voice in her thoughts. Crazy awesome, he'll think it's crazy awesome. The margaritas worked their magic, and Kathryn slipped into a long, deep night's sleep.

7

Of Dragons and Men
Spring - 1742 Isle of Skye

Mairi awoke to the smell of the peat fire and porridge. She washed her face in the basin of water by her bed and dressed. Her grandmother was setting bowls on the table, and her father sat with her brothers drinking coffee.

"Mornin', Mairi. You're up early this fine day," William said.

"Sit down by your brothers, child, and I'll fetch your porridge," Margaret said.

Mairi slipped in between Ranald and James and rubbed her eyes. She sat across from her other two brothers, Hugh and Donald. She was anxious for her father and brothers to leave for the morning, to check on the cattle. Mairi wanted to talk with her grandmother about her dream. The dragon had returned in the night to visit her, and she was sure her grandmother knew what her dream meant.

After breakfast, the men were off to work, and Mairi settled down next to her grandmother near the fire with some wool and spindles. Margaret was the first to speak.

"So, I can see you've somethin' on your mind. Go ahead, speak it."

Mairi lay the spindle down in her lap and reached to stir the fire. "I dreamt of the dragon again last night."

"Did you now?"

"Aye, and it is ever the same."

"Is this dragon friend or foe?" Margaret asked.

"It is friend. At first, I was afraid because I was not sure. But he changed forms."

"He—so, it was a boy then?"

Mairi set down the stick, as the flames leapt up the chimney. "No, Grandma. Tis a man. He is dark of hair and skin. His eyes are the color of the coffee in your cup."

"And, does he speak to you, this dark man?"

"Yes, his voice is strong and clear. He takes my hand, and he guides me through the forest to a village, where his clan lives. He covers me in the soft skin of a deer and sits me inside his hut to warm myself by his fire. I say hut because it is unlike any cottage I have ever seen. It is round, and the walls are made of skins of animals, but the roof is of thatch like our own."

Margaret took a sip of her coffee. "And what does he say to you, Mairi?"

"He tells me not to fear him, for he is the guardian of his clan. He tells me that his name is Uktena. What does this mean?"

"I have seen this dragon many times of late in my dreams. He is to guide you on a journey yet to be taken. When you meet him, Mairi, you must trust him." Margaret stood and walked to the window. "He will be a stranger to you, as will be his ways."

Mairi joined her grandmother at the window. "What journey is this you speak of, Grandma?"

Margaret put her arm around Mairi's shoulder and pulled her close. "This I do not know, child. I have not seen more than I've told you. I feel a sadness when I see this dream. My heart is heavy even now as we speak of it."

"Then I will not speak of this again. I do not wish to make you sad. There is sorrow enough in these days for all of us." Mairi went to her bed and brought back the snowdrop wrapped in fabric. "It's time for me to return this to the Fairy Glen. Then, there will be peace. I'm sure of it. You will see." Mairi smiled and kissed her grandmother on both cheeks. She reached for her bow and quiver and left for the glen.

When she arrived, the small trees were filled with songbirds announcing the spring rains making their way across the Minch Channel toward the isle. Mairi climbed the small hillside that held the rocky fairy castle. An ancient stone spiral adorned the ground atop the hill. She unwrapped the snowdrop and laid it near the center of the spiral.

"Mother, this is for you. We return this once beautiful flower taken from this sacred place as a remembrance and ask that any misfortune be withdrawn from our family name."

The wind began to move through the glen, carrying the salty scent of rain. Mairi could see the dark clouds moving in and climbed down to the tiny loch at the base of the hill. A damp chill hung in the air, but Mairi did not feel it. She felt nothing but the warm embrace of the glen and the presence of her mother. She ran back to the cottage ahead of the storm and arrived just in time for the midday meal. Her grandmother smiled as she saw Mairi's countenance.

"The flower has been returned, my penance accepted," Margaret said. "Thank you, Mairi."

A week had passed and family and friends had come together for

Beltane's Feast. After they all had their fill and gathered around the fire in the yard, Ranald called out for Mairi to finish the story she had begun the week before. At first, she protested and looked to Margaret for aid, for she had sworn never to speak of the dragon again. But all were carrying on in such a way, as was impossible to refuse.

"Go on with you, Mairi," said her grandmother. "I'll not ruin your story with my superstitious ways. Go on now. Tell us the end of your tale."

Mairi gave Margaret a hug and a kiss and turned toward the fire with a smile. "Gather in now, and I'll finish my tale."

Everyone moved close together, and all eyes were on Mairi as she looked into the flames.

"When last I left you, Morag had made her way into the green woods. She heard a sound that filled her heart with fear…" Mairi paused for effect.

"It was the dragon," cried one of her younger cousins.

"Morag turned, and there standin' over her was the very dragon she had seen sleepin' on the beach. His eyes were deep and dark, and she could see her frightened reflection in them. She stood like a stone, unable to move, unable to speak. She was even afraid to breathe for fear the movement of her chest or the stirrin' of the air by her breath might set him off. A deep rumblin' growl filled her ears, and all she could see were his sharp teeth." Mairi bent down and bared her teeth to some of the children around the fire and growled. They drew back and screamed. The adults smiled. She rose up and continued. "Suddenly, before her very eyes, he stood up on his hind legs and began to speak."

The children gasped, as did a few of the women.

"As he spoke to Morag, his shape changed into that of a man, with light brown skin and long dark hair the color of night, and his eyes—his eyes were as black as the deepest loch in winter. He was dressed strangely in the skin of a deer."

Ranald called out, "What did he say to her, Mairi?"

"Well, he told her his village was nearby and to follow him, and he would clear a path for her."

"Did she follow him, Mairi? Did he not eat her?" her brother James asked.

The young boys in the room began to call out. "She should slay him."

"She should run away, fast," a little girl cried out.

Mairi motioned for everyone to be quiet. "She did not run, and she did not slay him. She followed him, and he led her into a land of beauty and great magic—a land where she learned to speak to animals and ride a great dragon. He told her many things about how, in the form of a dragon, he lived to protect his clan. But now, I have moved ahead to other tales yet to tell.

"So, there Morag stood alone in the forest with only this dragon man. She knew there was nothin' else to do but to follow him. As he led her through the woods, he saw she struggled to walk.

'You have injured your leg,' he said, and before she could answer, he swept her up and carried her the remainder of the journey. When they arrived in his village, they were met by his clan. They were all clothed in animal skins, as were their round huts. Morag wondered if there were no deer left in the forest! They seemed curious at her strange appearance, but did not intend to harm her. The dragon man carried her into his small hut, placed her on a skin on the ground, and gave her another to cover her body, as she was now shakin' from head to toe." Mairi took a tartan and wrapped herself in it. "She asked him his name, and he told her it was Uktena, a name full of power and great magic. He then told her that her name would be Sea Maiden, for she had been delivered up to them by the sea."

The children all repeated "Sea Maiden" and giggled. She unwrapped the tartan from her shoulders and draped it over one of the children.

"I think this is enough for tonight, I see a storm's brewin' to the west."

"Please, please tell us more," cried the little girl sitting next to Mairi's grandmother.

"Tell us about the talkin' animals," a young woman said.

"I want to know how to ride a dragon," Ranald yelled.

But she held fast and would not continue. Truth being, she had not dreamed nor imagined the rest of the story. She tried on many occasions later to complete the tale. But always the dream never went beyond the first visit to the village. Mairi did not know that he would not be found again until she was much older and on a journey she had not thought possible.

As the rain began, everyone crowded inside the cottage and waited for the storm to pass. As evening fell and the rain lightened, the small gathering ended and everyone went home. Mairi and her grandmother fell asleep together that evening in front of the hearth. Neither dreamed of a dragon in a great wood, but rather of a tiny wren perched on a stone in the center of an ancient spiral, singing a song of thanksgiving.

8

A Box of Buttons

Kathryn awoke to the smell of coffee, and Beth singing in the kitchen. She sat up and instantly fell back onto her pillow holding her head. She vowed to never drink another margarita again. She lifted her head carefully off the pillow and sat up. Better. Must move slowly. She stood and walked to the kitchen.

"Morning, sunshine," Beth said.

"Please, no talking till I've had my coffee." Kathryn took a mug from the shelf near the sink and filled it with the dark roast and cream. "Thanks for making the coffee, Beth. And thanks for staying over. You may never take me to a place where they serve margaritas when I'm upset again. Deal?"

"Deal," Beth said. "I thought we weren't talking."

"What time is it?" Kathryn asked as she sat at the breakfast table and looked out at the pool, trying to bring her eyes into focus.

"It's eleven-thirty."

"What?" Kathryn looked at the clock on the microwave. "You're kidding me?"

"Nope. You needed to sleep." Beth grabbed a glass and the bottle of mango juice from the refrigerator and walked to the table. "Want some?"

"No, thanks. I'll just have my coffee." Kathryn pulled out the chair for Beth.

Beth slid into the seat and poured the juice into her glass. "What time will the boys be here?"

"Ian said around lunch when I talked to him on the phone yesterday." Kathryn took another sip of her coffee. "He called yesterday afternoon while you were in the shop to check on me. Always trying to take care of me."

"He's amazing. I can't believe he's graduating," Beth said.

"I know. An anthropologist."

Beth ran her finger around the rim of the crystal glass trying to make it sing. "So what does an anthropologist do exactly?"

"I'm not really sure. I think, goes to graduate school." They both laughed.

Kathryn grabbed her head and took another sip of coffee.

"What time are we going to Dad's in the morning?" Beth asked.

"Maybe leave around ten. Are you sure you can take the day off?" Kathryn asked.

"Yes. This is the advantage of being the owner of a business. Anyway, Mrs. P.'s niece is great and promised to come to work every day this week so I could…" Beth stopped.

"So you could babysit me?" Kathryn smiled.

"No. So I could *be* with you." Beth stood and walked to the refrigerator. "Are you hungry? Bacon and eggs maybe, or an English muffin?"

She opened the refrigerator and looked in the egg rack just inside the door. "Okay, so how about bacon and an English muffin?"

"Thanks, but I don't think I can eat anything just yet. I'm going to shower and get dressed. I'll bring you my cell phone in case the boys call while I'm in the bathroom." Kathryn stood and walked to the sink. She rinsed out her mug and loaded it in the dishwasher, moaning again as she stooped to set the mug on the rack.

Beth grabbed the latest edition of *National Geographic* sitting on the coffee table in the living room and walked out to the patio to sit in the shade by the pool. Kathryn brought her the phone and retreated to the bathroom for a long hot shower. She turned on the water and undressed. She brushed through her hair and thought all in all it had been a quiet first morning of her newfound freedom. Quiet, except for the occasional pounding in her head when she moved too quickly. Maybe she could do this after all, this life after…

The boys arrived in time for lunch, and as Ian promised, they all went to a nearby deli to eat. They spoke very little about the court hearing. Kathryn told them it went as it should have and the divorce was final.

"Your mom was awesome. Very poised. Very brave," Beth said.

"I'm sorry…" Ian paused. "Well, I'm just sorry, that's all."

"Me too," Sean said.

And that was the end of it. Kathryn steered the conversation toward going to their grandfather's house the next morning and celebrating his birthday. She said she had a surprise, but they'd have to wait till tomorrow to hear about it. After lunch, they returned to the house and relaxed around the pool the remainder of the day. Kathryn was glad to be surrounded by family. Her heart felt lighter.

Kathryn, Beth, and the boys drove the hour to her father's house in Splendora, a small town just north of Houston. When they arrived, Thomas answered the door in his grilling apron and welcomed them in.

"I've steaks on the grill. Come on inside. Settle yourselves in, I've gotta run out back and check on them," he said.

Everyone wished him a happy birthday, and there were big hugs all around. Beth followed her dad to the deck, and the boys went to the den and turned on the television. Kathryn climbed the stairs and walked into her old bedroom. Maybe she could move back home. Maybe just for a few months. What forty-eight-year-old woman moves back in with her father? The answer to that question made her nauseous. She would be *that* woman. People would talk about John living in London with his young intern and Kathryn living with her dad. She sat down at her old desk. All the furniture was painted an antiqued off-white. She pulled the chain on the metal lamp that sat atop her desk to see if it still worked. It did. The light shone dully through the beige- and green-striped shade. She ran her fingers along the tassels that hung along the bottom. The flowered quilt from her high school days still covered her bed.

Her mind drifted to her home in Houston—to her bedroom there. The one she used to share with John. She loved the furniture. They'd bought it early in their marriage on a trip to Asia. The heavy Burmese teak bed was covered with green silk bedding. A Korean chest made of rosewood and inlaid with mother of pearl held her clothes. John's giant chest of drawers was heavily carved with dragons.

The bed, along with all her other furniture, would soon be stored in a temperature-controlled room, waiting its fate. Even now, as she thought about their bed, she saw Courtney wrapped in John's arms. And Kathryn wondered, what do people do with all their—stuff? Memories of John were attached to everything in that house. He traveled often during their marriage, so the empty house seemed normal enough. And even though it had been nine months since he'd left, she still found herself expecting him back home, like he'd only been away on a long trip.

Kathryn's head began to pound around the temples as it always did when she thought about John. When would this end? She took a mental tour of her home in Houston, room by room, deciding what she would keep, what she would sell. John had taken a few pieces that belonged to his family. They were at his mother's house. With the brownstone in London fully furnished, he'd left with only his personal belongings. *So what will I do with all my things?* She pictured her Asian flavored bedroom in a Scottish stone manor. Doesn't quite work. She laughed and shook her head. *Come on now, Kathryn. You can do this. You're going to be just fine.* She could hear Beth's voice in her head. She loved Beth.

"Kathryn." Her father's voice carried up to her second-floor room.

She stepped out into the hall and answered. "Coming, Dad."

The smell of grilled steak and roasted potatoes wafted up the staircase. Even though it was his birthday, he'd insisted on cooking. He loved to grill, and no one could prepare a steak quite like he could. These were *his* words.

The dining table was set and as she walked into the kitchen, her father was filling five tall glasses with sweetened ice tea. Beth poured the croutons onto the salad and carried it to the table in the next room.

"Here, take these into the dining room, and I'll bring our plates," Thomas said.

"The dining room?" Her eyebrow lifted.

"Yeah, I thought we'd live it up today. It *is* my birthday."

Beth called the boys from the den, where they were busy playing Halo. A minute later they were seated at the table, anxious to dig into the large steaks covering their plates.

"These look amazing, Granddad," Sean said.

"Thank you, sir. Let me know if they need to be grilled a little longer."

"No such thing," Sean said.

"I'm sure they're all perfect, Dad. Thanks for cooking for all of us," Kathryn said.

"No problem. I get tired of cooking just for myself, so this was a treat. You sure you don't want to stay the night? There's plenty of room for all of you."

"We didn't come prepared for that. It's just an hour back into the city anyway," Kathryn said.

"So, Ian," Thomas said, "your big day is coming up and you'll be graduated. What are your plans for the future?"

Ian began to explain about the backpacking trip he and Sean would be taking, and then there would be graduate school. Conversation continued around school. Halfway through her steak, Kathryn noticed her father staring across the table at her.

"What is it?" she asked.

"I was just thinking. Only yesterday you were sitting there in braces and a ponytail complaining about Richard Newsome calling again to ask you out."

"Richard Newsome." Kathryn dropped her fork to her plate and laughed. "Good Lord, I haven't thought about him since high school."

"And rightly so. I just remember how put out you were with your mother when she announced at the dinner table that she'd accepted his invitation to the school dance *for* you. And what a nice boy he was. And how pretty you'd look in your new chiffon dress she'd bought at Hampton's Department Store."

"What was she thinking?" Kathryn cut another piece of steak and dipped it in sauce. "He was..." She looked at her father. "Well, let's just say I had to fight my way out of the car that night when he brought me home from the dance."

"Stop talking. Stop talking," Sean said, holding his left ear with one hand and taking a very large bite of steak with the other.

"We had no idea," Thomas said.

"No one did." Kathryn took a sip of tea.

"He seemed like such a nice guy," Thomas said and cut a piece of steak.

"Is no one listening to me?" Sean asked.

"Kathryn, you know Peggy meant well. You look so much like her. If she'd lived to be your age..." Thomas cleared his throat.

"If only." Kathryn took another bite of steak.

"We had some great times when you were young." He continued to stare across the table with a faint smile.

Kathryn looked up at him and thought how old he suddenly looked. "We did have a lot of fun together, Dad."

"You were the only eight-year-old girl, or boy for that matter, in Splendora who could hit the target with a long bow from fifty feet." He laughed. "The bow was as tall as you were."

"And you had to help me hold it and pull back the string." Kathryn leaned back in her chair and smiled.

"Yes, but you took aim and released the arrow all on your own. Which reminds me…ole Charlie Franklin passed away just last spring." Thomas took a quick sip of his iced tea.

"Charlie, how old was he? You know, I thought he was an old man when we used to go to his shooting range."

"The paper said he was ninety-seven when he died."

"Ninety-seven, really?" Kathryn forked several potatoes. "So, whatever happened to your bow?"

Beth raised her hand.

"It's okay, Aunt Beth. You can speak. We're not in school," Ian said.

"I'm not asking permission to speak, I'm saying I have the bow."

Kathryn cocked her head and raised her eyebrows. "You have it? What are you doing with Dad's bow?"

"I thought about joining a bow club. You know, competing maybe," Beth said.

"Competing?" Kathryn asked. "I didn't know you could shoot?"

"Oh yeah," Thomas said. "Beth's a fine marksman."

"Markswoman, Granddad." Sean looked at Beth and smiled, shrugging his shoulders, in a "you're welcome" gesture.

"Anyway,"—Thomas looked at Kathryn—"you know your sister. She collects things, and one day she decided to collect my bow and quiver of arrows." He took a big bite of steak and mumbled, "Does that bother you?"

"No," Kathryn said. "I'm just surprised that's all."

Thomas studied Kathryn's mood for a moment. "Would you have liked to have it?"

"Hey," Beth protested.

"No, no," Kathryn said. "I haven't really thought about it in years."

"You kind of gave it up once you got to high school for a volleyball," he said.

"Yeah, well, there wasn't an archery team at school, and I had to do something. So instead of shooting arrows at a target, I shot a hard rubber ball into the faces of my opponents across the front row of the court." Kathryn shifted in her chair. "It was my anger management tool."

"Does anyone else at the table feel like this is a two man—person—conversation?" Sean asked.

"Those were difficult years. Your mom lived in her own world most of the time…" Thomas exhaled a long sigh and leaned forward. "I'm sorry, Kate."

"It's okay, Dad. Long forgotten." Kathryn lied. She finished the last of her steak and potatoes and moved her chair back to stand.

"Kate." Her father paused.

"What is it, Dad?"

"I'm sorry for all you're going through with John. But I'm enjoying having you all here with me today. I didn't realize how lonely I've been since Beth left home."

"Dad, that's been years," Beth said.

"I know. I'm just sayin' I'm glad to have you all here. And, Kate, you're welcome to stay here if you need to."

"Hmm." Kathryn stood, grabbed her dishes, and walked around to her father. She gave him a quick kiss on his balding head and picked up his dishes. “Thanks, Dad. But there’s something I’ve been meaning to talk to you all about, and I think over dessert is the perfect time.”

Ian and Sean stood and cleared the rest of the table. “We’ll help get dessert,” Ian said.

Kathryn picked up the tray of brownies, then pulled the Blue Bell ice cream container from the freezer and carried them back into the dining room. The boys brought the bowls and spoons and sat back down at the table.

“Dinner was great, Granddad,” Ian said.

“Yes,” everyone else said in unison.

Kathryn stuck a single candle in her father’s brownie and lit it. They all sang “Happy Birthday” to him, and he blew out the candle.

“Thank you all,” Thomas said and took a bite.

Beth helped Kathryn serve up everyone else, and there was a long moment of “ooing” and “ahhing” over the dessert.

“So, what’s up, Mom?” Sean asked.

Kathryn set down her spoon and put both elbows on the table. “Okay, so I’ve been researching our ancestors lately. Actually, Mom’s ancestors, and I’ve made an amazing discovery.”

“That’s cool,” Ian said.

“You history dweeb,” Sean said to Ian.

“No, Sean. I’m an anthropologist.” Ian feigned a bow.

“Isn’t there a vaccination for that?” Sean laughed.

Ian punched his shoulder. “Shush. Mom is trying to tell us something.”

“Oh, was I talking?” Kathryn asked.

Beth finished her last bite of ice cream and brownie and dropped the spoon into the glass bowl. “All right, come on, Kathryn. Tell them.”

Kathryn sat up straight. “We are MacDonalds from the Isle of Skye. Isn’t that cool?”

"That is cool," Sean said. "Now, where's the Isle of Skye?"

"Are you kidding me?" Ian asked, punching his shoulder again.

"Hey, you're going to bruise my delicate skin if you keep that up, bro. And yes, I'm kidding. Skye…Scotland. See I was listening in geography class." Sean pointed to Kathryn's half-empty bowl. "Are you going to finish that?"

"Yes," Kathryn said. "Anyway, our ancestors came over in the 1700s."

"Go ahead, Kathryn. Tell them our ancestor's name," Beth said, smiling.

"Ranald, his name was Ranald," Kathryn said.

There was a moment of silence, then laughter broke out around the table.

"Ronald…MacDonald? Really?" Ian asked.

"You spell it with an 'a' not an 'o'." Kathryn took a quick bite of brownie.

"Oh, well that makes it all different," Sean said.

"You boys are just being mean now. Kate, I think that's fascinating," Thomas said.

"Thanks, Dad. Also, I discovered that most of Mom's ancestors from the 1700s were Scots. They were all septs of the MacDonald clan. Unruly clans it seems, so they were forced to emigrate to the Americas to get out of the king's hair." Kathryn looked directly at Ian and Sean. "Interesting, don't you think?"

"What's a sept?" Sean asked.

"Septs are a separate group of people, like a smaller clan, that are actually a part of a bigger clan like the MacDonalds," Ian said.

"You anthropologist, you. Learned that in school, did you?" Sean laughed.

"No, History Channel."

"Oh, cool."

Kathryn took her last bite of dessert. "And if that's not exciting enough, we have great-great grandmothers who were Cherokee and Chickasaw."

"This explains your skill with the long bow, Mom," Ian said.

"This explains a lot of things, Ian," Kathryn said. "And that is why, the week following your graduation, after I send you two off on your European backpacking trip, I'm going to the Isle of Skye."

"What?" Ian, Sean, and Thomas all asked in unison.

"Isn't that fantastic?" Beth asked. She stood and cleared the dessert bowls, carrying them into the kitchen.

"Wow," Ian said. "That's so cool."

"Yeah, I think it's awesome, Mom," Sean said.

"You deserve it, Kate," her father said, reaching to pat her hand.

Kathryn stood and walked to the kitchen. "Dad, you relax. Beth and I will clean up."

The three men retired to the den. Ian and Sean continued their game of Halo, while their grandfather read the paper. Kathryn and Beth laughed as they cleaned the kitchen together, replaying the dinner conversation.

After they finished in the kitchen, Beth joined the boys, grabbing a third controller. Thomas returned to the kitchen looking for Kathryn. She was drying up the last pan and putting it away.

He walked to an antique buffet in the corner and pulled a tin box from off the shelf. He set it on the kitchen table, pulled out a chair, and sat down.

"Kate, can you stop cleaning for a few minutes and sit with me? I have something I'd like to talk to you about."

She looked at her father and then at the box. She dried her hands and sat down across from him. "Last pan. What's up, Dad?"

He opened the box and moved it in front of her. "Do you know what these are?"

She looked into the box. "Is this a trick question?"

"No."

"Buttons. A lot of buttons," she said.

He reached into the box and pulled out a small pink button. "So, you don't remember anything about these buttons?"

"If you mean Mom's aversion to them, yes, I remember that."

He rubbed the top of his head, as was his habit when he was nervous. "Is there any coffee made?"

Kathryn stood and walked to the French press. "Yes, Dad. I'll get you a cup."

"Thanks." Her father breathed out with a sigh, a sigh that had been waiting to be released for decades.

Kathryn sat down and slid her father's coffee and a spoon toward him. "Okay, Dad. What's wrong?"

He grabbed the sugar bowl, dropped a spoonful into his coffee, then slowly stirred. "Kate, do you remember when you were young you never wore clothes with buttons? Always, zippers, or Velcro."

Kathryn thought for a moment. "Oh my gosh, yes. Mom and I had huge arguments about it when I got to middle school. By high school, she gave up trying. I always felt a little guilty about it, but who doesn't get to wear buttons on your clothes when you're a teenager? I know it all had to do with Tommy, but you guys never talked about it. Even now, I don't know why."

"I think I'm ready to talk about it. It's time." He set his right elbow on the table and rested his chin in his hand. "When you were five, your little brother, Thomas, Junior, swallowed a large fabric-covered button, and it lodged in his throat. Your mom was home alone with the two of you, and she slapped him on the back and did all she could, but it would not dislodge. She called me at work hysterical, and I told her to put you both in the car and drive to the hospital, I'd meet her there. By the time she got to the hospital it was too late, and he…"

Even now, thought Kathryn, after so many years, her father hurt from the death of his only son, his tiny namesake. He couldn't complete the sentence.

"I knew it was tragic. I just didn't know..." Kathryn paused.

"Anyway, your mother—she never fully recovered from it. And what mother could. But she developed a phobia to buttons. So, she tried never to buy you girls anything with buttons." He pulled several small buttons from the tin box. "If she did, she instantly removed the buttons and replaced them with snaps. She also took every button off every dress, jacket—anything she owned. This is her box of buttons."

"What about *your* clothes?" Kathryn asked.

"I refused to let her exercise her phobia on my clothing. It was always a point of contention between us. You were young and didn't pay attention, I imagine."

He stood and patted Kathryn on the top of the head, like she was eight again. "I just thought this might help you better understand your mother." He walked toward the living room.

"What brought this up? Am I asking questions about Mom right now?"

He stopped and turned. "No, Kate. She really loved you so very much. She loved all of us as best she could. I just thought you should know. That's all." He returned to the den and his newspaper. The conversation was over.

Kathryn sat in her father's kitchen and filled the table with rows and rows of buttons from her mother's tin box of terrors. When the final button lay in the final row, memories washed over Kathryn like a rogue ocean wave, toppling her already fragile world—and she wept like a little girl.

The next two weeks were filled with Kathryn securing a realtor to sell her house—packing, sorting, and storing or selling all her earthly belongings. And then there was Ian's graduation. Courtney chose not to come, which relieved a lot of potential stress. Beth whispered

"*Braveheart*" when John first walked into the reception, and Kathryn managed to treat John with a coolness that seemed to unnerve him. Ian graduated with honors, and the boys were soon off on their backpacking trip. The three days after their departure were filled with shopping with Beth, and hours of packing for her trip. The day finally arrived for Kathryn's flight. Thomas and Beth drove her to the airport. Her need to escape and hope of finding the stone manor and her ancestors had overcome her fear of flying, or so she hoped. Beth handed her a Sudoku book to distract her, in case of turbulence, real or imagined. And their father pulled a tin box from a small paper bag.

"I want you to take this with you."

"Why?" Kathryn took the box.

"You'll know what to do with it when the time is right." And with that he gave Kathryn a father-size hug, one he hoped would last her through whatever journey lay ahead.

So, with tin box and laptop in hand, wearing her newly cleaned plaid skirt, Kathryn boarded a plane for the "Misty Isles."

9

A Prince and a Promise
Summer – 1743 Isle of Skye

After a restless night's sleep, Mairi was up early to meet the sunrise. She listened to the stillness of the house in her brothers' absence. They were off on clan business with her father, William. *Here I sit,* she thought, *with the old folks tendin' whatever there be to tend.* After a small meal of trout and leek broth, she grabbed her bow and quiver and headed off to the Fairy Glen with the sheep.

Her mother's presence was very strong that morning in the glen. Mairi had once asked her grandmother how she found the Fairy Glen after the massacre. After a long silence, her grandmother said she was destined to birth Anne in that special place.

It was Mairi's grandfather, Hugh, who found Margaret lying unconscious by the pristine stream with newborn Anne wrapped in a piece of what little remained of her nightgown. He picked them up and took them home to his cottage nearby. A female presence had not graced Hugh's home since the death of his wife six years earlier. She had died giving birth to the youngest of his seven sons, William. Hugh took Margaret for his wife and raised Anne as his own daughter. Her grandmother claimed, were it not for some mystical presence, they would have died in the glen. She always believed God sent Hugh to find them. It was their destiny.

Although William was only six, he loved Anne from the moment he saw her lying in her willow crib. On her eighteenth birthday, they married. It saddened Mairi that she never knew her mother. She must have known the mysteries the Fairy Glen kept hidden from normal folk. Mairi wished that her mother could have braided her hair just once with the bluebells that bloomed in the summer. This shared grief bound her to her father like the willow branches woven together for her crib.

Her father always said Anne was the most beautiful woman he had ever seen, with long auburn hair and eyes the color of the stream beside which she was born. They were married seven years before Ranald, their first son was born. Then every two years for the next six she delivered a son: Hugh was second, Donald third, and finally, James. Four years later Mairi was born. Finally a daughter, but Anne had fallen ill just before Mairi was born and was too weak to live beyond the delivery. Mairi had always thought it a cruel joke to give a woman four sons to love and raise, and then when she was finally given a daughter, Fate cut the string that held her life in the balance.

As the skylarks sang, a gentle breeze carried the sweet aroma of the rowan blossoms through the glen. Mairi drew an arrow from her quiver, took aim at a nearby mountain ash, and let the arrow fly. It hit the trunk dead center, startling a flock of ravens resting in the branches. The sound of the rustling leaves set in motion by the flapping wings cascaded across the glen, swishing and swooshing like the water breaking across Bride's Veil waterfall in spring.

Mairi sang a song she had heard that very morning while walking through the glen. She had been given many songs in the Fairy Glen. However, this one was different. This one spoke of love's first kiss. At fifteen, she had often pondered such things. She imagined a pirate prince invading the glen and carrying her away across the sea to exotic lands of silk and spice.

Mairi raised her bow and aimed with a second arrow but was startled by a noise behind her. With bow and arrow drawn, she swung around and saw a young man on a white horse just across the stream. She felt a strange flutter in her chest.

The young man held up his hands and said, "So, you draw me in with your song, and then I am to be your prey. I gladly surrender; I am your humble prisoner."

Mairi smiled, let down the bow, and lowered it to her side. Her cheeks turned as red as her lips.

The young man, who appeared a bit older than her fifteen years, slid off his horse and let it graze nearby. He leapt across the stream and came near Mairi.

"Hello. My name is Alexander, Alexander MacDonald. By what name are you called?"

Mairi looked into his face and thought he was the handsomest boy she had ever seen. She imagined he must be kin of the Lord of the Isles himself. And *he,* riding up on that beautiful white steed. *Haven't I dreamed this very thing.*

She shuffled her feet and ran her fingers through her hair, "My name is Mairi MacDonald. I live just over the glen there. Why is it I know you not? I know all my kin. You're not from here then?"

"No, I'm from Glen Rowan," Alexander said, pointing east. "I was restless; I took off ridin'." He frowned and rested his right hand in his sash, fitted loosely around his waist. "You see, my brothers are all off fightin' on the mainland. I've been left to tend the home place and my mom and sisters. I told my father I was ready to go with the others, but he wouldn't hear of it."

"Off fightin'," Mairi said. She looked away toward her home. "My father told me they were off on clan business."

"Well, I guess you could say tis clan business. There were some cattle thievin' charges raised against the MacDonalds in Glencoe, and a war was stirrin'. Anyway, why should a wee lass like yourself care about what they are doin'?"

Mairi held up her bow and quiver and said, "I'm tired of tendin' sheep. I'm as good a shot as any of my brothers."

Alexander leaned toward Mairi and brushed her hair back from her eyes. "I thought I couldn't take another moment of womenfolk, but I'm guessin' I was wrong now."

They smiled and then laughed, sending echoes through the glen. Sitting by the stream, Mairi and Alexander spent most of the day talking of their families and their passion for adventure, which they were sure could never be found this side of the mainland. A wren sat in a rowan tree nearby and watched.

"You know, I thought it was a fairy song that lured me into the glen," Alexander said.

"It just might have been that indeed," Mairi said. "They do live here, you know."

Alexander laughed.

"You're laughin' at me, are you? So you don't believe in fairies then?"

"I'm sorry. I didn't know you were bein' serious. My mum believes in the devilish creatures fair enough." Alexander picked up a small stone and threw it across the stream and into the wee loch.

Mairi smiled.

"I was just thinkin' how you've obviously never spoken with a man who's had an encounter with a *leanan sidhe*. I've heard it's quite unforgettable." Mairi plucked a bluebell from the grass next to her.

"What's a *leanan sidhe*?"

"Why, a fairy mistress, of course. Don't tell me you've never heard of them?" Mairi turned facing Alexander. "Didn't your mother or grandmother…or someone tell you stories about the *leanan sidhe*?"

"I'm afraid my upbringin' has not been as…enlightenin' as yours, Mairi."

She raised the flower to her nose and gasped.

"What's wrong? Is there a bee in it?" Alexander asked and leaned closer to her.

"I took this flower. I wasn't thinkin'. Oh, this is awful." Mairi looked around the glen.

"I don't understand. It's only a flower. No one will mind."

"This, Alexander, is the Fairy Glen. It's named that because it belongs to them. And everyone who knows anythin' about fairies knows you must never take somethin' that's theirs without permission." Mairi looked at Alexander and her face softened. "You think I'm crazy."

"Carried away by the fairies, I'd say." Alexander smiled back and touched the tip of her nose. "But I don't mind it, Mairi. You're the most interestin' girl I've ever met. And you're the only girl I've met who can truly shoot with a bow."

"And you, Alexander, are the first boy I've met with a white horse."

He looked at the sun setting low in the sky. "I think it's gettin' late. I've a long ride back to the manor. Can we meet again?" he asked.

"Yes, I'd like that very much."

"So it doesn't worry you to meet me here alone? Without an escort?" Alexander asked, as he stood and held out his hand for Mairi.

"Oh, but we're never alone here." She took his hand and smiled.

Alexander and Mairi met often in the Fairy Glen, and their friendship grew into a deep love, their two souls bound together, like intertwining vines of the primrose, by the magic of the glen. In the early months of their love affair, Alexander pledged himself to Mairi until their last breaths. This was not a pledge given lightly, but a vow made with every intention of it being kept. Only the glen knew it was never to be.

10

Homecoming

Kathryn boarded the plane and found her place. She buckled her seat belt, then looked at the vacant seat next to hers and hoped her traveling neighbor would be friendly. She closed her eyes, leaned back against the headrest, and tried to remember the reassuring faces of her father and Beth. Her heart was racing, and her throat tightened. Kathryn opened her eyes and took a deep breath. *One…two…three.* Then a slow exhale. *One…two…three…four.* She repeated this several more times and began to relax just a little.

A man in an Italian suit sat down next to her and smiled. "Hello. You traveling alone?" he asked.

Were she not so panicked, she might have noticed his perfect white teeth or the way his hair had a hint of gray around the temples. Kathryn cleared her throat and tried to appear calm. "Yes, I'm on my way to Scotland."

"What takes you there? Business?"

"No, not exactly. I'm just doing some research." She reached out a shaky hand. "My name is Kathryn."

"My name is Charles." He shook her hand firmly.

Oh no, what was I thinking? Do strangers exchange names on an airplane? Does he think I'm too forward? He's still staring. Say something, Kathryn. Something—smart.

"I'm sorry. Was that awkward exchanging names like that? I mean, I don't mean anything by it. I'm from Texas, you know. Friendly and all. Really, I always introduce myself to strangers." *Stop, stop now before he asks to get off the plane.*

The cabin steward came by and took Charles's coat and offered them a glass of champagne. Kathryn declined the offer, but Charles took another look at her and told the steward to bring them both a glass. Before she could open her mouth to protest, the steward was gone.

"You seem a bit nervous. A glass of champagne is just what you need." He buckled his seat belt and turned back toward Kathryn. "Have you flown much?"

"Yes, just not alone in a very long time. Does it show?"

"Well, maybe a just a little. Your knuckles are white from the tight grip you have on the armrests. And you're just a little bit pale."

A bit pale. Oh no, what if I pass out? Kathryn released her grip and rubbed her hands. "I admit, I am nervous." She took a deep breath. "You're not from Houston, are you?"

"No, Los Angeles. I was here on business," Charles said. "And you?"

"I'm from Houston. Although I just put my house on the market. Not sure where I'm going to be living," Kathryn said.

The steward brought their champagne. Kathryn took her glass and turned to look out the window. Over the intercom a voice gave safety instructions as the plane backed away from the terminal.

Charles reached over and gently touched Kathryn's arm. She turned toward him, and he held up his glass. "Here's to an uneventful trip. Cheers."

She raised her glass. "Here, here. Cheers."

"You said you were going to Scotland to do some research?"

"Yes," Kathryn said, sipping her champagne.

"Do you mind if I ask what kind?"

"No, I don't mind. I'm researching my ancestors. They're from the Isle of Skye. I'm just not sure where exactly, or why they immigrated to America." Kathryn took another sip of champagne and brushed a wrinkle from her skirt. "Sounds kind of lame, doesn't it?"

"No, I think it sounds fascinating. I don't know the first thing about my ancestors. I haven't really thought much about it. But hearing you talk about yours...well, I'd like to know more about my own." Charles cleared his throat and shifted in his seat. "So, do you have a family?"

"Are you asking if I'm married?"

Charles smiled. "Hmm, right to the point. I like that."

Kathryn blushed. "Oh Lord, I'm sorry. I'm afraid I haven't had a conversation with a man in a very long time."

"You only talk to women?" Charles asked.

Kathryn pointed to Charles and shook her head. "See I'm terrible at this. What I meant to say is...I'm recently divorced. I have two sons in college. Well, one just graduated, and they're on a backpacking trip around Europe. I thought this would be a good time to take a trip, for myself."

"I'm sorry about your divorce. I've been there myself. And just for the record, I've enjoyed our conversation so far." Charles took the last drink of his champagne.

"Thanks," Kathryn said. "So what takes you to London?"

"I'm meeting a friend there." Charles became quiet.

"For vacation then?" Kathryn asked, and she finished her champagne.

"Yes. She lives in London?"

"Oh that's nice."

Just then, the pilot came over the speakers and announced they had been cleared for takeoff and were next on the runway. Kathryn grabbed the armrest and tried to take a deep breath, but her throat was too tight. Her head began to spin, and panic set in. She leaned forward and grabbed a book from her bag she'd stored under the seat in front of her.

"And by the way, thank you for talking to me. I know you were just trying to distract me so I wouldn't be so freaked out. It helped. Well, that and the champagne."

"You're welcome, Kathryn. If you feel like talking again, I'm right here." Charles smiled and began looking through the movie options on his TV screen.

After takeoff the plane leveled off, and the engines settled into a steady hum. Kathryn looked out the window and gasped quietly. Charles looked over, and she smiled, pointing to the sea of clouds outside the window. He shrugged his shoulders and nodded. Obviously, not so impressed with the view. Kathryn looked back out the window and felt her anxiety ease. They had just broken through the clouds, the darkness gone. Nothing but blue sky above and what looked like a sea of cotton below. It was beautiful.

Time passed and the darkness returned, but this time from the sun setting and night approaching as they flew east toward London. Dinner had been served and the cabin was quiet. Kathryn was unable to sleep, but did drink a glass of red wine and felt fairly calm. She'd been reading the novel Beth had given her to pass the time, *Pride and Prejudice*. Beth said Jane would make for a great companion on the flight.

Just as Mr. Darcy was telling Louisa that Elizabeth Bennet's dirty petticoat had quite escaped his notice, a sudden loud noise broke over the hum of the plane's engine, accompanied by a short shaking of the plane itself. All the sleeping passengers stirred, and several stewards and attendants hustled to the front of the plane.

Kathryn's heart once again raced, and she put down Mr. Darcy and Elizabeth Bennet.

Charles had been watching a movie and noticed her panic. "So how's the book?"

"It's wonderful. *Pride and Prejudice*. Have you read it?"

"No, I haven't," he said.

Suddenly, an announcement from the pilot interrupted their conversation. "This is the captain speaking. I guess everyone heard the loud noise a few moments ago—yeah, well, we are not really sure what it was." Long pause. "We think it was probably just luggage shifting in the hull of the aircraft. But we have called ahead and are asking for directions on what we should do next. Please remain calm. The aircraft appears to be perfectly fine. No problems. We will let you know if anything new arises. Try and get some sleep, we're about four hours from London. Thank you."

The first class steward appeared. Kathryn ordered another glass of wine, and Charles ordered a gin and tonic.

"So, are you okay?" Charles asked.

"I think so," Kathryn said. "Thanks."

The remainder of the flight was uneventful, and after her second glass of wine, Kathryn relaxed and went back to reading. A light breakfast was served an hour before they were scheduled to land, just as Kathryn was nearing the final chapter of the book. Finally, the plane touched down and taxied to the gate. Kathryn and Charles wished each other a great onward journey as they gathered their belongings and disembarked the plane.

After a two-hour layover at Heathrow Airport in London, Kathryn boarded her final leg of the flight to Scotland. Her anxiety level was not quite so high on the second takeoff. She had decided it was due to the nearness of Scotland and the possibility of finding the stone manor of her dream. Though upon further reflection, she knew she could not rule out the two glasses of wine.

After landing in Glasgow, Kathryn rented a lovely silver Volvo and headed north for the Isle of Skye. With each passing mile, she felt the return of freedom and confidence she had allowed time to steal. Guilty thoughts over what she should have done differently in her marriage fled into the wild Scottish landscape.

She could hear Beth's voice in her head encouraging her to throw herself into this Highland adventure like a pig running into a mud hole. Beth told her to wallow around in it. Let herself be covered in it from head to tail, and who cared what people back home might think or say. Kathryn told Beth that a lovely bluebird in a birdbath might have been a more appealing metaphor, but she got the point.

If only Ian and Sean could see me now, Kathryn thought, driving through the narrow roads, twisting and turning along the lochs and through the glens—and all this on the wrong side of the road. She used to be so adventurous. When had that Kathryn disappeared?

She looked at the rugged mountains and thought how different they stood in contrast to the lush mountains of Indonesia. Her mind carried her back to a time when life was filled with hope. She smiled as she remembered a visit from her father her last year there…

Steam rose from the wet pavement of the narrow road that led from Jakarta to Bandung. Kathryn breathed in the thick air as her father clutched the roll bar of the green Land Cruiser, his knuckles as pale as the whitewashed buildings that lined the roadside.

"Isn't Indonesia beautiful, Dad?" Kathryn shifted down into second gear as they skidded around another hairpin curve on the narrow road to Bandung. "What's wrong? You look a little nervous."

"I'm fine. You just keep your eyes on the road."

"Doesn't this look just like a *National Geographic* shoot?" Kathryn grabbed the camera from the back. "Here, start taking pictures. It'll take your mind off the road."

"Watch out for that produce truck."

"Wow, they think they own the road. I love this drive from Jakarta. We'll stop just a few miles up the road at a great little restaurant in the middle of a tea plantation."

Kathryn pointed to the mountain peak ahead. "It's the best view in all of Java."

At the restaurant Kathryn ordered two chicken and rice dishes served with a peanut sauce while her dad took pictures from the patio of the restaurant. One roll of film later, he returned to the table.

"You're right, Kathryn. This view is amazing. I wish Beth could have come. We just couldn't afford two tickets right now." Her father took a white cotton handkerchief from his pants pocket and wiped the sweat from his forehead. He sat down at the table and put the camera on the empty seat beside him.

The waiter brought their lunch out to them and quickly left again.

"It's okay. I'll be home in a few months, and she and I will have lots of time together planning the wedding. These last three years have passed so quickly." Kathryn ran her finger across the white linen tablecloth. "I'll really miss my students."

Her father pointed his fork at Kathryn, puffy rice kernels falling to his plate. "Beth has been watching the classified ads in the newspaper. She says the high school is hiring for next fall."

"Beth's dreaming," Kathryn mumbled through a mouthful of *sate*. "John will never agree to live in a small town. We'll be in Houston or London. Prepare yourselves."

Kathryn had met John her second year in Indonesia in a restaurant in Jakarta. She had driven up to the capital to visit friends. Dressed in a black silk business suit, he sat facing her at the next table. Every time she looked in his direction he stared back. By the end of the evening, he introduced himself to Kathryn and her friends. She agreed to meet him the following day for lunch, which turned into dinner. For the next two years, they had a standing date every three months, when John would return on business. Their relationship was filled with romantic dinners in expensive restaurants and train rides through the lush countryside to the southern coast for weekends together. John lavished her with flowers, imported chocolate, and expensive jewelry. Kathryn innocently imagined life would always be this way when she said yes to John's proposal of marriage.

An hour into the drive to Skye, Kathryn saw a road sign: Loch Lomond 2 miles. Just a bit past the village of Luss, she found a place to pull off to the right of the road. The deep blue loch stretched as far as she could see. As she made her way down to the water she heard a bagpipe playing the haunting Highland air, "On the Bonnie, Bonnie Banks of Loch Lomond." Standing along the shoreline was a man dressed in full Highland gear, kilt, bagpipe and all. Kathryn looked around. They were alone. She'd seen the sign to the Thistle Bagpipe Works and wondered if he was advertising it. She listened, enchanted by the cry of the pipes.

A tale of love and war made famous through song drifted through her thoughts. Two Scottish prisoners, held by the English in Carlisle on the border of Scotland and England, had fought on the side of Bonnie Prince Charlie at Culloden and were wounded and captured. One was to be released, and the other executed in the same hour, not an uncommon practice in those days. The words of the doomed young Highlander, Donald MacDonald became immortalized in verse.

Kathryn closed her eyes and imagined the ghost of the young prisoner returning to his true love in this very place. She soon found herself singing, her voice carrying across the loch stretched out before her.

O' ye'll take the high road
and I'll take the low road,

and I'll be in Scotland afore ye,
but me and my true love will never meet again,
on the bonnie, bonnie banks o' loch Lomond.

Quiet fell over the loch as Kathryn realized the piper had stopped. As she opened her eyes and turned toward him, he had disappeared along with his music. Kathryn walked quietly back to the car. In a country full of legend and lore, where tall tales were mixed with history, how was one to know what was real and what was imaginary? She pulled out the map she had bought at the market on her way out of Glasgow. *What else am I to find on this drive north? Yes.* An hour and a half farther up the road she'd be at Glencoe. More history, more tragedy, more adventure.

Hunger overpowered Kathryn as she reached the immense landscape that was Glencoe. She pulled into a gravel carpark and grabbed the bag of food and the MacDonald tartan she'd bought at the shop in the airport. Kathryn walked toward a nearby stream. Skylarks sang to the sound of the water as it broke across the rocks, running through the glen. Clouds had formed, and the smell of rain hung in the air. Kathryn zipped her raincoat as she reached the stream and laid the tartan on the heather-covered ground. She leaned back on her elbows looking across the glen and thought strawberry jam had never tasted so delicious on a slice of bread.

Kathryn felt a sudden sense of sadness as dark clouds rolled down the steep slopes of the mountains into the harsh and untamed landscape of the glen. No phantom bagpipes played, only the faint sound of voices weeping, as a chilly breeze slipped over the mountainside and across the moor.

The cool mist turned to a cold rain. Kathryn pushed the voices away as her thoughts turned to her escape to the Isles. Hope filled her heart and lifted the gloom of the glen.

Kathryn enjoyed the next three hours of her journey toward Skye. The azure blue lochs and the heather-covered glens were breathtaking. The land was rugged and wild, and the smell of salt filled the air, luring Kathryn ever closer to the sea. Only once had she taken off on the wrong side, albeit the right side of the road. This she quickly corrected, and all was well.

As dusk fell, the hills reflected the sunset-colored sky. Kathryn rounded a sharp curve and saw the Skye Bridge stretching across the water like a great sleeping dragon, with the mountains rising up beyond it. She pulled to the side of the road for a moment and sat staring at the majestic view. It was more beautiful and magical than she had imagined. This was going to be a great adventure, indeed. As she crossed Loch Alsh, Kathryn left the mainland of Scotland and entered the Misty Isles.

Tired, but too excited to sleep, she called Alastair MacDonald, the owner of the cottage she'd leased, and asked where she could find dinner before checking in. He recommended the Ardvasar Hotel Restaurant. He told her to take the A851 and drive southwest along the Sleat Peninsula until she reached the small village of Ardvasar. It was only a few miles down the road from the cottage.

As the narrow road wound between the Sound of Sleat and the wooded hillsides, Kathryn noticed the flickering lights of Mallaig across the sound in the eerie twilight that had settled on the island. A mile farther and she found herself in the village of Ardvasar, so small that you could drive completely through it by the time you pronounced its name. Like most buildings on the island, the restaurant and hotel had whitewashed walls and a black roof, with black window frames and shutters. Inside the small restaurant, a cozy feeling from the warm wood walls, floors, and tables greeted her. *How is it possible to feel so at home in a place I've never been before?* Seated at a table looking out over the Sound, she ordered fish and chips and asked for a local beer. When the waitress returned with her drink, Kathryn toasted the air with a smile and took a sip. *Beth would love this place.*

"Your first time to Skye?" the waitress asked.

"Yes. Not my first time to Scotland, though."

"Ah, I beg to differ. You've not been to Scotland if you've not been to the Isles. A taste maybe, but not a full bite." She laughed and said, "*Fàilte.* Welcome to Skye, and how long will you be stayin' with us?"

Kathryn looked around the restaurant filled with strangers and realized she wasn't afraid. Somehow in these foreign surroundings she felt at home. "Indefinitely, I'd say." She introduced herself to the woman who looked to be her peer. "Hello, my name is Kathryn Trent...ah, Silverton." *Another adjustment to make.*

"Hello, Kathryn. My name is Sarah. And what brings you to Skye, if you don't mind me askin'? A bit early for a holiday?"

"Well, I was doing some family research, and I found an ancestor from the Isle of Skye." Taking another drink she continued, "That, and a recent divorce brought me here."

"I'll not ask about the divorce, that'll be your own private matter, but an ancestor from Skye? Really now? What was the name?"

"Ranald MacDonald—" Kathryn began, but was interrupted before she could finish.

"The MacDonalds. Oh my," Sarah said. She folded her hands as if to pray and bowed her head, her red hair falling forward across her freckled face.

"Ah—yeah," Kathryn said, one eyebrow raised. "He was born somewhere on Skye. I came here to find out what part of the island he was from and why he left."

"I wish you good luck with that. You know, the Isle was at one time covered with MacDonalds. They were the Lords of the Isles. Truth be told, they are the heart and soul of all that is Scotland.

'Course I might be just a wee bit biased, eh? Bein' as I'm a *Sgiathanach* myself, a Skyewoman." Sarah smiled at Kathryn. "I'll leave you here to consider your ancestors while I look to your food."

A few minutes later, Kathryn's fish and chips arrived steaming hot. Hunger numbed her sense of etiquette as she devoured her meal. She was too tired to see if anyone else was eating with their hands. With warm grease sliding down her wrists and the smell of smoke and hops in the air, Kathryn thought about Beth again and wished she had come with her.

Sarah returned and asked if she needed another beer. Kathryn told her she'd had her limit and just needed the bill. "Well, I hope you find what you're lookin' for, Kathryn, and I hope you come back to eat often in our place."

"Thanks, I'm sure I will."

"So you're sure you've never been here before?"

"Yes, I'm sure. Why?"

"I don't know. You just look familiar, that's all. Well, do come back."

Kathryn walked to the car and laughed at the inexplicable feeling of connection she had about this place. During the short drive to the cottage she had leased, near the Clan Donald Centre, her excitement gave way to sleep-deprived exhaustion. It had been thirty-six hours since she'd left Houston, and she found herself too tired to even remember why she'd come. She turned off the rock road that led to her cottage and into the driveway. She stepped out of her rented Volvo and drew in a deep breath of the sea air. The cottage sat off the main road and looked out across the Sound. With just enough energy to carry her bag and laptop, Kathryn found the key in the window box just as she had been instructed.

The cottage had two bedrooms with a small kitchen and living room. It was bright and cheerful with whitewashed walls and plenty of windows to bring the beauty outside into full view. A vase full of fresh-cut bluebells and wild garlic blooms sat on the table. Kathryn walked into the bedroom that held a view of the Sound of Sleat and the Sea of the Hebrides, set down her suitcase, and fell onto the bed, traveling clothes and all. A light rain fell as the last hint of twilight slipped behind the barren mountains and into the sea.

As sleep threatened to overtake her she sat up and began rummaging through her suitcase looking for her pajamas and toothbrush. She came across the wooden box Beth had given her and leaned away from the bed to set it on top of the dresser. Her reach was not quite long enough, and the box tumbled to the floor. As it hit, the white stone popped out of place, and a tiny compartment appeared. Kathryn swore under her breath and sprang from the bed, hoping the box hadn't been damaged. As she bent down and gently lifted it from the floor she noticed the white stone was missing, revealing a tiny compartment. She sat down on the edge of the bed and noticed a piece of cloth stuffed into the now open drawer. Kathryn reached in and carefully removed what turned out to be a tiny bag. Inside the bag she found a carved malachite bead hanging from a silver chain. She pushed the small compartment back into place, but it would not hold shut. She looked around until she found the white stone lying on the floor next to the dresser. She picked it up and pushed it back into place. *Genius.* Kathryn tried to remove the stone again, but it was stuck firmly in place. She set down the box and admired the necklace, running her finger across the carved bead. It was a Celtic love knot. The silver chain was tarnished, and the bead appeared to be crudely made, but beautiful all the same.

Kathryn clasped the necklace around her neck and walked to the window. She leaned her forehead against the glass and for a moment thought she saw the faint image of a stone manor rising up across the moor. As the image disappeared, she realized her hand was clutching the necklace. *How long has this been hidden away inside the box? What must have happened to cause someone to hide it there anyway? A hidden love perhaps? Or maybe, a love compromised?*

Kathryn's exhausted mind turned to John. Did he wonder if she was hurting? Was he sorry? Her thoughts drifted to the tiny village of Ardvasar, and a sense of contentment came over her like the feeling that comes from belonging. Somewhere deep inside, Kathryn knew she was at home on Skye, in shadows and mist. Where what *is* looks very much like what once was.

11

Faith or Fairy
Winter – 1745 Isle of Skye

The wind and rain blew across the moor and beat against the cottage where Mairi and her grandmother sat huddled near the peat fire. A pot of porridge hung by a heavy chain over the flames, and hard bread sat on the table near the middle of the room. The small flock of sheep and hens were bedded down in the lean-to attached to the cottage.

Mairi's father had traveled to the next croft hoping for word of the battles taking place on the mainland. Her four brothers were still away fighting for their beloved homeland and for freedom, along with other men and boys of the Isles. The clan chiefs of Skye had refused the prince when he came looking for support against King James, but a number of the men followed later on their own to the mainland; among them were Mairi's brothers.

The harsh landscape dictated life on Skye. Few enjoyed a life of privilege. Mairi had watched her father's countenance take on the darkness of a winter's storm, his complexion weathered like the rocky shores along the North Sea. She knew rejuvenation would only come about with the return of her brothers. And if what they had heard was true, it could be another long winter away.

Mairi looked deep into the flames of the fire and saw her own heart burning with love for Alexander. Snow had fallen twice on the hills since they first met in the Fairy Glen. Mairi smiled as she thought of him. In the midst of the sorrow that surrounded her, he was her hope—her joy—her future. They were bound together heart and soul. They planned to marry as soon as his father and brothers returned from the fighting.

Her grandmother saw her smile, and as with all grandmothers, knew what secret thoughts stirred her soul. "Mairi, what are you thinkin' of, or should I ask whom?"

Mairi drew closer to her grandmother and laid her head in Margaret's lap. "Tell me again about Grandpa findin' you and Mother in the Fairy Glen. You know, I never tire of hearin' that story."

Margaret laughed and stroked Mairi's hair. "Yes, child. I love tellin' it as much as you love hearin' it, I think." Margaret paused and stared into the glowing hearth. "I can't tell you how I found the Fairy Glen except that I was called there. The Maker knew the kind of man your grandfather was and that he was in need of a mother for his children and I, a father for Anne." Margaret picked up the stick that lay next to her and stirred the peat on the fire. Sparks popped and danced up from the burning embers toward the chimney.

"There are those who still believe in the ancient ways, as well as in God."

Mairi raised her head and asked, "And are you one of those, Grandma?"

"Yes, child, I am." Margaret placed her hands gently on Mairi's face. "It is said that when a fairy longs for somethin' they cannot have, it will bring on their death. They look for the place of their birth, or as near it as possible, and there they lie down, enfolded in their own wings, and die."

"It's a good day for tellin' sad stories. But what's this to do with my mother?"

Margaret took the woven tartan and wrapped it around the two of them and continued, "Mairi, I believe the place where your mother was born, beside the stream in the Fairy Glen, was just such a place. You see, it is also said that when a fairy dies they are born into the world of men in that very place and that very season."

Mairi sat up and stared at her grandmother. "What are you sayin'?"

"I'm sayin' I believe a fairy died where your mother was born and her spirit became tied to your mother's."

Mairi's mind drifted away to the glen. Her mother a fairy? Could this be true? Surely it must be if her grandmother believed it to be so.

"What do you think the fairy longed for so strongly that it caused her death?" Mairi asked, moving a length of hair from her face.

"I think as she walked near the glen and saw your father and his brothers playin' there, she began to want a child of her own—a human child. And the longin' was more than she could bear. Fairies are known to die of such a longin'."

The door opened, and the wind blew the vase of dried heather off the table and onto the flagstone floor, where it shattered. Mairi's father walked in with a sad look and weary shoulders. Margaret stood and poured him a cup of hot tea, while Mairi walked to the shattered vase and began picking up the broken shards of clay.

Margaret handed him the tea and helped him off with his wet woolen wrap. "What did you hear, William? Anythin' of the lads?"

William walked to the circle hearth of stone and warmed himself by the fire. "No, nothin'. But I know there will be word soon, and it will be good news. We must have faith, aye, we must have faith." He bent near the fire and looked toward Mairi. "I'm sorry about the vase, dear."

"It's fine, Father," Mairi stood and put the broken pieces in an empty basket that stood by the doorway. "It's only made of earth. It can be replaced."

Margaret poured herself and Mairi a cup of tea, and they sat in silence around the fire. Mairi's scattered thoughts held images of fairies, of men fighting, and of Alexander in the glen. Alexander fought his way to the front of her thoughts. She closed her eyes and held the necklace Alexander had made between her two fingers. She traced the endless knot charm carved into the malachite bead and remembered the pledge he'd made to be hers until their last breath. His tall image stood out in her mind. His eyes, blue as the midsummer sky, smiled at her. She could see his long, wavy hair blowing in the sea breeze, kissed by the sunset, a hint of red surrounded by darkness.

The day Alexander gifted the necklace to her the sun was shining in the glen as she waited for him to come. Her brothers had taken the sheep to another area to graze, and she was free for the whole day. She and Alexander had met once a month on the first *Di Luain*, Monday, once the long winter ended. It was on one such day a year past that Alexander brought a gift for Mairi to the Fairy Glen. He held out a small fabric bag, tied at the top with a red piece of yarn.

"Here, I have somethin' for you."

Mairi stepped forward and took the bag. She smiled and began to untie the yarn. "What is the occasion? My birthday has long passed."

"I know. I'd thought to give it to you then, but I didn't finish it in time. So, what do you think? Do you like it?"

Mairi pulled a small necklace from the bag. On the chain hung a hand carved malachite bead in the form of a love knot. "Oh, Alexander, it's beautiful!"

Alexander took the necklace and fastened it around her neck as she held up her hair. "I made it for you, Mairi. It's my promise to you, that I'll be yours 'till we die."

He kissed her gently on her neck just as she was dropping her hair. They embraced and slowly lay down on the mossy glen floor by the spring. Mairi stopped him before he carried their lovemaking too far.

"Alexander, please wait."

"Wait?" He continued stroking her body. "You and I, we are already wed in the eyes of the glen. No one else matters. We've waited long enough. It's so hard to only see you a day here and a day there. I burn for you, Mairi. You must know that."

Mairi slipped from his gentle grip and sat up. She held the necklace in her hand and smiled. "I accept this as a token of your promise to me, but there'll be no collectin' on such a promise till we stand before our families on my weddin' day. Have you told your family yet, about us?"

Alexander put his hand to his forehead and sighed. "Seas be cursed, Mairi, stand with me now, here in the glen. We'll say our vows, and it'll be all right."

"I'll have no secret weddin', Alexander. You haven't told your family then?"

"No, but I will, and soon, to be sure. You know, Mairi, a man can only take so much of bein' with you and not go crazy. You're my *leanan sidhe*. A fairy mistress, come to tempt me and drive me mad."

"So you believe in them now, do you?" Mairi laughed and kissed him. "I love you, Alexander. So, will you talk to your father or no?"

Alexander ran his fingers through her hair. "Yes, my love. I will talk to my father before the next time we meet, and I'll come for you at your home and not the glen, so that I might speak with your own father as well."

Two weeks later, she was sitting at the table with her family eating a bowl of hot porridge when there came a knock on the door.

Her father opened it, and Alexander stood with a bundle of wildflowers in each hand.

"Good mornin' to you, sir." Alexander bowed slightly. "I've come to speak to Mairi, if I may."

Mairi's father turned and looked at her, whose face was brighter than he'd seen it in days. She stood quickly, but her grandmother gently took her by the wrist and held her in place.

William held out his hand. "My name is William MacDonald, and I am Mairi's father. What business do you have with my child?"

"Child?" Mairi protested.

"Excuse me, sir," Alexander said, the flowers visibly shaking in his hands. "Let me introduce myself. My name is Alexander MacDonald of Glen Rowan."

"Glen Rowan? You're the son of Donald of Glen Rowan?" William asked.

"Aye, I am, and I've come all this way to speak to your daughter, Mairi. If I may?"

Margaret released Mairi's wrist and nodded for her to walk to the door.

"Father, we met in the Fairy Glen while I was tendin' the sheep, two years past."

"Two years past, you say?"

"Aye, and he's come to speak to you today." Mairi couldn't contain the joy she felt, and a broad smile spread across her face.

Alexander handed her a small bouquet of wildflowers and held the other one out to her grandmother. Margaret rose and took the flowers, thanking him. William stepped back and motioned for Alexander to enter the house. Mairi's brothers rose from the table and walked over to extend their hands in greeting.

"So, Master Alexander, how is your father?" William asked.

"My father and brothers have left this very mornin' for the mainland to fight alongside the prince."

William studied the excitement that showed on his son's faces. "My own sons are leavin' this day as well. They'll be joinin' up with your family. And, why is it you're not goin' yourself?"

Alexander's face burned red. "I begged to go, but my father said I was to remain behind to look to the land and the womenfolk."

"This is a wise father, yours. To keep a son back in case—" William stopped short. "It seems my own sons are too old to keep back." William reached for his pipe. "So, Mairi says you wish to speak to me?"

Alexander looked first to Mairi, then to her father. "Aye, I had intended to come askin' for Mairi's hand in marriage."

"Had intended?" Mairi asked.

"Aye, but with my father's mind so predisposed to leavin', I couldn't see clear to speak to him of such things as marryin' just now."

Mairi dropped the flowers onto the table. "And why not?"

"Mairi." William held up his hand. "I agree with your young man. It would be best to wait till they return safely from the fight to speak of such things."

William turned to Alexander and extended his hand. "I know of your father. He is a fair and great leader of our clan. I'll give my consent as soon as you have his blessin'."

Alexander took his hand and shook it hard. "Thank you, sir. May I have your permission to take Mairi for a ride on my horse? 'Tis a fine day outside, and we have things to speak of."

"I would not usually say yes to such a thing before you were betrothed, but under these circumstances, I'm willin' to yield. Take care with her, though. She's my only daughter and the joy of my life."

"I will, sir." Alexander reached his hand out to Mairi. "Shall we go then?"

"Aye, let me get my wrap." She grabbed her tartan and reached for her bow.

"Mairi," Alexander said. "I think you'll not be needin' that today. I'll take care of the both of us."

She was about to protest but saw him look toward her father and brothers and chose to let him keep his honor in front of her family.

"You're right. I'm in your care now."

The young couple left the cottage, and Alexander mounted his white steed first. Mairi jumped up onto the horse and threw one leg over, no ladylike pretense. The fact that it didn't cross her mind to sit sideways on the horse spoke to Alexander of her spirit, wild and innocent at once. He leaned back into Mairi's warm body as she sat straddled on the horse behind him. It was one of the many things that set her apart from any other girl he had ever met. When he looked into her eyes he saw other worlds. Worlds he hoped to explore for the rest of their lives.

Mairi broke the silence as the horse galloped across the moor, heading north toward the sea.

"Where are we going?"

"You'll see soon enough. There's someone I'd like you to meet." Alexander slowed the horse down and looked back at Mairi. "I want you to know, I appreciate what you did back there in front of your menfolk."

"What do you mean?" Mairi asked, feigning innocence.

Alexander smiled. "Aye, you know. Leavin' your bow and sayin' you'd put yourself under my protection. I know if we ever found ourselves in need of protectin', you'd be fightin' alongside me."

"Alongside you?" Mairi asked.

"Aye, it would please me if you'd stand alongside me and not in front."

They laughed, and she held him tight around his waist, leaning her head against his back.

"You know, I was mad when I heard you hadn't told your father, but then, when you asked my father and he agreed, my heart melted straight away." She kissed him gently on the back of his neck. "I've never been so happy."

Alexander flipped his leg over Mairi's head and turned facing her. The horse continued on as if his master always rode toward the back. Alexander gently grabbed Mairi's legs and wrapped them around his waist. He pulled her toward him, and they kissed. The breeze from the sea blew her hair so that it wrapped itself around Alexander's head. They were too heated by their embrace to feel the chill in the air. The sun shone through the occasional clouds, and the skylarks sang from the trees as they passed through the moor, finally coming upon the road that led into the village of Uig. The horse stopped as it stepped onto the dirt road, rutted from wagons that traveled from the crofts.

Mairi pulled back her hair and wrapped her tartan around her head to keep the brisk sea air from piercing her ears. Alexander gave her a quick kiss on the forehead, faced forward, and headed down into the village.

"You've still not told me where we're goin'." Mairi said.

"We'll be there in a few more minutes. Patience, my love."

They passed through the village. Fishermen were sitting along the shore sorting through their catch from the night before, and local women were busy buying food for the day. A young man who looked to be their age sat mending a net. He nodded and smiled as they rode by.

The horse climbed the steep road that led up out of Uig along the barren coast of Skye. Alexander turned down a small path that led to a wild wood inland. It was known as Druid Wood, and most thought it to be dangerous—inhabited by malevolent spirits. The farther into the forest the darker it became. Mairi tightened her grip around his waist and felt her heart race, thrilled at the wildness of the woods. She heard a distant roar ahead. The path began to lighten as the trees thinned toward an opening, and the thunderous noise became louder.

Alexander stopped his horse just short of the opening and jumped off. He reached up to Mairi, and she fell forward into his arms.

"We're here," he said.

"Here where?" Mairi asked.

He laughed. "Patience, Mairi."

"You keep sayin' that. I'm about to burst."

"Now, close your eyes and hold tight to my arm." Alexander walked Mairi slowly to the opening in the trees. His horse followed behind. Mairi felt the sun full on her face as she stepped out of the woods.

"Look, Mairi. We're here."

Mairi squinted as the brightness of the sun flooded her eyes. She lifted her hand to her brow and sheltered it. Her mouth fell open, and she let out a tiny gasp as she walked forward, dropping her grip on Alexander's arm. Before her lay a beautiful waterfall, surrounded by green ferns and wildflowers. Wild purple rhododendrons bloomed along a path that led to a cave opening beside the waterfall. At the base of the falls was a wee loch, clear and deep. The water was a beautiful shade of turquoise.

Alexander walked up behind her and whispered. "There is someone I'd like you to meet."

She followed him into the cave opening. The air was damp and smelled mossy. A warm light glowed ahead in the darkness. The stone-walled path wound to the left and led into a large room that opened into the backside of the falls. The tiny pool flowed into the opening and provided a watery floor for half the room. They walked deeper into the mountainside, climbing higher and higher.

The light became brighter as they walked into a small room roofed with dirt and large roots from the woods that sat atop the cave. A small opening at the far side of the room let in sunlight and fresh air. The sweet smell of incense burning on a large root, used as a table, in the far corner of the room filled the air and overpowered the musty dampness of the cave. Lit candles of all sizes and shapes cast light and shadow throughout the room. Something stirred under a floral silk spread that lay on a bed ornately carved with mythical animals and beautiful winged creatures.

Mairi reached for Alexander's arm and held tight. He patted her hand and smiled. The covers drew back, and a woman sat up. Mairi thought she was the most beautiful woman she had ever seen. Her long golden hair hung to her waist, and her turquoise eyes glistened like the pool outside the cave.

"Who dares to enter my sanctuary uninvited?" she asked.

Alexander went down on one knee and pulled Mairi alongside him. "Rhan, it's Alexander. I've brought her to you."

Rhan stood slowly and walked toward Mairi. She placed her pale hand under Mairi's chin and lifted her to her feet. They stood eye to eye. Rhan ran her long nails around Mairi's pale face three times and repeated words in a tongue Mairi had never heard.

"You do not fear me, my dear?" Rhan asked, stepping back and admiring Mairi as though she were a masterpiece.

"No," Mairi said truthfully. "Why should I fear you? You're—beautiful."

"Aye, your innocence is evident. But you are wrong not to fear me. All humans fear me, or do you not know who I truly am?"

"Alexander called you Rhan."

"Every name has a meaning, does it not?" Rhan asked.

"Yes," Mairi answered.

"Mine is an ancient name, because I am ancient. It means fate." Rahn walked to Alexander and took his hand motioning for him to rise. "She is all you have said. I will spare her as you've asked."

"Spare me? Spare me from what?" Mairi asked, taking Alexander's hand.

Alexander began, "I met Rhan at my grandfather's deathbed when I was but five. No one else saw her. As she left the room, I followed her to this sanctuary here in the mountain. I stayed with her for three months, listenin' to her stories and songs. One day I remembered my mother and asked for her with tears. Rhan chose to return me unharmed to my family who believed I had wandered off in the woods where I miraculously survived alone for months. No one knows what actually happened to this day. No one but you, Mairi."

"But what has that to do with me?" Mairi asked.

"Findin' you in the Fairy Glen was not an accident. It was fate. Rhan sent me to you." Alexander said.

"What do you see when you look at me, daughter of man?" Rhan asked.

"I told you, I see a beautiful woman—with long flowing hair the color of spun gold." Mairi looked to Alexander. "Is this not true?"

Alexander turned to Rhan confused.

She took Mairi's hand and led her to a mirror in a far corner of the room. They stood together side by side and stared into the mirror. Mairi fell back and gasped.

"What did you see?" Rhan asked.

"I saw—an—old—hag standin' next to me," Mairi said, carefully enunciating every word.

"What you saw in the mirror is my true reflection. But your eyes are enchanted. Just as your mother's were."

"My mother's?" Mairi repeated. "What do you know of my mother's eyes?"

"I was with your mother when she died."

"But, how?"

"It was her fate. I was sad to take her at such a young age. But she wished to go. Her spirit was too strong to remain bound by her human body." Rhan walked to the table and lit another stick of incense. She turned and looked at Mairi. "It is often the case with fey children."

"I don't understand. What do you mean?" Mairi asked.

"You've heard your mother in the Fairy Glen. She has called to you. She sings to you, does she not?"

"Yes," Mairi whispered, as she stepped forward and stood next to Rhan once again.

"It is how you were able to see the door to the cave."

"Alexander, leave us." Rhan saw the concern in his eyes. "I will send her to you soon enough. Trust me."

Alexander looked to Mairi, and she motioned for him to go on ahead.

"I'll be waitin' right outside by the falls," he said, and he bowed to Rhan.

"Come sit with me for a few moments. I have something I need to tell you." Rhan led Mairi to her bed, and they sat together.

"I wish to speak to you of the dragon you have seen many times in your dreams. Your grandmother has seen it as well, has she not?"

"Yes, she has, but she will not speak of it. I think she's afraid."

Rhan reached for the necklace that hung around Mairi's neck. She tapped it with her nail.

"This was a gift from Alexander, I suppose. It is beautiful."

"Thank you. Yes." Mairi reached for the necklace and clutched it tightly in her palm.

"Malachite is a powerful stone of protection, but even more, it is a love stone. Wear it close to your heart to bring you balance." Rhan leaned closer. "Do not take it off, you will need its protection. Mairi, I have agreed to spare you from an early death, but I cannot spare you from the pain that is about to pierce your heart and fall upon you like a dark shadow. You will think you cannot survive it. But, know this, you must look for the dragon. He will be your deliverer from the dark woods and lead you into a spacious place full of light.

You must follow him. You must not fear him." Rhan held her finger gently to Mairi's trembling lips. "Do not speak of this to anyone. Not to Alexander, not to your grandmother. It is your destiny. It is your fate."

"I—I don't understand." Mairi suddenly felt cold and afraid.

Rhan stood and extended her hand to Mairi. "Come, it is time for you to leave. Alexander is waiting for you. I will speak no more."

As Mairi took her hand, the smooth, pale skin turned weathered and gnarled. And she watched as Fate lost her beauty and became an old woman, ancient and wise. Rhan walked to the great room.

"I will go no farther." Rhan released Mairi's hand.

Mairi walked down the stone-walled path toward the light outside. She had seen fate—faced her, and lived. But, what did she mean? What dark shadow would she have to endure? Oh well, she was not afraid. Alexander would be at her side. They would fight this darkness together. Whatever it might be. No, she would not be afraid. It was her destiny. It was her fate.

Alexander sat by the pool waiting for Mairi. When she emerged from the cave, he jumped to his feet and ran to her. "Are you all right? What did she say to you?"

"I'm fine. I can't say, except that she spoke of my destiny," Mairi said. "I do have a question for you, though."

"Only one?" Alexander asked.

"How is it you have lived with Fate herself and seen and heard things most humans do not, yet you told me you do not believe in the fairy folk?" Mairi asked, both hands on her hips.

"I'm sorry for that, Mairi." Alexander smiled. "I suppose I was havin' a bit of fun with you. That, and I had to be careful, not to speak of her."

"It was cruel of you tease me so, Alexander. But I can't fault you for wantin' to keep your secret. Will we come visit her again?" Mairi asked.

"I don't know? Only if she calls to me," Alexander said. "I

should take you back home now. Your father will be wonderin' where we've gone. Remember, you can tell no one."

"I know. I'll not say a word. I promise," Mairi said. *There are things I can't tell even you, my love.*

They mounted the horse and rode back through the woods toward Uig.

"Why did you bring me here?" Mairi asked.

"She asked me to."

"Do you visit her often?"

Alexander looked back over his shoulder at Mairi. "Yes, since I was five. She speaks to me in my dreams as well. She told me to bring you to her before your eighteenth birthday."

"Why?"

"After I met you that first time in the glen, I began havin' a dark dream. I saw you covered in a white shroud, dead. I told her about this dream, and she said your fate had been set. I pleaded with her to spare you. Each time I asked she said no. I wouldn't relent, and she finally agreed to change your ill-fated death. Then, she told me to bring you here."

"What do you mean she changed my ill-fated death?" Mairi felt her body tense as she asked the question.

Alexander felt her muscles tighten. "Don't worry, Mairi. Everything will be fine. I will take care of you. Remember?" He turned and looked at her over his shoulder, then lifted the side of her mouth into a half smile.

Mairi let her anxious thoughts fall to the ground like dead leaves from a tree in winter. "She said we musn't speak of this to anyone." She rested her head against Alexander's back.

"Rhan was right about one thing," Alexander said.

"What's that?" Mairi looked up at him.

"Your eyes. They are enchanted. You have bewitched me with them, Mairi, and I shall never be free of you. I never want to be free of you." He turned and kissed her tenderly.

The fire popped and Mairi jumped. Heavy snows had kept her and Alexander apart since that day in the Druid Wood near Uig. Mairi counted each passing day, longing for spring and the return of Alexander. As Mairi sat near the fire embraced by her thoughts, a warmth covered her body and soul. *He will return. And this horrid war will end and my brothers will return, as will his father and brothers, all safe and sound...and there will be much celebration. And there will be a wedding in the Fairy Glen.*

12

School Days Revisited

A summer storm blew in from the Atlantic and decided to make itself at home directly atop Kathryn's cottage. Three days had passed without a single glimpse of the sun, and her mood had slipped in the mire that surrounded Sleat. This was not how she'd planned to spend her first three days on Skye. Kathryn had only left the shelter of her cottage on daily trips to buy groceries. She'd kept a fire burning and a pot of hot water on the stove for tea. Any other time this might seem quaint and relaxing, but Kathryn was anxious to get out and explore. She'd chatted with Beth daily on her laptop and texted once with the boys, who were backpacking through Portugal.

It was now the morning of the fourth day, and a knock sounded on the cottage door. Kathryn answered holding a cup of tea. A young woman stood in the doorway holding a basketful of supplies with one hand and a stack of sheets and towels in the other.

"Hello. My name is Molly MacDonald. My parents own the cottage, and I'm here to tidy it up for you."

Kathryn waved her in. "Please come in out of the rain." She closed the door behind her. "You know, you don't need to clean up after me. I can take care of it myself. Besides, it's only been three days."

"No, it's part of the cost of the cottage. I'll come twice a week and change your towels and sheets and restock the paper in the kitchen and the loo." She smiled and took a roll of paper towels from the basket and set it on the kitchen counter.

"So, do you think this rain will let up soon?" Kathryn asked.

Molly laughed. "You know, it could rain most every day here. Not all day like with this storm, though. Just a shower here and there, usually."

"Oh," Kathryn said. "I guess I don't need to wait for the storm to blow over to get out then?"

"No, no. This is pretty normal for Skye. Though if we're going to have sunny weather, this next week is a good one for it."

"Okay. Thanks," Kathryn said. "Will it bother you if I sit here on the couch and read?"

"No, not at all," Molly said.

Kathryn walked to the sofa, grabbed her stack of ancestral charts sitting on the lamp table, and sat down.

She looked over at Molly and thought she must be in her early twenties. Her wavy brown hair was pulled back in a ponytail, and she was wearing a fleece jacket and jeans. She possessed a natural beauty that required no makeup. *I wonder if Ian might like her. She's quite beautiful.* It was a mother's prerogative to be on constant lookout for just the right girl for her sons. Sean had managed to find Isabella on his own while at the university. Ian didn't seem to be particularly concerned one way or the other. Kathryn thought a sweet, young lass might make for an interesting match.

Molly turned to walk toward the bedroom. "Would I be in the way if I change the bedding and picked up a bit? I'm quite fast."

"Thank you. Go right ahead. Would you like a cup of tea or a soda?"

"No, thanks. I'll get right to it then." And Molly walked into the bedroom and began to clean.

Kathryn laid down her papers, stood, and followed her into the room. "Would it bother you if I hung out and chatted with you while you clean? I've been cooped up for a few days and would love to have someone to talk to."

Molly smiled. "I'd welcome the conversation. Thanks." She stripped the sheet off the bed and began pulling the clean one in place.

Kathryn stepped forward to help. "So what do you do when you're not cleaning the cottage?"

"Oh, thanks." She tossed the other half of the sheet to Kathryn. "I study music at the university in Glasgow during the rest of the year. I came back home for the summer to help my parents. That, and I sing in a local band."

"Really? What kind of music?"

Molly grabbed the duvet and smoothed it over the sheet. "A mix of traditional Celtic and rock. You're welcome to come hear us. We'll be at a small pub in Kyleakin a week from this Friday. We start at about eight o'clock."

"I'd love to come. What's your band called?"

"We're called The Green Bairns. I'll write down the name of the pub and the directions before I leave."

"The Green whats?"

Molly smiled. "Bairns. It means children. The Green Bairns, as in fairy children."

"Hmm. Sounds enchanting," Kathryn said.

Kathryn loved Molly's smile. It was sincere and altogether friendly. For the next hour, as Molly cleaned, they talked about everything from where to find good local food to where to shop for traditional Celtic artwork on Skye. When Molly's work was done, she sat down at the kitchen table with a soda and listened to Kathryn talk about her two sons. Before leaving, she wrote the directions to the pub as she'd promised. Kathryn placed them next to her laptop on the desk and walked Molly to the door.

"Thanks for letting me talk your ear off while you worked. And thanks for tidying up the cottage. It looks great."

"No worries. I enjoyed the company, it made the time go faster," Molly said.

"I'll look for you at the pub," Kathryn said.

"All right. See you." Molly opened the door and her umbrella.

"Goodbye, Molly," Kathryn said and closed the door. The cottage was quiet once again.

Kathryn ate a small cheese sandwich and packed up her laptop. With no end of the rain in sight, she drove to nearby Armadale Castle and met Jane MacDonald, the genealogist for the Donald Library, and Molly's cousin, twice removed. Jane was tall like Kathryn and just as pale. She wore her hair short, and it was dark brown like her eyes. After a quick tour of the grounds, the two sat down with all of Kathryn's papers spread out atop a table and began to piece together the puzzle of her past. Jane told her the research would be difficult due to the fact that her ancestors had immigrated to America in the 1700s, a time when few written records were kept on Skye. But Jane loved a good challenge and was ready to help in any way possible.

On the drive back to the cottage, Kathryn's phone rang. It was Ian.

"Hey, Mom. How's it going?"

"Great. I've just been doing some research at the Donald Library. Didn't have much luck yet, but the woman who works there is great. Oh, and I met a girl today who I think you'd like."

"Always on the lookout for me, are you?" Ian asked.

"Sorry, I can't help myself. I'll always be your mom. So how are you guys? How's Sean?"

"We're doing great. Portugal and Spain were awesome. We're in France. Paris, to be exact. We found a hostel near Notre Dame," Ian said.

"Are you both eating?" Kathryn asked.

"Yes, Mom," Ian said. He laughed. "Look, Sean and I want to come to Skye and spend the last two or three weeks there with you. What do you think?"

Kathryn gasped with excitement. "Oh yes. I'd love it, and I know you guys will love it here."

"Cool, we'll get details later when it's closer to time to come. I love you, Mom. Sean wants to say hi."

"Love you too, Ian."

Sean took the phone. "Hey, Mom."

"Hi, Sean. How are you?"

"Great. Paris is awesome. So, how's Skye? Found any ancestors yet?" Sean asked.

"Haven't found any yet, but I'm determined to keep up the search. I've rented a nice Volvo to get around in."

"Nice."

Kathryn continued. "Skye is beautiful. You guys will love it. I can't believe you're coming. That's so great."

"Yeah, we thought it'd be fun, and we miss you, Mom."

"Aww, you guys are the best. I miss you both, too," Kathryn said.

"Love you, Mom, and we'll talk again soon."

"Love you too, Sean. Bye-bye." Kathryn set the phone on the seat next to her as she pulled into the cottage drive. She parked the car and sat looking out across the Sound to the hills of Knoydart. *Life is as it should be for the first time in months,* Kathryn thought. She leaned her head back against the seat and smiled. Her sons were coming in a month. There would be much to talk about, she felt certain of it.

After a week of research through countless parish records and rent receipts, Jane suggested Kathryn consider taking a class on the history of Skye at *Sabhal Mor Ostaig*, the Gaelic college. They offered special summer classes in English for people holidaying on Skye. All other classes were taught in Gaelic.

Early the next morning, Kathryn drove the two minutes to the campus and registered for History and Culture of the Inner Hebrides. It was a small college and several professors were on hand to help with questions. Victoria Nicolson, the professor of the history class, recommended Kathryn take a beginner's Gaelic class, as well, and introduced her to the Gaelic professor, Donald Gunn. Kathryn registered for his class, and after a short conversation about what she'd need to bring to class the first day, she said goodbye and drove back to the cottage. In a matter of ten days, Kathryn had made more friends on the Isle of Skye than she'd had for the past thirty years in Houston. Beth would be proud.

Kathryn found a seat the first day of class and looked around the room. There she sat, alone again in a roomful of people, but this time she was determined to make the most of it. She felt stronger now, more confident—this would be different. Her thoughts wandered as she waited.

When Kathryn's oldest son, Ian, reached school age, John insisted they enroll him in an exclusive private school. John moved comfortably in high society—when he was around to move. Kathryn grew up in small-town society and never felt quite in step with the other mothers. Most of the moms in their Houston neighborhood had live-in housekeepers and nannies for their children. When John had insisted she hire a nanny, she managed to put it off long enough that he ultimately forgot about it.

Kathryn's feelings about being out of place worsened as the boys grew older. In the winter of Ian's senior year, Kathryn sat alone in the bleachers watching him and Sean passing the basketball back and forth as they warmed up for the final game of the season. She looked around at the other moms sitting with their husbands, dressed as though they were attending a fashion show rather than a basketball game. Kathryn was tired of being at the bottom of the food chain at every social event.

Alexis Drummond waved and motioned for Kathryn to join her and her husband, Edward. He was an executive with a major oil company. Alexis, much younger, was president of the Junior Forum and a member of the Daughters of the Confederacy. With no way out, Kathryn moved to the middle of the pack.

"Where's John?" Edward asked.

"Away on business," Kathryn said. She kept her eyes focused on the boys, hoping to deter further conversation. She failed.

"Kathryn, honey," Alexis said, "how *do* you do it? We never see John anymore. How do the boys feel about that?" Alexis leaned closer to Kathryn and whispered, "It must be humiliating to sit here at the final game all alone."

The bleeding had begun. Soon the others would catch the scent and be on her like lions on a wounded zebra.

"It can't be helped," Kathryn said. She moved away from Alexis and sat on her un-manicured hands. "This is John's busy time of year. The boys understand."

She was lying. The bleeding was out of control.

"Will you and John be at the Waterford's dinner party Friday?" Alexis smiled. Her teeth appeared to be pointed.

"I didn't know there was a dinner party."

Alexis slowly lifted her hand to her mouth. "Oh, I'm sorry. How embarrassing. I just assumed you'd be invited." Alexis giggled. "You know what they say happens when you assume."

Kathryn thought that statement had never been truer, but refrained from responding. Determined to watch her son's last game,

Kathryn tuned out Alexis droning on and on about the latest gossip. After what felt like the longest game of her life, the final buzzer sounded. They'd lost by two. Could this night get any worse? The boys came out of the locker room and said the team was going to the assistant coach's ranch overnight. She drove home alone.

Kathryn devoured every word spoken in Victoria's class. She loved history, and having ancestors from Skye made it even more fascinating. Gaelic, however, wasn't going so well. Words did not roll off the tip of her tongue, but rather stumbled past her teeth like drunken sailors. Donald noticed Kathryn was struggling in class and offered private tutoring. Since she was desperate to be able to speak a few words of Gaelic, she agreed to the offer.

In addition to being a noted linguist, Donald was also an accomplished chef. He invited her to dinner and tutoring at his home on Thursday. Kathryn accepted, glad to spend an evening out and not alone in her cottage. He offered to pick her up, but she insisted on driving herself there. Somehow it made it feel more like a tutoring session and less like what it truly was, a date. Donald wrote down his address in Ardvasar and drew a primitive map. His house stood two doors down from the hotel. It had been a church several hundred years earlier, and he had converted it into a house.

Kathryn arrived that evening with her books and the wooden box from Beth in a bag. She intended to ask Donald about it. She hoped he'd know about the carvings. He met her at the door, dressed in a brown corduroy jacket and a light blue sweater and jeans. It had been raining all day, and the evening was quite cool. He took her jacket and showed her into the kitchen where he'd already begun preparing dinner. She set down her bag and walked to the counter.

"What's this?" Kathryn asked.

Donald walked into the kitchen after hanging up her jacket and stood next to her. "First, let me say, you look lovely, Kathryn."

Kathryn looked down at her green sweater dress and black tights that clung to her body and blushed. "Oh, thank you. I've been living in jeans since I arrived and I just thought…" Kathryn stopped, shrugged her shoulders, and smiled.

"Well, you thought correctly," Donald said. "We'd best turn our attention to this beautiful piece of fish. I went to the market after class and picked up fresh trout. Here, give me your hand, and I'll show you what to do with it."

"What?" Kathryn blushed.

"The fish, Kathryn, dear. The fish."

"Oh."

Kathryn noticed how he towered over her in the small kitchen. She reluctantly reached out her right hand and watched it disappear in his as he demonstrated the proper way to fillet trout. His touch sent heat through her body. She felt surprised by the stirring inside her. But fear held it at bay. With the trout in the oven, Kathryn noticed the way Donald's wavy, strawberry blond hair was haphazardly tucked behind his ears as he leaned over the pan mashing potatoes and turnips. The heat returned.

After dinner with a glass of wine in hand, they walked into the living room and sat on the sofa. The lesson began.

"So, Donald, I was really happy when I read there were only eighteen letters in the Gaelic alphabet. I thought that would make it easier to learn. Then, you introduced the fifty-plus sounds they make, and now I'm lost." Kathryn set down her wineglass on the lamp table and pulled the Gaelic text book from her bag. "Look, a *d* at the start of a word is pronounced as a *d* in English, elsewhere in a word, as a *t*, unless it's followed by an *h*, then it's pronounced like a *gh*, which is a blurred version of *g*, which is a voiced version of *ch*." Kathryn tossed the book on the coffee table and threw her hands up in the air.

Donald laughed, picked up the book and moved closer to

Kathryn on the sofa. A fire crackled in the hearth, but it was not the heat from the flames that was causing Kathryn to feel warm from head to toe. She tried to convince herself it was a hot flash, or maybe the wine, but she knew better. Donald set the book on the lamp table next to the sofa and put his arm around her.

"Why don't we just sit here in front of the fire and enjoy each other's company for a bit? Let our dinner settle."

Kathryn jumped to her feet and grabbed her wineglass.

"More wine, Donald?"

"No, thank you, I'm quite content. But let me get you another glass."

"No, no. I can get it. Just sit tight," she said.

Kathryn went into the kitchen and poured herself another glass, hoping to stall long enough to catch her breath. Why hadn't she seen this coming? She wasn't ready for this, not yet.

Kathryn grabbed the book as she sat down next to Donald and opened it to the first chapter. "You know, my sons will be here in a couple of weeks, and I'm determined to be able to speak at least a little bit of Gaelic for them."

"A couple of weeks? I think we've plenty of time to relax in front of the fire, don't you?" Donald asked.

"Maybe we can relax next week. I think it's too soon really. In fact, I'm thinking we really shouldn't relax until about Chapter Three. What do you think?"

Donald smiled and took the book from Kathryn. "Chapter Three, is it?" He turned to the chapter and read. "In this unit you will learn how to ask what someone wants, say what you want, and say please." He leaned against Kathryn. "You're right, Chapter Three might be just the right time."

The atmosphere was relaxed, and Kathryn felt very much at ease once Donald turned his attention to their lesson. For the next two hours, she stumbled through pronunciation and some basic vocabulary. At the end of the lesson, she put away her books and pulled out the wooden box.

"I was wondering if you'd take a look at this and tell me what you think about it?" Kathryn asked.

Donald looked at the animal carvings for a moment, then flipped the box over.

"Aha, this is fantastic. Where did you find this?"

"My sister gave it to me. It came from the East Coast of the U.S. We thought it might be antique."

Donald ran his fingers over the markings on the bottom of the box. "You see these carved notches and dots just here? These are actually letters from an ancient alphabet. If I'm seeing it correctly it appears to be a name. M—A—I—R—I." He took a pair of reading glasses from his front jacket pocket and held the box closer. "There are initials here in the corner, but I can't quite make them out. Maybe a U, or V, or even a W. The second letter looks to be an M. Probably the person who made the box."

"Do you think it's old then?" Kathryn leaned close to Donald and turned the box over in his hands. "What about these animals, what do they mean? Or do they mean anything at all?"

"First off, yes, I think this box is quite old. And as for the animals, they each one carry a special meaning in Celtic culture. The first one appears to be a bird of prey. Possibly a hawk or an eagle. The shape favors a hawk, which might elude to the connection between this world and the Otherworld."

"Otherworld?" Kathryn asked.

"Yes, it might be a place where souls go when they die, or even more often it is a realm in which those who aren't human live. You usually go there by invitation only. They can be found under the western seas or on a specific island. Also, sometimes you can enter through caves or openings in mounds of earth." Donald pointed to the otter. "This is an otter, I think, a very popular symbol on Skye.

They were considered very magical, were protectors of people, and could help you find wisdom."

Kathryn ran her fingers across the last of the three animals. "What about this little bird, what is this?"

"Hmm. Aye, this one, I'm afraid, I'm not quite sure of. There are countless small birds it could be. I'll have to do a little research to figure this one out." Donald held the box up to the light. "This white stone here looks like Skye marble, but it could be any number of stones from anywhere, I'd wager."

Kathryn looked at the clock on the mantel. "It's getting late. I should probably go."

He handed her the box, and she placed it back in her bag as she stood. "This has been a wonderful evening, Donald. The food was delicious, and hopefully, I'll be better prepared in class now. Thanks for all your help." She dug in her bag for her car keys.

Donald stood and moved close to her. "It sounds like rain outside. You're more than welcome to stay the night, where it's warm and dry."

"Thank you, but I don't think I'm really ready for this," Kathryn moved toward the door.

Donald smiled. "I have a guest room. I was just offering it for the night. Truly."

Kathryn stopped short of the door and turned toward him. "I'm sorry. I just thought..."

Donald put his finger to her lips. "Shh." He took her hand and gave it a gentle kiss. "I'll be dreaming of Chapter Three. I think you should do the same."

Kathryn smiled. "I'll consider it."

It was Friday, and Molly would be singing at the pub at eight o'clock. Not wanting to go alone, Kathryn had invited Victoria.

They agreed to meet at the Ardvasar Hotel Restaurant for dinner at six and drive together to the pub afterward. Kathryn spent the day at the Donald Library reading through several old books about Sleat, the southern region of Skye where the library and her cottage were located. She'd hoped to find some lead about her ancestors but nothing surfaced. She drove back to the cottage, showered, and dressed for dinner. At seven o'clock she drove the short distance to the restaurant, parked and went inside to look for Victoria.

Kathryn saw her already sitting at a table overlooking the Sound. It wouldn't be dark for hours, but the sun was seated low enough in the sky to reflect many shades of red to orange across the water. Sarah arrived with the menus and recommended the wild salmon. So, they ordered two. Dinner conversation moved from their history class to more personal interests.

"How was your tutoring session with Donald?" Victoria asked, lifting her glass of wine.

"Hmm. Well, he's a great cook. And we did talk about Gaelic. But I must confess, it was not the only thing on his mind last night." She raised her glass of wine, and they toasted.

"Here's to a man of many talents," Victoria said.

"Are you speaking from experience?" Kathryn asked. "Because that could be quite awkward."

"No, no." Victoria laughed. "Just an observation."

"Well, I've already had to explain that my interest was in learning Gaelic at the moment."

"Ouch," Victoria said. "How'd that go over?"

"He was quite the gentleman. I did dangle a carrot out there, however."

"I must say, you're crafty Kathryn. But be careful. He'll expect you to keep your promises, if you're making any."

"No, I didn't make any promises—I don't think," Kathryn said.

"I've known Donald for over twenty years now. He's originally from Inverness. But he may have told you that already. He's quite handsome, don't you think?" Victoria took a sip of wine and waited for an answer.

"Yes, he's very handsome. But I'm just coming off a divorce, and I'm not looking for a relationship. I don't think I'm ready to start dating." Kathryn shook her head. "I haven't been with anyone but my husband for the last twenty-five years. Do you have any idea how scary that is?"

"You know, I wasn't really thinking about a relationship, Kathryn. I was just thinking you've been alone for a while, and you might be interested in—well, like I said he's quite handsome. I hope I'm not speaking too frankly here."

Kathryn was now the color of the sunset and shifted in her chair. "You sound like my sister Beth."

"Sounds like I'd like your sister," Victoria smiled.

"Yes, you would. Everyone likes Beth." Kathryn smiled. "So, Donald and I didn't really talk about anything personal last night. Has he been married before? Does he have a family?"

"He's been divorced for about three years now. He has two daughters living in London. There aren't a lot of options on our small island for *social* prospects, are there?"

"And what about you? Do you have family?" Kathryn asked.

"Well, I've one son, working in New Zealand and a daughter living in Portugal, with her father. They're short and red-headed like me. They love the out of doors, like their father. He's a writer, and we've been divorced for a very long time. I've had several love interests since then, but nothing lasting." Victoria set down her glass of wine. "There, how's that for my life?"

"So, do you know anyone who's not divorced? I'm wondering if that's even possible?" Kathryn asked.

"Oh sure, I know a lot of people who've stayed together. Let's see there's Jane at the Donald Center, and your landlord and his wife.

That's two couples. Hmm. Well, enough of this dreary subject. It's Friday night, and we've a Celtic band to hear later. Let's talk about what else you've done this week, besides going to class and dinner with Donald."

Sarah brought out their dinner and set it in front of them. "*Bon appétit.*"

"Thanks," they both said in unison.

"Let's see," Kathryn said. "When I wasn't in class or studying, I've been researching at the Donald Center or driving up and down every road in Sleat, paved and rock, in search of a stone manor." Kathryn cut a piece of salmon and took a bite. "Mmm, this is delicious."

"You know the island is full of stone manors. Are you looking for one in particular?" Victoria asked.

"Yes, actually I am." Kathryn wiped her lips with her napkin and placed it back in her lap. "You're going to think this is crazy, but I've had this recurring dream since I was eighteen of a stone manor. When I found out about my ancestors on Skye, I decided to come looking for it."

Victoria smiled and leaned back in her chair. "Fascinating. So, you think this dream manor has something to do with your past, or your family's past, I should say?"

"Okay, well this is where it gets a bit crazier. Not sure we've known each other long enough for me to be able to say this and not freak you out. But hey, here goes." Kathryn took a sip of her wine, while Victoria leaned forward on one elbow in anticipation. "In this dream, I hear a voice with a Scottish accent telling me I will find true love in the manor. I've even seen a man standing near the manor in the misty darkness."

"This is like a scene out of a movie," Victoria said.

"I know," Kathryn said. "What do you think? Crazy?"

Victoria took a bite of salmon and pointing her fork at Kathryn said, "Yes, crazy and fascinating. This island is full of tales, some believable and others fantastic." She raised her wineglass. "Here's to hoping your fantastic tale ends up to be true."

After a toast to finding the stone manor, they continued talking and eating for another hour. When they had finished and settled the bill, Victoria offered to drive them to the pub to hear The Green Bairns. They walked to the parking lot and climbed in her Mini Convertible. It was red, like Beth's.

"My sister, Beth, drives this same car. How funny," Kathryn said.

"I hope to meet her someday. She sounds amazing," Victoria said. They both laughed.

The summer twilight formed an ominous frame around the dark hills of Knoydart across the Sound. The sea gulls called out to one another, and the diminished waves lapped at the rocky shore as Kathryn and Victoria climbed into the car for the short drive to the pub. Several small fishing boats sat anchored in the small cove, and the smell of salty sea and fish filled the cool night air. Victoria gave Kathryn a mini lesson in the history of Celtic music on Skye as they drove to the pub.

When they arrived, the small parking lot was filled with cars. Kathryn heard a beautiful voice, high and pure, floating on the breeze as they walked toward the pub from the carpark. She wondered if it might be Molly. A fiddle and a flute harmonizing accompanied the rich female voice. Once inside, they ordered a beer and took the only two seats left in the pub in the back left corner. It *was* Molly singing, and Kathryn marveled at the music.

"This might be the most beautiful music I've ever heard. What's the name of the song?" Kathryn asked.

"It's called '*An Gille Ban*' in Gaelic. I can see it speaks to your soul, Gaelic or no," Victoria said. "It's in your eyes. Look around the room. You've the same expression as everyone here. Oh, look."

Victoria pointed to Molly. "She's smiling at us. She sees it too, I'm thinking."

"It's so crazy. I don't have any idea what the words mean, but I feel something—like a stirring inside when I hear it. Is that weird or what?" Kathryn patted her chest with the palm of her hand.

"You're a Skyewoman, my friend. *Fàilte*—Welcome. But you know, Kathryn, this song speaks to you because of what you've just gone through, I think. It's about someone whose love has been unfaithful, broken his vows. But though she's been deceived and the tears are flowing and her heart is bruised, she will chant her love's praises."

"Hmm. I was with you until the chanting my love's praises. No more chanting for me," Kathryn said. "A romantic notion put to haunting music, but impossible to live out, I think."

The evening went late, and the music was magical. Kathryn didn't want it to end. But end it did, and after a hearty congratulations for a fantastic performance, Kathryn asked Molly when she'd see her again. Molly said she'd be back by the cottage on Monday morning. They agreed to have lunch together after she finished cleaning and said their goodbyes. Victoria drove Kathryn back to the restaurant to get her car.

"It was a lovely evening, Kathryn. I'll see you in class Monday afternoon. Call me if you need anything over the weekend. I'll be around," Victoria said.

Kathryn climbed out of the Mini. "I had an awesome time too. Thanks for coming along. See you in class."

She waved as Victoria drove away and turned to unlock her rented Volvo. Kathryn looked up at the Mini Convertible as it drove away and decided it was time she found a different car. She would begin looking for something else, something more worthy of a woman descending from Skye MacDonalds and possessing a dream of a stone manor.

Kathryn lay in bed that night with a Celtic tune singing her to sleep. It was two in the morning. She would sleep in and then do a bit of exploring along the southern coastline of Sleat. Hopefully, in a new rental. This had been a very good day.

The next three weeks were filled with long drives around Sleat in her newly rented Land Rover, lunches at a nearby pub with Victoria—discussing everything *but* history—cups and cups of hot tea with Jane in the library at Armadale Castle, two days a week talking about music and life with Molly, and cozy dinners practicing Gaelic with Donald.

Kathryn explained to Donald in English when they arrived at Chapter Three that what she wanted was more time. More time to get to know each other without doing anything that would complicate an otherwise lovely relationship. He understood her English perfectly, although it was American, and the dinners became less and less cozy as her Gaelic improved.

13

Sons, Songs, and Skye

Looking up from the screen of her laptop, eyes bloodshot and wrists aching, Kathryn extended her arms over her head and dropped them gently down her back until her sternum popped. *How long have I been working*? Kathryn wondered. I've been here a month already. How is that possible? Her cell phone rang.

"Mom, it's Ian. We just landed in Glasgow. We'll be taking a train to Skye."

"Oh, wow. That's great," Kathryn said and stood to stretch.

"What are you doing?" Ian asked.

"I've been busy writing this morning, lost in the moors, you know. How has your time been in England?"

"Great, we've seen a lot of cool stuff, and Dad took us to a couple of shows." Ian cleared his raspy throat and continued, "Sean and I only have a few minutes to find the right train. They said it's about three hours to the ferry at Mallaig, and then a twenty-five-minute ride across the Sound. Can't wait to see you. We'll tell you all about our trip when we get there."

"I'm really excited too. Call me when you get to Skye, I'm just minutes away from the ferry dock."

"Okay, Mom," Ian said. "Oh, Sean says top o' the mornin' to you."

"Hmm, so he thinks we're in Ireland." They laughed and said goodbye.

Kathryn grabbed her cup of lukewarm tea and stepped outside the cottage. The hills of Knoydart were visible across the Sound. She hoped for a whale sighting but so far was disappointed. The proprietor of the cottage had assured her when she headed to the northern shores of the island she'd be sure to see whales, as well as dolphins. She finished her tea, took a deep breath of fresh Isle of Skye air, and retreated back into the cottage.

She sat down to write but found it difficult to concentrate. At Victoria's urging, Kathryn had begun writing a novel about her ancestors and the stone manor. She found it to be a great way to relieve the frustration of not finding answers; filling in the holes of her family history with fiction was quite fun. She was so excited the boys were on their way. She had much to tell them, and she knew they'd love the exploring that lay ahead. Closing her laptop, she decided to refill her cup of tea and take a walk through the moors.

Her cell phone rang. The boys had landed on Skye. Kathryn grabbed her keys to the green Land Rover and headed out the door. It was a two-minute drive to the dock, and as she pulled into the carpark her excitement rose. Straight ahead on the platform was Ian, standing tall like his father, toting a duffel bag and backpack. Sean, a little shorter, just under six foot, leaned over a stone wall near the water's edge capturing the rugged shores of Knoydart in the distance with his camera. The Land Rover skidded to a halt, throwing gravel into the air. Kathryn hopped out, threw her arms open, and ran toward the boys.

"You're finally here." She grabbed Ian, then Sean, and gave them each a big hug and a kiss.

"Mom, you've been cooped up in that cottage too long," Sean teased.

"No, really I'm just glad to see you both. Sounds like your trip has gone well so far. You can tell me about your favorite places over lunch. There's a great little pub near the Skye Bridge. It's called Saucy Mary's. You guys will love it. There's nothing quite like fresh fish and chips and a hearty Scottish beer to warm the heart."

"Hey," Sean said as he loaded the bags into the back of the Rover, "I think I dated a Saucy Mary my freshman year."

They laughed.

"The trip's been awesome so far," Ian said. "We were in London all last week. We stayed at the brownstone with Dad and…" Ian stopped and looked at Sean. "Anyway, Dad took us to a couple of shows the first two days we were there, then he had to leave for Singapore."

"Really? What shows did you see?" Kathryn asked.

Sean closed the back hatch and walked to the passenger side of the Rover. "*Les Miserables*, because why wouldn't we, and *Mama Mia*."

Kathryn laughed. "*Mama Mia*, that doesn't sound like something you guys would want to see."

"Well,"—Ian began—"it's Courtney's favorite, I think."

"Oh. Oh, sure." Kathryn pointed to the Rover. "Let's get in and head to lunch."

Ian jumped into the driver's seat and started up the Land Rover.

"So, I guess you're driving?" Kathryn said, smiling. She climbed into the front passenger seat.

Sean jumped into the back. "Oh, yeah. This is a sweet ride. I thought you'd rented a Volvo."

"I traded it in for this. I just woke up one morning and realized the Volvo belonged to the old Kathryn. By the way, she pretty much doesn't live here anymore."

Sean leaned forward from the back seat, extended his hand, and said, "Hi. My name is Sean. I don't believe we've met?" Kathryn grabbed his hand, and they laughed.

"So, how's Courtney? Did you guys hang out while your dad was gone?" Kathryn tried to seem interested in a non-threatened, pleasant sort of way.

"She tried to make us feel at home, but it was really weird, Mom," Sean said.

"All right. Well enough about that." Kathryn said and buckled her seat belt.

"Have you taken it off-road yet?" Ian asked, as he pulled away from the platform.

"Yes, for picnics and such—Ian, watch out!" Kathryn yelled, as they weaved around an oncoming car. "Remember—you drive on the left, Son."

"Sorry, Mom."

The drive across Sleat was tranquil. The green rolling hills covered in heather lay in contrast to the dark blue of the sound. Sheep were in abundance; a casual attempt had been made to hold them to the pastures by an occasional rock wall. Sean hung out the back window taking one photograph after another. Kathryn was careful to take note of each and every glen and creek-bed, moor and mountain, all fodder for the novel she had decided to write. She felt quite inspired on Skye, and between her dream and her research, a story was beginning to form. Besides, Beth said that's what women did when they were nearing fifty. What could that mean?

Soon they arrived at the pub. Kathryn noticed Donald seated alone and introduced him to her two sons as her professor and friend. He invited them to join him at his table, and they agreed.

"So, Mom," Sean said, "you never said anything about going to school here. First, the Land Rover, now college classes. This is awesome. What are you taking?"

"I'm sure I told you guys about my classes," Kathryn said.

"You did, Mom," Ian said. "Sean just wasn't listening."

"Hey," Sean protested and gave Ian's head a slight shove from behind.

"It's okay. You guys have been busy with your own adventure. I'm taking beginning Gaelic with Donald." Kathryn nodded toward Donald and smiled. He feigned a bow. "And I'm taking a history class about the Isles. They're really interesting." Kathryn paused and added with a half smile. "Besides, I figured if I went back to college Courtney and I would have something to talk about. There's no sorority to join, though. So that'll be different."

The boys laughed a nervous *are we supposed to be laughing* kind of laugh. Kathryn bit her lip and just as quickly as the words had escaped her mouth, she wished she could suck them back in. It was the old insecure Kathryn who had made the tacky comment about Courtney, but it was too late to take it back.

Donald, trying to relieve the tension, commented about the oddity of her sons being named the same.

"I know, I know. I just loved the names and only later found out they were each a form of John. Who knew?" Kathryn laughed. "And to make it even crazier, their father's name is John."

She made a reference to George Foreman, which only her sons understood, and the subject was dropped. Midway through the meal, everyone in the pub broke out in "The Skye Boat Song."

"Have you heard of the Bonnie Prince?" Donald asked.

Sean glanced at Ian and smiled. "Wasn't that your nickname in college?"

Donald yelled above the singing. "This song is a tribute to him because he escaped with his life to the Isles after his defeat at Culloden."

Donald leaned close to Kathryn. "The singing is for the tourists. Shall we join in?"

Speed bonnie boat like a bird on the wing,
Onward, the sailors cry.
Carry the lad that's born to be king
Over the sea to Skye.

"Ian, take a bow, dude, this song's for you," Sean said.

Donald looked confused, and Kathryn told him not to ask. They finished their meal, and as they said goodbye he asked when their next tutoring session would be. The boys walked out elbowing each other. Kathryn took Donald by the arm as they walked outside.

"I'll be taking a break from class and tutoring for the next several weeks while the boys are here," Kathryn said.

"A break?" Donald asked, patting her hand. "I'm not sure that'll be good for your Gaelic."

"I promise to practice every chance I get until I return to class." She gave him a platonic hug and stepped into the car.

As Kathryn and her sons drove to the cottage, a light drizzle was falling. Her mind filled with thoughts of the next day. After several weeks of digging through the Clan Donald Library with Jane, they had discovered Ranald was from the area near Uig, on the northeastern end of the island. The following day she and the boys would drive north in search of ties to her past.

They arrived at the cottage, and the boys settled into their room. The three spent the remainder of the day talking about all they'd seen and done on their trip. In addition to their studying at the university in Austin, Sean and Ian played together in a band. They told Kathryn they hoped to catch some of the local music while on Skye.

"Oh, perfect," Kathryn said. "There's a fiddle and accordion festival next weekend in Portree. We'll definitely go. And I've met a girl about your age who sings in a local band. I've already gone to hear them. We can find out when they'll be playing again."

"You've been really busy since you got here," Ian said.

"I have. It's been great. I'm also writing," Kathryn said and pointed to her laptop on the kitchen table.

"Writing? I didn't know you could write." Sean paused and shook his head. "Wait, that didn't come out right. You know what I mean."

Kathryn smiled. "I do know what you mean. I haven't written since you guys came along, really. I don't know why I've waited so long to get back to it. Maybe I just didn't have anything to say till now."

"I doubt that," Ian said. "And I mean that in a good way, Mom. What are you writing?"

"It's a novel about a stone manor and our ancestors from Skye. I've just slowly taken what I'm discovering in my research here and pieced together a story. It's been really fun."

"Is this the stone manor in your dream? The one you talked about at Granddaddy's?" Ian asked.

"The very same," Kathryn said.

"Well then, you have to promise to write us in," Sean said. He stood, turned his head and looked toward the ceiling, placing his hands on his hips. "I could be your inspiration for the lead character."

Ian laughed. "She's not writing about Peter Pan."

Sean lowered his hands and sat down next to Kathryn on the sofa. He put his arm around her shoulder. "I can fly, you know."

"You know that just might come in handy. I'll take it into consideration." Kathryn stood. "Anybody want a snack or something to drink?"

The boys said yes, and Kathryn made a plate of nachos and poured everyone a Coke, no ice. After all, they *were* in Scotland. By ten o'clock, the sun was making its final descent behind the mountains into the sea, and the sky radiated pinks, oranges, and yellows against the darkness still being held at bay. Adventure beckoned the boys, and they decided to take an evening walk through the moor. Kathryn found them a flashlight and made sure they took their phone. After they left on their hike, she sat down at her laptop, too excited to sleep. She worked late into the night until the voice of reason reminded her she needed to be alert enough to drive the boys around Skye in just a few short hours.

Ian and Sean had returned at midnight and had been sleeping for several hours when she finally closed her laptop and retired. The soft sound of rain and the song of the skylark in the distance soothed Kathryn, as she crawled into bed. Skye had refreshed her body and soul. She had found peace here. She reached for the malachite necklace that hung around her neck, her talisman, and prayed this newfound peace would last. The rain came down harder, and the window rattled as the wind picked up. Thunder sounded in the distance. Peace. Such a fragile thing.

14

When Forever Ends
Summer – 1746   Isle of Skye

After a long year of fighting and a tragic defeat at Culloden, the few men and boys who were left alive fled home to their families and safety. A small number of those who survived were from the Isles.

Only two of Mairi's brothers survived, Ranald and James. The week following their return was filled with tending to their wounded bodies and souls, and mourning the loss of Hugh and Donald. They talked of how every man not killed in the battle, fled and was hunted like an animal. Many who'd fallen wounded in the field were given no mercy, but put to death on the spot where they fell. Ranald and James, by the grace of God and the kindness of Highlanders along the way, had found their way home. Mairi worried for Alexander's family and wondered if they had survived. She had been to the glen each day, but he had not come. Maybe tomorrow would be different.

None of Alexander's brothers had survived, only his father. All had fallen at Culloden or on the run back to Skye. As the sun rose the morning after his father's return, Alexander thought of Mairi and her brothers and wondered how they fared. He was about to leave for the glen when his father, Donald, stopped him.

"Alexander, we need to talk, lad."

Alexander stopped at the door and came back inside. "Yes, Father, what is it?"

"Alexander, you are my only son now. You must marry and bring life and blood back to our name. There's been word the king has taken away our chiefs and outlawed our tartans and our music. It is an attempt to weaken the clans. All he has left us is our name."

"But, Father," Alexander asked, "surely his arm doesn't reach to the Isles?"

"Even now, I have been called to Portree to relinquish my arms. Captain Ferguson is sailin' up the coast in the *Furnace.* General Campbell is aboard ship. And the Isle is full of redcoats led by Allan MacDonald arrestin' or shootin' those who fought for the prince at Culloden."

"Father, let me go to Portree in your place. They'll arrest you."

"No, son, I will not be arrested."

"But how can you be sure?"

Donald placed his hand on Alexander's shoulder. "Alexander, I have procured an agreement with Lord MacLeod."

" An agreement with the MacLeods? You know I will stand and fight, Father. Just tell me what to do."

"Alexander, for now the fightin' is over. I've spoken to Rory MacLeod, and you're to wed his daughter, Fiona, in a fortnight. They withheld aid to the prince and have favor with the Crown. This I need you to do, Son."

Alexander quietly protested, "Father, you can't ask me to do this. Ask me anythin', even ask me for my life, and I'll gladly give it. But this I can't do."

His father removed his hand, and with temper and voice raised, he said, "What do you mean, you won't do it? You have no choice.

We have no choice. It is our only hope to retain our lands and possibly my life." Donald took in a deep breath. "Besides, I've seen Fiona, as have you. She's easy on the eyes and hearty as well. She'll make you a fine wife and will bear you many sons."

"But, Father, there is someone else. While you were gone—her name is Mairi MacDonald. She lives near the Fairy Glen. I made a promise."

"I can't help what promises you made as a boy. You must be a man now and do this. There will be no more talk of it. I have given my word, Alexander, and you will marry Fiona MacLeod. It is your duty to your dead brothers and to me. Would you leave your good mother without home or husband?"

"But what about *my* word, Father?"

"A boy's promise, nothin' more." And with those words, Alexander's father left the house.

Alexander sat down by the hearth and with his head in his hands wept as he thought of Mairi. She would not understand why he was bound to do what his father had asked, and he would not be able to explain it to her, though he intended to try.

Mairi met Alexander in the Fairy Glen with the sun gently climbing up the eastern sky. As he came near she could see the pain written across his face. They moved close and embraced.

Mairi looked into Alexander's moist eyes and asked, "What is it, my love? I have never seen you look so sad. Is it news of your father and brothers?"

Alexander held her shoulders tightly and moved her an arm's length away. "My father is home, but he returned home alone. Not one of my brothers lives."

Mairi moved toward him, "Oh, Alexander, I'm so—"

Before she could finish her lament or come any closer,

Alexander interrupted. "Wait—before you say another word, I have somethin' else to tell you." He looked, and tears began to pool in his lower lids. "Mairi, I thought losin' my brothers was a sadness so great I couldn't bear it. But—there is a sadness beyond words that has overtaken me." He looked up and continued. "Mairi, my father has arranged for me..." Alexander took a deep erratic breath and wiped the moisture from his eyes.

Mairi took his hands and said, "What is it that has caused this dark cloud to pass over your soul? I am afraid. Please, tell me what it is so I can share the burden of your sorrow."

Weeping, Alexander fell to his knees and wrapped his arms around Mairi's small waist. He pressed his face against her chest and cried, "Mairi, you are right when you say you will share this burden. Even now, I can't find the words to tell you."

Mairi took Alexander's face into her hands and raised his gaze to hers. "My love, tell me what it is. There is nothin' we can't endure if we are together."

"We will never be together again, not after today. That's what I have come to tell you."

Mairi dropped her hands from his face and asked, "What are you sayin', Alexander?"

"My father has arranged for me to marry in order to secure our lands and his safety. He has commanded it. I have to obey him."

Mairi pulled away from his embrace and stepped back. "Who—who has he arranged for you to marry?"

"Oh, Mairi, it's not important who, I don't even know her, really. All I know is it's not you." Alexander tried to reach for her, but she moved away. "Mairi, listen to me, I told him about us, about our promise, about our love, but he wouldn't hear it."

"Well, make him hear it. You must."

"Mairi, I tried. You don't understand what this all means."

"We could run away then. We could board a ship to the Americas." Mairi's mind was already planning their escape.

"I can't," Alexander said softly.

"What do you mean you can't? How can you stay and marry someone else, someone you don't love?" Mairi would have left family and home to be with Alexander. How could he not feel the same as she?

"Maybe we could find a way to still be together," Alexander said, as he slowly rose to his feet.

"How could that be if you're to have a wife?" Mairi rubbed the tears from her checks and stood tall.

"I don't know. We could secretly meet somewhere."

"Secretly? Like criminals? Or worse." Mairi frowned.

"I can't be without you, Mairi."

"Are you asking me to be your mistress then?"

"It's a common practice. Great men have done it before us."

"Do you not honor me in any way, Alexander? I'll be your wife, or I'll be nothin' at all."

"I don't mean to dishonor you. I'm desperate for you, Mairi. But you don't understand. I'm the only son left, and there are things takin' place that we can't change. It's for the safety of our people, my father. Your brothers, Mairi, they too are in danger." Alexander moved close and said, "I have thought about this as I traveled here to tell you. It isn't fair, but I have no other choice. I don't expect you to understand. I just want you to know"– he paused and took her hand –"I will always love you, Mairi. There will never be anyone else who has my heart but you, I promise."

"No more broken promises, Alexander. I can't bear it." Mairi shook her hand free and ran from the glen. She could hear Alexander calling her, but she didn't stop, she couldn't stop. Alexander mounted his white steed, took one final look at the Fairy Glen, and rode away, disappearing into the mist.

15

Ancient Voices on the Wind

A light rain fell on the cottage. The strong winds blew west from the Minch as raindrops tapped a wake-up call on the window panes. Kathryn stood at the window sipping her morning tea, gazing across the heather-covered moor northward.

She was ready to venture out to the northern part of the island. She had held off exploring the north part of Skye until her sons arrived. She and the boys hoped to find clues to their past and maybe even a stone manor.

"Rise and shine, men," Kathryn yelled. "The hour has come."

She opened the door to the boys' room. "Hey, come on. There are ancestors waiting to be discovered."

An hour later, with disheveled hair and sleep still in their eyes, Ian and Sean dragged themselves out of the cottage. Kathryn sat waiting in the Land Rover. She had two thermoses full of coffee—one black and one with fresh cream, three mugs, and a map. Molly walked up, basket in hand, with a pile of extra sheets and towels.

"Hey, Molly. Come meet my sons," Kathryn said.

The boys quickly tried to tame their hair, but it was not to be. Ian extended his hand first. "Hi, my name's Ian."

"Hello, I'm Molly." She smiled, and Kathryn watched.

"Hey, what's up. I'm Sean."

"Nice to meet you," Molly said.

Kathryn stepped out of the Rover. "Victoria told me you'll be singing in a concert at the college tomorrow, along with other Celtic bands."

"Aye, I don't sing 'till after lunch. Around two o'clock." Molly reached for the door.

"We'll be there. I thought the boys would really enjoy the music. And if you're not busy afterward, maybe we can go get something to eat. Or, at least a beer." Kathryn's eyebrow raised.

"Okay, sounds great. I'll see you then. Have a fine day."

"We will, we're off to the north part of the island in search of ancestors."

Molly waved. "Have fun."

They said their goodbyes and climbed into the Rover.

"So, Mom," Ian said. "Who's Molly?"

"She's the landlord's daughter, and she sings in a band—in Gaelic. She's amazing. She's the one I was talking about at the dock when I picked you up. You guys should hang out." Kathryn smiled.

"Matchmaking, are we? And we just got here," Sean said.

"Hey, no complaints from me," Ian said.

"Thought as much," Kathryn said.

Driving along the eastern coastline of Skye, they saw surfing seals and playful dolphins near the shores of the Inner Sound. The rain stopped, and the sun made a rare appearance. Kathryn took this as a good omen. They drove north through Portree, stopping only for a moment to pick up a flyer about the music festival at the local tourist center, then they took the smaller road northeast, into the Trotternish Peninsula. Kathryn marveled at the rugged landscape, with the Trotternish ridge on the left, its jagged peaks and pinnacles piercing the Highland skies, and the Sound of Raasay on the right, separating the Isle of Skye from the mainland of Scotland.

After several hours of exploring one-lane roads through the sparsely populated area, they came upon a heather-covered glen near the harbor at Uig.

"Stop," Ian shouted. "This is it."

Kathryn came to a skidding halt on the rock road. "What's it?"

"This is the perfect spot for our Highlander picture."

Sean laughed and said, "You're right, dude. This is perfect."

"What are you guys talking about?" Kathryn asked.

Ian grabbed the camera. He and Sean jumped out of the Rover and ran to a knee-high patch of heather. A sharp breeze blew in from the Minch, overpowering the sweet smell of the heather with the salty sea air. The isolated glen was just what they'd been searching for. Not a house in sight.

"Mom, you keep a lookout for cars," Ian yelled.

Kathryn walked toward the boys. "Why?"

"Stop right there, Mom," Ian said, taking off his shirt and wrapping his plaid scarf around his chest like a sash.

"Me first," he said as he unbuttoned his jeans.

Kathryn turned away toward the Rover, "What on earth is going on?"

Ian dropped his jeans, revealing plaid boxers, then stood with one hand on his hip and the other fist raised high, lifting his head up toward the sky with his profile in full view of the camera.

Sean laughed and said, "That's it. That's perfect." He took several shots, and they exchanged places.

Kathryn turned in time to see Sean standing in his plaid boxers and sash, knee deep in heather. She fell to the ground laughing. "So, I guess this means you're not waiting 'till we find a kilt."

"They're too expensive," Ian said. "We decided this would do. What do you think?"

Kathryn shook her head as she watched her sons standing in the glen in their plaid boxers. Their jeans were around their ankles, halfway hidden in the heather.

"Let's not tell Molly about this, okay?" Ian asked.

"Our secret," Kathryn said.

A light rumble echoed across the glen floor as a truck drove toward them from the east. The boys grabbed their jeans and pulled them up. They picked up their shirts from the ground and ran to the car. The truck passed, and an old man waved and smiled. Kathryn wondered if he had done something similar when he was young. Probably not.

"I'm going to walk to the top of the hill and check out the view," Kathryn said. The wind had picked up, and she felt a bit chilled. "Sean, throw me the tartan there on the back seat."

Kathryn wrapped herself in the wool tartan and walked up the hillside. She stood next to an ancient stone on the edge of a cliff overlooking Uig Bay. From the island of Harris, dark clouds moved across the Minch toward Skye. Kathryn watched as small boats sailed into the bay ahead of the storm. Voices from ancient times were carried along by the wind, and Kathryn stood still and listened for her name.

Duncan MacDonald sat at the stern of his boat and steered across the bay toward Uig, racing the storm to reach a safe place to anchor and ride it out. Conn stood near the bow and barked. It was not unusual for Conn to bark at the wind or passing gulls, but his bark took on an urgency that caught Duncan's attention.

"What is it, lad?"

By this time, Conn was running along the deck from bow to stern and barking toward the shoreline. Duncan tried to settle him, but he would not be consoled. Duncan looked to the hills along the coastline and saw a distant figure atop the cliff near *Clach Ard Uige*, the High Stone of Uig. He grabbed his binoculars and looked through them. He could see it was a woman.

"Is that what you're barking at?" Duncan lowered the binoculars and looked at Conn, who was standing next to him, tail wagging, now silent. He looked again, and as he pulled the woman into focus, he lost his grip on the binoculars, and they fell to the deck. On the hillside was the Lady. He had not seen her for over thirty years, and now there she stood. He reached for the binoculars and looked back toward the shore. She had disappeared. He looked up and down the coast, but she was nowhere to be found.

"I've lost my mind, Conn. I've not made it to the pub yet, and already I'm seeing visions. It's worse than the sirens near Benbecula."

Conn sat next to Duncan as they sailed into the bay, both silent as the rain began to fall. The waves were white-capping as the wind picked up. Only the thunder and the voices that rode the westerlies could be heard. And Duncan listened for her name.

16

The Storyteller

It began to rain again as Kathryn walked back to the car. They all agreed it was time for lunch and a pint, so they headed for Uig. Just east of town, they found the Lady of the Glen Pub. They stepped inside the small whitewashed building and found a table. The proprietor came over and handed them each a menu.

"*Fàilte Girbh.* A welcome to you all. My name is Angus MacQueen. You look as though you've just crossed an ocean to get here. Parched, are you now? What can I get for you?"

"Is there a local beer you'd recommend?" Sean asked, always ready to try something new.

"Aye, Red Cuillin, a medium bitter ale or maybe, a Black Cuillin, a dark strong brew. Not at all like your American beer. Well now, that's not really a beer now is it? That's more like a lager. Beer is supposed to be black with a head on it and is only properly experienced in a pub." Angus smiled, his smoke-stained teeth showing through his reddish-gray beard. He placed his hands on Sean and Ian's shoulders and looked across the table at Kathryn.

"So, what'll it be? Three Black Cuillins all around?"

Kathryn looked at her sons. They nodded. "Yes, sounds great," she said.

"Do you think it'll quit raining soon, Mr. MacQueen?" Ian asked.

"Oh, please lad, call me Angus. You know we've a sayin' here on the Isles. *If you can see the glen . . . it's a gonna rain. And if you can't see the glen, it's a rainin'.* I'll be back with your beers in a minute now. Will you be havin' a bite to eat as well?"

"Yes," Kathryn said. "Any recommendations?"

"We're close to the bay here. Any of the dishes with fish would be a good choice if you're wantin' local fare."

They each ordered a different item from the menu as a sampling. As Angus walked away to the bar, Kathryn tried to imagine his medium frame fitted in a kilt and boots. His long salt-and-cayenne-pepper hair and rugged appearance made it easy to visualize.

Angus returned with the frothy glasses of black beer, set them on the table, and pulled up a chair of his own. "Your food will be out shortly. Do you mind if I join you for the first pint? It's a local custom."

"Please do," Ian said, and the three introduced themselves.

"So, Angus, who is the Lady of the Glen?" Sean asked. "I noticed the pub is named after her." He sipped the froth from the top of his glass.

"Aye, the Lady of the Glen. Now that be a tale worth both the tellin' and the hearin', if you have the time for it."

"Oh, Angus, please tell it. We love a good story," Kathryn said.

"I will at that, Kathryn, dear. I think it'll be of special interest to you in particular."

"Me? Why would you say that?"

"Just a feelin', that's all."

Like many Skyemen and women, Gaelic was Angus's heart language. Heavily accented, his words drifted off his tongue like a Highland reel—mysterious and haunting, yet full of life. He took a big gulp of his beer, set down the glass, and began.

"In the days long after the MacDonalds were Lords of the Isles, there lived a young girl of sixteen. Her name was Mairi MacDonald. She lived at the edge of the Fairy Glen, which can nearly be seen from this very pub on a day when the sun shines. Mairi lived with her grandmother, father, and four older brothers. She, being the youngest and the only daughter, helped spin the wool and tend the sheep that grazed in the glen.

"Now Mairi passed her days herding the sheep through the mists of the green Fairy Glen. It was just such a day when the young Alexander MacDonald rode his young steed through the glen, breaking into her dreams. He thought her a fairy at first glance. And until the day she left the Isles, even though her name was MacDonald, he never knew but what she might truly be of the fairy folk." Angus winked and put his finger to the side of his nose.

"Mairi thought Alexander was the fairest young man she'd ever beheld and thought he must be a descendant of one of the Lords of the Isles. A friendship bloomed, and they both knew one day they would wed.

"Two years passed and Mairi blossomed, while Alexander's deep voice announced his manhood was complete. With the return of the men of the clan who survived the disastrous battle of Culloden, fear spread across the Isles. But amid the fear, many a child was conceived and alliances were made, as was bound to happen after the men had been away fightin'—if you don't mind me tellin' it so plain. The English king meant to put an end to the clans and their chiefs and their ancient way of life once and for all. For you see, though the Lords of the Isles no longer ruled and reigned, the clan chiefs were still powerful, and the Highlands and islands lived and died by their words. We have always been a troublesome lot." Angus tapped the table, and Kathryn noticed his chest swell with pride.

"It was at about this time that Alexander MacDonald's father announced to the whole northern clan that his son was betrothed to Fiona McLeod of Dunvegan, as a sign of peace between the clans and as a penance for the part he and his boys played in the battle of Culloden, fightin' on the side of the Bonnie Prince. The weddin' was to be held at the winter solstice, and there was nothin' could be said to sway him otherwise." Angus leaned in, folded his short, stocky arms and set them firmly on the table.

"On the day of the weddin', Mairi MacDonald walked the ten miles through the boggy moors and climbed the hill that overlooked the weddin' takin' place at Glen Rowan, the home to Alexander MacDonald. As the moon began to rise over Ben Edra and the mist turned into snow, Mairi sang an ancient love song as the hills of the glen wept.

"The story goes, Mairi lay down on the hillside. The snow fell a'heavier and heavier until it covered her body like a soft blanket.

"Now here's where the story gets a bit confusin'. I've heard tell her brothers found her near death and carried her to home. Soon after, they all boarded a ship for the Americas, and they were never heard from again.

"That's probably the truth of it, but the story we like tellin' around these parts is that she was found the next mornin' by a young shepherd. Her spirit had left sometime during the night and made its way back to the Fairy Glen, where it is said on occasion she can still be heard a'singin the ancient song."

Angus raised one eyebrow and smiled. Kathryn and the boys burst into thunderous clapping, breaking the spell of Angus's tale.

"That was a beautiful story, so sweet and sad," Kathryn said.

Angus noticed the necklace that hung around Kathryn's neck and continued. "You know," he said, "that's not the end of the tale."

"This sounds interesting," Ian said. "Go on, Angus."

A young woman brought out their food and set it in front of

them. Angus took another swallow of his beer and leaned back in his chair.

"Wow, this looks awesome," Sean said.

"Do you mind if I continue while you eat?" Angus asked.

"Not at all," Ian said. "Tell away."

"Tell away?" Sean asked.

Kathryn elbowed Sean. "Please continue, Angus."

"There is an old MacDonald manor built on a hillside near Glen Rowan. The family has lived there for generations."

Kathryn dropped her fork onto her plate. "Sorry."

"They've seen Mairi's ghost?" Sean asked.

"In a manner of speakin'. The laird of the manor, Duncan MacDonald, lives there today with his younger widowed sister. He never married." Angus glanced at Kathryn, who was leaning so far forward in her chair, he worried she might fall onto the floor.

"Did you say manor?" Kathryn asked.

"Yes, I did."

"Is it built out of stone?"

"Most are, I think," Angus said.

"Oh, of course they are. Sorry," Kathryn said.

"He never married?" Ian asked. "What's the word for an old maid in man terms?"

"I believe it's called impossible." Sean smiled.

Angus laughed. "Now, I didn't say he never left the manor like a monk in a monastery. I just said he never married. Were you here a little later in the day you might meet him yourselves." Angus shifted forward and took another drink of his beer. He wiped his bearded mouth with the back of his hand and continued, "As I was sayin', story goes, when he was a lad of nine years, he heard a fairy song floatin' across the glen from the hill where Mairi MacDonald had last been seen. He walked to the knoll, which was shrouded in mist, and standin' on the crown of the hill was Mairi herself. A blessin' attend her departin' and travelin'." He quickly kissed his thumb and pressed it to his forehead. "They spoke, though no man, woman, nor child knows the words that passed between 'em. She appeared to him again when he was eighteen. It was then that he painted her portrait, and it hangs in the Great Hall of the manor to this very day. You should drive out that way. It's a short drive from here. Take a left from my pub and the first rock road to the right. Drive about five miles, and you should come upon it."

The three looked eagerly at one another. Kathryn thanked Angus for the wonderful meal and the great story. He got up to walk back to the bar.

"Kathryn, dear," Angus said.

"Yes," she answered as she cut her last bite of white fish.

"You know, 'twas the Lady that brought you here to the Isle and even to this very pub. 'Tis who you are, lass."

Kathryn smiled and waved. "Okay. Thank you, Angus."

"Mom"—Ian said, finishing his last bit of sandwich as well—"what if this is the manor in your dream? Maybe that's what he meant when he said you'd be interested in the story."

"But how does he know? I never told him about my dream, or even what we were doing here. He just told me the Lady brought me here. Angus is crazy."

"It's the Misty Isles, Mom. Home to fairies and trolls and stuff," Sean said, then shot her a huge smile and a mischievous wink.

Kathryn laughed, dismissing Angus's words as a storyteller's ploy. She walked to the bar to pay the bill. Angus totaled it up and handed her the ticket. She counted out the money and a small tip and laid it on the bar.

"You talked about the Fairy Glen. Is it easy to find? I think I'd like to go there. It sounds lovely," Kathryn said.

Angus took a small piece of paper from the drawer in the bar and drew a map of the road to the Fairy Glen and for good measure added the road to the MacDonald manor as well. "Here you go now. I hope you come back to visit us again. I'd like to hear how it goes for you at the Fairy Glen *and* the manor."

Kathryn looked at the map and smiled. "Ahh, I see. I think you've read my mind, Angus. And I'm sure we'll be back. Thanks again for your Skye hospitality."

Kathryn walked to the door, while Ian and Sean headed over to the bar to say goodbye to Angus.

"One last thing, lads. I'd like to teach you a wee bit of Gaelic," Angus said. He raised his fist into the air and yelled, "*Cha Gheill*."

Ian and Sean repeated the words with fists in the air.

"What does it mean?" Sean asked.

"It's an ancient Gaelic war cry "Never give up," Angus said. "You'll be teachin' it to your mother now, won't you?"

"You bet," Ian said.

The boys reached across and shook hands with Angus, then walked out of the pub and to the Land Rover. Kathryn climbed into the driver's seat and started the car. She looked at the map and laid it on the small dash.

"Angus drew me a map to the manor and the Fairy Glen. I think we'll start with the manor. What do you say?" Kathryn asked.

"Let's do it," Sean said.

"I'm in," Ian said.

Kathryn turned left from the rocky parking lot and headed north. Her heart beat faster as she turned right onto the small rock road that led to the manor. With each passing mile the smile on her face broadened. After all these years, could it really be the stone manor she'd dreamed of? One more mile and she'd know.

17

The Fairy Glen

The tiny rock road twisted and turned like a snake through the heather. Sheep grazed on the hillsides, and only those occasional rock walls broke up the pastoral landscape. The long road took a familiar turn to the left. Kathryn glanced at her sons and raised both eyebrows. As they turned the corner, below on the right stood the MacDonald Manor. She pulled the Land Rover to the side of the road and stopped short of the drive. Kathryn threw her arms to the top of her head and gasped. And then there was a long silence. She lowered her arms and grasped the steering wheel.

"So, what do you think? Is this the mysterious dream manor?" Sean asked.

"Yes," Kathryn said. She felt she could hardly breathe. After all these years, she had found it! After a few moments of silence, she said, "Okay, this may be about the craziest thing I've ever done."

"You know, I think this might rank right up there at the top," Sean said, looking in Ian's direction.

"Crazy as it sounds, I didn't come all this way just to look at it from the outside." She paused. "But what am I supposed to do? Knock on the door and say, Hello, my name is Kathryn Tre— Silverton, Kathryn Silverton." She stumbled over her name for a moment and then recovered. "I'm from Texas, and I've had this dream about your home since I was eighteen. Can I come in?"

"I like it," Ian said smiling. "I say we do it? And by the way, Sean and I can come up with a few other crazy things you've done."

"Oh, yeah we can," Sean said laughing. "You ready?"

Kathryn took a deep breath. "As ready as I'll ever be." She pressed slowly on the accelerator, turned off the main road, and crept down the driveway. After parking, the three stepped out of the Rover and stood in awe of the medieval manor. It sat majestically grounded on the side of the hill overlooking Glen Rowan. The expansive house was built of huge gray stones. It had several turrets, which gave it the appearance of a castle. An iron eagle was perched atop one, as though it were a guardian.

After admiring the stone manor from a distance, they walked to the front door, made of massive carved wood with a heavy iron knocker in the shape of an unsheathed sword. Kathryn reached up, grabbed the knocker, and gave it a good pounding. They waited for a moment. No one came to the door. She knocked again, and again no answer. Ian had wandered off to the right toward the stables.

"Ian, I don't think anyone's home. We should come back later," Kathryn said.

"Let's take a look around. Maybe they're outside somewhere," Sean said.

Kathryn called Ian again, and he stopped at the entrance to the stables, peering in through an open window. She walked to the Rover, turned, and said, "I don't feel comfortable looking around if no one has come to the door. Believe me no one wants to explore this place more than I do, but I think we should wait. Don't want to get shot for trespassing."

"We're in Scotland, Mom. Not Texas," Sean said.

"I know, I know. Just kidding. But really, I'm not comfortable walking around if no one's here. We can come back first thing in the morning and try again. It's early afternoon, maybe we should start at the beginning of Angus's story, in the Fairy Glen. What do you guys think?"

"Cool," Sean said, climbing into the front seat of the Rover.

Ian had made his way back to the car. "I peeked into the stables. There are some beautiful horses in there."

"Hop in. We're off to the Fairy Glen," Kathryn said.

Ian climbed into the back seat, and they drove away. When they reached the main road, Kathryn turned left, and they drove up the coast. Just before they came to the Uig Standing Stone, she saw the sign to Sheader.

"Here it is. I think we're close now," Kathryn said.

The road narrowed into a single track lane, barely wide enough for one car. A moment later they came to a sharp curve in the road. Just around the bend, there before them lay the Fairy Glen in all its magical splendor.

They had never seen anything quite like it. Small pinnacles pierced the glen floor, the whole moor covered in an intense deep green with patches of purple heather strewn here and there, like brush strokes of paint across a canvas. One peak actually looked like a wizard's steeple hat.

Kathryn imagined Mairi tending her sheep and her first meeting with Alexander MacDonald. It was obvious how love's spell could be cast in this mystical place. She sat down among the heather by the stream that seemed to appear from nowhere and then emptied itself into a miniature loch. The boys sensed she was lost in thought and wandered off to explore on their own.

She lay back and looked up at the passing clouds. Kathryn thought of how unpredictable life could be. This was not how she had imagined her life at forty-eight. Many times in the past months she had thought of how she might have contributed to her failed marriage. She had tried to find both reasons and excuses for the part she had played. But the fact remained, John had chosen someone else. Broken promises. Ever since she arrived in Scotland, she had sensed something was out there waiting for her—her future. A smile broke across her face as she wondered what adventure lay ahead.

She sat up and looked at her two sons as they climbed over the small hills. She had always thought they were her future, her life. She had discovered on the Isle that life was much bigger than that. Kathryn wondered how she could ever regret the past; it had given her two of the people she loved most in all the world, and here they were in the Fairy Glen.

Yes, thought Kathryn, *life is good. I'm here in this mystical place with my two sons and driving a Land Rover.* She picked up a pebble and skipped it down the stream and into the loch. A wish—a hope—a promise.

A heavy mist began to move across the glen from the direction of the sea.

"Time to go," Kathryn called to the boys, and they hurried back to the Rover before the mist became too dense to find their way, not an uncommon problem on the "Misty Isles."

As they climbed in, Kathryn suddenly looked at her watch. "You guys hungry?"

"Always," Ian said.

"By the time we drive back across the island to Sleat, it'll be dinner time. It may be slow going. Hopefully we'll drive out of the mist when we turn inland," Kathryn said. She started the engine and pulled back onto the lane. "I'm so disappointed no one was at the manor. It's going to be hard to sleep tonight."

"It's okay, Mom," Sean said. "This is all part of *the plan.*"

"*The plan.*" Ian laughed. "What plan?"

"I don't know," Sean said, "but whatever it is, this is part of it."

"Dude, the fog has muddied your brain. *The plan.* You sound like crazy Angus."

"Hey, Mom has the dream. I have—*the plan.* And you have..." Sean rubbed his chin. "Not sure what you have."

They all laughed and speculated on what *the plan* might be on the slow drive back to the cottage. Kathryn was relieved as they pulled into the drive just before seven o'clock. She told the boys they'd be leaving soon for dinner. She called the restaurant at the Ardvasar Hotel to be sure there was an available table. They assured her they'd have one waiting for her when she arrived.

Kathryn opened her laptop and checked her email. There was a message from her Realtor. An offer on the house. So soon, she thought. That's a good sign. The threads that held her tattered life together were now woven into a new tapestry. A tapestry of wispy clouds floating across a sea blue sky. A tapestry of misty-covered moors and mountains. A tapestry of angel wings and a fairy song.

Kathryn finished reading the email and smiled at her two sons who were rummaging through the refrigerator and cabinets in the kitchen. "There's an offer on the house."

"That's great, Mom," Ian said.

Sean set down the bottle of milk he'd grabbed from the refrigerator and leaned against the counter. Ian walked past him toward the living room and gave him a gentle pat on the back.

Kathryn didn't notice and walked through the front door and out into the moor. A light mist was falling. Kathryn closed her eyes and listened to the distant sound of the sea breaking on the coast. She took a deep breath and filled her lungs with the moist, salty air. As she stood there the mist turned to rain. Kathryn raised both hands in an expression of surrender to what destiny had brought her. She thought she heard a faint fairy song as she twirled in circles with arms open wide. The rain stopped suddenly, and an eagle circled overhead, imitating her dance of deliverance.

As the sun peeked through the thin clouds, Ian stood ready at the door with a hot cup of tea and a towel. Sean was nowhere in sight. Kathryn thanked him and dried off quickly. She headed to her room and told Ian thcy'd leave for the restaurant in half an hour. She needed to call Beth and tell her about their day.

He walked into their room and found Sean on his cell phone talking quietly.

"Hey, we're leaving in half an hour to eat dinner," Ian said.

Sean waved him off and continued talking. Ian assumed it must be Isabella, his girlfriend, and left the room to give him some privacy.

Kathryn sat on the bed and phoned Beth's cell, hoping she'd still be on her lunch break at the shop. As luck would have it, she was.

"Hello, Kathryn, is that you?"

"Yes, Beth. It's so good to hear your voice. Have you got a minute to talk?"

"Absolutely. How's it going? I've been hoping you'd call. I leave for another buying trip in a couple of days and wanted to talk to you before I left." Kathryn heard Beth telling Mrs. Podhorzki she'd be on the phone with her for a few minutes. Mrs. P. sent her love and Beth continued. "I've enjoyed your emails, but they've been short and sweet. Not enough information. Tell me all about your Gaelic professor. I need to know everything."

"Oh, Beth. There's so much to tell. I don't know where to start," Kathryn said.

"Let's start at the very beginning. It's a very good place…"

Kathryn interrupted. "Please, Beth, don't break into song just yet."

"Sorry," Beth said. "Got carried away. Go on."

"Okay, so about Donald. I've been taking Gaelic, not going so well by the way. He's been tutoring me, and he's an amazing cook."

"Did he hit on you?" Beth asked.

"Yes."

"I knew it. I knew this would be a great trip for you, Kathryn," Beth said.

"Slow down. There's really nothing more to say about Donald. I told him I wasn't interested in anything more than tutoring."

"What? Are you crazy?" Beth asked.

"Beth, come on. I didn't come here to jump into another relationship."

"Who said anything about a relationship, Kathryn? I'm talking about just jumping in."

"Hey now. You know I'm not the jumping in type."

"Oh. That's right. That would be me."

"Beth, I've found the stone manor. And I've found out about our ancestors. There's the manor, and a portrait of the Lady of the Glen, and Duncan MacDonald and—"

"What? I need to know everything, Kathryn," Beth said.

For the next half hour, Kathryn told Beth all she'd discovered about their ancestors with Jane, and about the conversation with Angus in the pub. She told her about the stone manor and the portrait and the Fairy Glen. By the time the conversation ended, Beth told Kathryn she would be on the first flight she could take after her trip to Tunisia. Beth agreed to call Kathryn the minute she booked a flight and let her know the details. When Kathryn lay down her phone, she fell back on the bed clapping. Beth was coming. The adventure was about to become even more exciting. Was that even possible?

Kathryn freshened up and told the boys it was time to go and by the way, their Aunt Beth would be coming in a week or so. There was much applause. They got into the Land Rover, Sean at the wheel, and drove to the Ardvasar Restaurant and Pub for a bowl of haggis and a beer. Kathryn had been told the way to tell a true Scot was if they ate haggis. They were about to see if they could pass the test. The boys were excited. Kathryn had extreme doubts.

When they arrived, the small restaurant was crowded with a mixture of locals and tourists. Sarah met them at the door and quickly led them to a table. Kathryn had become a regular during her month-long stay on Skye. Ian and Sean smiled as many of the locals called Kathryn by name while they walked through the pub area. After they were seated, Sarah took their orders for haggis and a beer all around.

"Have you had haggis before?" Sarah asked, smiling.

"No, but we're up for the challenge," Ian said. "We're trying to prove our MacDonald heritage."

Sarah laughed and said, "If you want to really prove you're a MacDonald, you need to be here for the Haggis Hurlin' Contest in August at Loch Lomond."

"Haggis hurling?" Sean asked. Unable to pass up the opportunity for a joke, he said, "Mom, that sounds like a contest you might able to win. Possibly tonight."

Kathryn laughed, tying to hide her apprehension.

"So, Sarah," Ian said, leaning back in his chair, "what exactly is haggis?"

"Well, you take a fresh sheep stomach and rinse it well. Then, you boil the lungs, heart, and liver 'till they're tender. Now some folks cut the windpipe away from the lungs, others just leave it hangin' over the pot to drain into a bowl while it's boilin'."

Kathryn raised one hand in the air and the other to her mouth. "You know, I don't think I can do this."

"Mom, you have to," Sean said, leaning toward her and whispering, "it's part of *the plan.*"

"Okay, well no more details about how it's made then," Kathryn said, closing her eyes and shaking her head.

"Do you like oatmeal and nutmeg?" Sarah asked, placing her hand on the back of Sean's chair.

Kathryn opened her eyes. "I *love* oatmeal and nutmeg. I'll take that."

Sarah laughed. "No, dearie. I meant do you like it? 'Cause it's in the haggis."

"Oh."

"I'll be a bringin' three orders of haggis with bashed neeps and tatties."

"Excuse me?" Ian asked.

"Bashed neeps and tatties, that's what you eat with haggis, don't you know. Neeps'll be turnips and tatties are what we call potatoes."

"Sarah, bring it on, but I might need two beers prior to boost my courage." Kathryn crossed her arms on the tabletop, laid her head down, and moaned.

After a sufficient amount of stout beer, Kathryn, Ian, and Sean ate haggis, neeps, and tatties. Kathryn did her best, but only managed a couple of bites. She was determined not to win the "hurling" contest that night in front of all her new acquaintances.

As the three stood to leave their table and head home, the locals at the tables around them broke out in a round of cheering and applause. A hearty "well done" was shouted in Gaelic and English. Kathryn waved and smiled as she walked toward the front door. Ian and Sean raised a fist and shouted "*Cha Gheill.*" Angus had taught them well.

The ride back to the cottage was full of bragging and laughing over their successful haggis adventure. Ian built a fire in the hearth when they arrived, and Kathryn put on a pot of coffee. The three stayed up late into the night talking about all they'd seen and heard on the Isle of Skye. They purposely avoided discussing life back home and the past. This night was about the amazing adventure the three of them had found themselves a part of—and *the plan.*

18

A Fairy's Tale

The door to the pub opened and Conn appeared, looking as regal as his namesake, followed by his master. Angus looked out across the bar and yelled for them both to come on in. Duncan was a regular patron of the pub, as was Conn, his dark brindle companion. It is said that a dog and his owner often begin to resemble each other over time, and Duncan and Conn were a fine example of this oddity.

Days earlier, Angus had found an advertisement in the paper and read it aloud, announcing to everyone in the pub it was a personal ad for Duncan.

> Large, massive, powerful, symmetrical and well-knit frame.
> A combination of grandeur and good nature, courage and docility.
> In general outline, giving a square appearance.
> Broad, deep, long body, powerfully built.
> Muscles sharply defined.
> Eye colour hazel-brown.
> Weight 15+ stone.

Only after reading the ad did Angus reveal it was describing a mastiff stud for hire.

Duncan walked to the bar and sat down. His faithful mastiff took a guard position at his feet, then lay down and closed his eyes. Angus handed Duncan a beer and was trying to remain calm as he began telling him about the American who had visited the pub earlier.

"Well, Duncan, you missed 'em."

Duncan brushed the loose-hanging strands of hair from his face and took a long drink of his beer. "Missed who?"

"I've seen her, Duncan," Angus said, leaning across the bar. "She was here in the pub. Had you come sooner, you'd have seen her for yourself, man. Where've you been?"

"I sailed back in today from Harris and then took Flora to Portree to pick up a dress she'd ordered. Is that all right with you? You planning my schedules these days?" Duncan asked.

"No, no. You just missed her, that's all."

"Angus," Duncan said, pointing his finger and smiling, "how many times do I have to tell you? I'm not interested."

"No, you don't understand. 'Twas *her.*"

"It was her? Her who?" Duncan took another sip of his beer and leaned down to pet Conn.

"It was your Lady, Duncan." Angus slapped the counter with his hand. "As surely as me dear, dead mother, Christ be praised, rests in the ground, she is here on Skye."

Duncan sat up and laughed. "Angus, is this another of your pranks?"

The smile left Duncan's face, and he studied Angus, looking for a hint of mischief in his eyes. The image of the lady on the shoreline of Uig Bay flashed across his mind.

"No, mate, I'm a tellin' you. She was in here for lunch, with her two sons. They're from America." Angus drew himself a beer and took a big gulp. "Duncan, she looks like Mairi come back to life. A bit older maybe, but she looks like the paintin'."

Duncan decided to humor his old friend. "An American? That's impossible. I've been waiting all these years—for an American? So, how old do you think she is?"

Angus shrugged. "I dunno, old enough to have two grown sons." Then he quickly added, "But the Lady has kept her lookin' young enough. Though I'd say there'll be no one accusin' you of robbin' the cradle."

Duncan began tracing the rim of his glass with his fingers. "You said she was here with her two sons. So she's married then."

"I can't say, but there was no man with her."

Again the image of the lady on the hillside at the bay passed through his mind like an unrelenting visitor. "I never thought about her having married. I guess I thought—she would've waited." Duncan looked at Angus. "Where is she staying?"

Angus lowered his eyes and began wiping down the counter.

"Angus—I said, where is she staying?"

"I dunno. She didn't say. But I told her about Mairi and Alexander. I told her about you and the portrait in the manor. I guess I thought she'd just run along and find you."

Duncan shook his head and began to laugh under his breath. "Fate continues to mock me." He stood, and Conn jumped up, leaning against his leg. "I—first of all, I don't believe in the Lady. This is all madness. I'm—"

Angus interrupted. "Duncan, don't panic. Now you're talkin' out of your head. She is as real as your own breath, man. You saw her. You talked to her, did you not? A vision maybe, but 'twas Mairi. Vision or no, the woman today was as real as you and me." He reached across the bar and firmly grasped Duncan's arm. "Sit down, friend. I'll not speak of it again. Let's enjoy our beer together."

Duncan reluctantly sat back down, followed by Conn. "I'm a fool, Angus. I saw a ghost when I was boy. A ghost from one of my grandfather's stories and let my childish imagination carry me away to a world that only exists in myths and legends." Duncan took another drink of his beer. "I've waited my whole life—for what? An American woman—with two sons. I pray she's not the one." Duncan looked out across the pub. "How in the name of Saint Columba would that be fair?"

"Well, if you saw her, you might think fate was a bein' more than fair." Angus leaned against the counter, his yellowed teeth breaking through his lips in a boyish smile. "I tell you the truth, Duncan, if fate was half as kind to me, I'd be standin' on the top of this counter and crowin' like a Red Bantam cock, I would."

Duncan and Angus let out such a boisterous laugh that Conn jumped to his feet again. "It's all for naught, Angus. No matter, I'm leaving in the morning."

"Leavin'? For where?"

"I've a commission to finish for the gallery in Edinburgh, and there's another storm brewing in the Atlantic. So, I'm off to the outer Isles. The threatening sky'll make a great backdrop for the paintings. I sailed over today to check it out."

Angus drew them both another pint and said, "I don't mean to rattle on like a loose shudder in a storm, but you're no fool, you know. You're the envy of every man on the island. The Lady spoke to you and no one else. If she told you to wait, it must be worth the waitin', and if this be her, she'll be here when you return."

"All right," Duncan said, raising his glass to Angus, "enough talk of ladies and legends and loud crowing cocks."

Angus raised his beer and said, "Aye—to stormy seas and sturdy sails."

The remainder of the evening was filled with local gossip and reports of the good fishing off the coast. A few tourists came and went, but the pub was mostly filled with locals. Duncan walked over to a painting of a raging sea off the Isle of Lewis. He'd sold it to Angus many years back, when he first opened the pub. It hung on the west wall, near the flashing neon Red Cuillin sign. Angus had asked for a replica of the Lady, but Duncan had refused. He'd told him it was too personal to hang in the pub. She wasn't to be displayed for the world to see.

Duncan looked around the pub at the men and women he'd known all his life. Even though he loved Skye with all his heart, the Isles to the west lured his soul away, like sirens across the Minch. He only hoped the storm would hold off until he could make his way around to the Atlantic.

As darkness finally fell upon northern Skye, Duncan said his goodbyes, and he and Conn headed for home. A heavy rain was falling as Duncan drove to the manor, the darkness pierced only by the lights from his truck. The vision of the Lady on the hillside kept interrupting his thoughts. *Could that truly have been her?*

After the short drive from the pub, Duncan made his way up the stone stairway to his suite in the west wing of the great manor. Flora had lit a fire in the fireplace while he was at the pub, and Conn curled up next to the hearth, grateful to be home. As the rain gently pelted the glass, Duncan raised his arm to the pane of his bedroom window, leaned his head against it, and looked across Glen Rowan toward the hillside. *Where was she?* He closed his eyes and the memory came washing over him like a flood, as if it were yesterday.

In the coolness of the afternoon, Duncan lay in the deep grass alongside the rushing brook that carved a path through Glen Rowan, his eyes fixed on a pair of eagles that soared overhead, rising higher and higher on the swirling currents around the top of Ben Edra. Nine-year-old Duncan imagined himself mounted on their wings. He had sketched the glen and laid his pad on his chest. His thoughts were lost in ancient tales told to him by his grandfather.

A mystical melody drifting on a breeze sank lower and lower

into the glen, until it reached Duncan's ears. It was sung by a voice so soothing he thought it must be a fairy. He sat up and looked toward the hillside to the west. The mist had been rolling in from the sea and was creeping down the slope into the moor. He thought he saw movement on the hilltop. Duncan stood up and walked toward it to get a closer look. As he climbed, the melody became clearer. When he reached the top, a young woman stood in a white flowing gown, her long tea-colored hair waving gently in the breeze, and a malachite stone hanging from a small chain around her neck.

"Hello," said Duncan, hands in his pockets.

"Hello, lad. What's your name?"

"Duncan MacDonald. And yours?"

"I am Mairi MacDonald." She smiled, reached out, and stroked his dark chocolate hair. "Do you live here in the glen, lad?"

"Aye, there on the hill." Duncan pointed toward the manor, then turned and asked, "I've not seen you before. Where do you live?"

"Well, a very long time ago I lived near Uig and the Fairy Glen." A gentle smile graced Mairi's face. "I am now without a home, you might say."

"Without a home?" Duncan looked puzzled.

"Aye, lad. My soul has been wanderin' for many years." Her smile faded like the colors of sunset at dusk.

Duncan's eyes brightened, and raising his hand to his mouth he whispered, "I know who you are. My grandfather told me about you. But—but I thought it was only a tale. You—are—the Lady of the Glen?"

"Aye, I am," Mairi said, the faint smile returning but only to her eyes. "I have come lookin' for someone."

"Who are you looking for?" Duncan placed his hand back in his pocket and rocked back and forth on his heels.

"Alexander MacDonald. Do you know him?" Mairi asked.

"Sorry, ma'am"—Duncan laughed—"but there are many Alexander MacDonalds around here. Which one?"

"He lives in this very glen," Mairi explained and looked past Duncan toward the valley below.

"Oh, no, ma'am," Duncan said. He followed her gaze across the moor. "There's no Alexander in Glen Rowan." Duncan turned back around, but she had disappeared. He called for her and wandered around the hilltop in search of the Lady, but could not find her.

Both confused and excited, he ran home. He found his mother in the kitchen mending clothes. Duncan told her about Mairi, but she dismissed it as his imagination, nothing more. She told him he had listened to his grandfather's tales too many times. He knew it was not his imagination. He also knew his protests would fall on deaf ears. So, he kept their meeting tucked away in a special place inside his soul.

Duncan caught his reflection in the windowpane and thought of the more than thirty years that had passed since he last saw her. *Where was she?* He turned and walked toward the hearth. He picked up the poker, then stirred the fire and stared at his first sketch of the Lady sitting on the mantel. He had forgotten the sound of her voice, but not the words she had spoken. He sunk into his high-backed leather chair, closed his eyes, and heard a voice, a whisper. . .

Nine years passed since he'd first seen the Lady, and Duncan had taken over much of the responsibility of running the manor. His father had died the past winter, and although he was the youngest, he was the only man left at home. On a midsummer's day, while returning home from gathering the sheep, he thought he heard a woman singing. The sound was so faint he first thought it to be a songbird perched in the branches of the yew tree on the bank of the stream. As it grew louder, he recognized the song. There to the west of the hillside she stood, the Lady. Leaving the sheep in the moor, Duncan ran to the top of the hill.

He couldn't believe his eyes. There she was, just as nine years before. She had not changed, though he was no longer a boy, but a man.

"My lady," Duncan bowed.

"Duncan, I've been waitin' for you to become a man and here you stand." Mairi opened her arms wide. "You're the image of Alexander himself. He towered above every other man in his day."

"Alexander? My lady, what are you saying?"

"Duncan, you and you alone will be my salvation. You will lay my soul to rest after all these years." She smiled and reaching up, stroked his hair, just as she had done when he was nine years old.

"How can I do such a thing?" he asked, drawing her hand to his chest.

"I have come to tell you that you must wait for true love to come to you, Duncan MacDonald. My Alexander could not wait, but you must promise me, here and now, that you will wait. And she will come, I have called to her this very day in a dream." As she spoke, a thick mist began to roll in across the hillside and down into the glen. The intoxicating smell of the rowan blossoms drifted on the fog.

"But—how will I know her?" asked Duncan.

"Neither your eyes nor your heart will deceive you. Listen to them both." Mairi moved toward Duncan and kissed him softly on the cheek. She then stepped back and said, "I will not see you again. Remember, you must wait." With her last word, she disappeared into the mist.

Duncan stayed on the hilltop and contemplated what she had

said. The fog lifted, and he watched the sun set behind Ben Edra. With her image still fresh in his mind, he returned to the manor and retired to his room. He opened the cedar trunk at the foot of his bed and retrieved his sketch pad and pencil. Seated at his grandfather's oak desk, he drew the Lady of the Glen.

Over the next several months, Duncan transferred the sketch with his paintbrush to canvas. When completed, he hung the portrait over the mantel of the fireplace in the Great Hall. Those who saw the portrait were captivated by the Lady's beauty and the mystery found in her sea green eyes.

Duncan stood up and walked back to the window. Fear hovered in the back of his mind. He wondered had he been a fool all these years. What was he waiting for? No, *who* was he waiting for? He thought of his trip in the morning. He knew the week would pass far too quickly, for he loved the outer Isles, the wind and the waves, and the fierceness of the weather as it hit the seaward shores on its long journey from the Americas. The Americas. An American woman. Oh, Lady, surely not. As he looked across the glen through the mist and the rain, he heard a fairy song. He knew he had to wait.

19

Painters and Pirates

As the sun rose over the Minch, Duncan quickly loaded all his supplies and equipment onto his sailboat, the *Leanan Sidhe,* and he and Conn set off for the Isle of Benbecula. He had sold more than one painting of his rendering of Flora MacDonald and Bonnie Prince Charlie crossing from Benbecula to Uig. Duncan looked at the Minch as it rolled out before him. He loved the salty sea air in his lungs and the wildness of the waters. He often thought he was born in the wrong century.

He would gladly trade in his truck for a stallion and his cell phone for a falcon. Better yet, had he been born during Mairi's day, he would have surely been a pirate sailing the seas on a galleon. *A pirate,* he thought as a smile spread across his face, a painter—a pirate, not quite the same. *I steal a view from nature, capture it on canvas, and sell it for a profit. Aye, maybe 'tis a pirate I be after all.*

Kathryn rose early; the sun was unusually bright that morning. The cottage lay as still as the boys asleep in their beds. As Kathryn sat at the kitchen table looking out over the moor, her cell phone rang, startling her. It was Jane at the library; she had found more on the family of Ranald MacDonald.

"Hello, Kathryn. It's Jane. I've some exciting news for you. Can you come in today?"

"I'm not sure I'll be able to make it today, but if not, then tomorrow. What have you found?" Kathryn asked.

"It seems your ancestor, Ranald, had three brothers and a sister. Sadly, I've only been able to find the names of one of the brothers and the sister. The other two brothers were killed at Culloden in 1745, but their names are illegible. It looks like a water stain on the ink maybe," Jane said. "The brother who lived was named James, and his sister's name was Mairi."

Kathryn rose to her feet. "What information do you have about his sister?"

"You know, I couldn't find anything beyond her name. Though I've heard a story about a Mairi MacDonald from the Uig area. Some say she immigrated to the Americas. Others say—well—something different."

"Is it about the Fairy Glen?" Kathryn asked.

"Yes, that's the one. Have you heard it then?"

Kathryn's mind was racing almost as fast as her heart. "Jane, do you think this could be the same Mairi?"

A long pause.

"I can't really say, Kathryn. I'm a genealogist, and I look at documents and oral history and try to piece things together."

Kathryn could hear the sound of papers rustling.

Jane continued, "It's the right area and the right time. It's entirely possible. If you'd like to come by later I could show you what I have."

"Oh Jane, this is so exciting. I can't come in today, we're off to the Uig area. I'll be in tomorrow morning first thing, though. Thank you so much for your help," Kathryn said.

"My pleasure, Kathryn," Jane said. "I'll look for you tomorrow then."

"Sounds great," Kathryn said. "And thanks for calling."

Kathryn set down her cell and stood for a moment looking out across the moor. The excitement from this new discovery welled up inside her until it exploded. She raised her fist in the air and at the top of her lungs yelled, "*Cha Gheill*." She heard a loud thud, then another, and the boys came running out of their room rubbing their eyes and stumbling toward her.

"What is it? What's wrong?" Sean asked, his blond hair falling across his half-opened eyes.

"Jane, from the Donald Centre, just called and told me that Ranald, our ancestor from Uig, had a sister named Mairi." Kathryn was smiling ear to ear. "It's the same time period as the Mairi in Angus's story." She paused and looked at the confusion on the boys' faces.

"Come on, guys, don't you get it? We might be related to the Lady of the Glen. How cool is that?"

"Are you serious?" Ian asked.

"Dude, brush your teeth." Sean pinched his nose and backed away. "You've got haggis breath."

Ian slapped Sean's shoulder and blew in his direction. A friendly scuffle ensued, which Kathryn hardly noticed; she was too caught up in thought.

She walked into the kitchen. "Get dressed, gentlemen. We're off to see the manor."

Sean smiled as he skipped toward his room and sang, "We're off to see the manor—the wonderful manor of Uig."

Ian slapped him again. "Hey, will we be back in time to hear Molly sing?"

Kathryn stuck her head out of the kitchen and smiled. "Oh yeah, I almost forgot. Of course, we'll make sure we're back by two. Now hurry and get dressed."

As they drove back up to Uig, Kathryn looked at her two sons and smiled. Life had become—interesting again. A mist still hung heavy at times in her mind, but those days were fewer now than when she first arrived on Skye. The wildness of the landscape and the mysterious mist had dispelled the ordinary from her life. Kathryn felt her own soul taking on the personality of the Isle.

"So," Kathryn said, breaking the silence, "I want you both to know how glad I am you're with me. And I also want you to know that I'm okay, and I'm going to continue to be okay. I can't really explain it, but I belong here. I can just feel it."

"We know, Mom," Ian said. He gently touched her shoulder. "We could see it in the Fairy Glen yesterday."

She looked in the rearview mirror and saw a troubled look on Sean's face. The remainder of the drive to Uig was unusually quiet. The sun was shining, and Skye had never looked more beautiful. In spite of the sunshine, Kathryn felt troubled by Sean's silence. He had seemed in a great mood earlier. *Could it be something I said?* she wondered. *What did I say anyway? I'm glad they're here. I'm okay—I belong here. Maybe he doesn't agree.*

Finally, they turned onto the road to the manor. A man was leading a flock of sheep across the road. Kathryn stopped, and Sean grabbed his camera and began shooting. The man's dog herded the last sheep into the adjacent field, and Kathryn continued driving. They rounded a corner, and there sat the stone manor. A smile spread across her face, and her heart beat faster as she pulled into the drive. The three stepped out of the Rover and walked to the door. Kathryn once again gave the door a loud knock, stepped back, and waited.

Moments later, the door opened, and a woman with long auburn hair and pale green eyes, who looked to be a bit younger than Kathryn, greeted them in Gaelic. She had a tall full figure and was dressed in a jumper made of a highland weave. Kathryn thought she noticed a look of surprise in the woman's face but decided she might not be used to strangers knocking on her door. A small red-headed boy hid behind her; his eyes widened when he saw Kathryn. He turned and ran down the long corridor.

"Hello," Kathryn began. "I know this is going to sound crazy, but my name is Kathryn, Kathryn Silverton, and these are my two sons, Ian and Sean." Everyone nodded politely and she continued. "We've been looking for a stone manor that has appeared to me in a dream, and I think this just might be it."

The woman smiled and calmly asked them to come inside.

"My name is Flora MacDonald. That was my grandson, Charles, hiding behind me. I think you startled him a bit."

"I'm so sorry. I know this all seems really crazy," Kathryn said.

"No, no. Not at all. Why don't you come in for a cup of tea? If you'll pass this way, you can wait in the Great Hall while I hurry off to the kitchen. It's a rather large room. I think you might find it interesting."

They followed Flora, admiring the tapestries that lined the large entryway leading to the Great Hall. Kathryn could feel the hair standing up on her arms as though lightning were about to strike. Breathless with anticipation, she glanced at the boys. She had seen the same expression on their faces when they were small on Christmas morning. It seemed her excitement was contagious.

Flora opened a massive wooden door and extended her arm. "Please, wait in here. I'll return in just a moment with our tea."

The three felt dwarfed by the greatness of the room as they entered and stood in the center of the sunlit hall. The sun had returned to the Isle, a good omen indeed.

Directly in front of them was a great stone fireplace, and hanging on the wall above the mantel was a portrait. Kathryn took several steps forward and stopped. Of all the stories she had hoped to find and write, this was beyond even her wildest imagination. Before her—captured on canvas for all to admire—was a life-size portrait of Duncan MacDonald's Lady of the Glen, just as Angus had told them, and around her neck hung a malachite bead with a Celtic love knot.

Ian moved forward, slipped his arm through hers, and whispered, "Mom, she looks like you."

Sean stepped forward and took Kathryn's other hand. "I'd say we've found the ancestors."

20

Landscapes and Dreamscapes

The Minch was rough, the anxious waters tossing and turning, announcing the brewing storm. By midmorning Duncan had reached Benbecula and sailed north along the eastern coastline of North Uist. He crossed the Sound of Harris and moored his boat in Leverburgh at the south end of the Isle of Harris. Duncan picked up a rented car and made the short drive to the west coast of the island, with Conn as his co-pilot.

A hearty wind blew from the west. The sky was unusually clear for the Outer Hebrides, but as he topped the final hillside, billowing storm clouds rose above the horizon. The Atlantic lay before him, its turquoise blue waters rising and falling, then crashing upon the sandy shore. Farther out, he could see the deep, dark waters bracing for the tempest. His timing was perfect. He pulled the car to the side of the road and stepped out to photograph the storm making its way toward shore. Conn leaped out of the car and took off across the hillside for a romp of his own. For the next several hours, Duncan took photograph after photograph, capturing the ever-changing light, the different moods of the sea, and the thunderous clouds moving in.

The wind grew fierce, and the first raindrops fell as Duncan stepped back into the car calling for Conn. They headed toward 4 Horgbost, the bed and breakfast where he had rented a room for the week. He stayed there often because of the spectacular mountain and ocean views. As he arrived, he saw the Neolithic cairn in the front garden of the house and wondered, as always, who was buried there and what story they had to tell.

Duncan grabbed his bag and stepped into the entry, Conn close on his heels. He rang the bell at the desk and was greeted by Mrs. Morrison.

"Duncan, you've arrived just in time for the storm. Your usual room is ready for you. Here's the key." She gave it to Duncan and leaned over to pet Conn. "Conn, you're looking fitter than ever." She looked back at Duncan. "If you need anything just let us know. Breakfast begins at seven. Will that be early enough for you?"

"That'll be just perfect. Thank you. We'll see you in the morning."

As Duncan settled in, he watched the storm break onto the shore in full force from the refuge of his bedroom window. Squall after squall screamed ashore like a banshee. Duncan glanced down at Conn sprawled out on the braided rug at his feet. Man's best friend. The perfect companion. Hours might go by without a word of conversation—and that was fine. They shared a special bond. Duncan knew that Conn would not hesitate to defend him to his last breath. He sat down next to him and began to stroke his massive back. Conn raised his head and laid it on Duncan's knee.

"So, my old friend, what do you think? Is it possible after all this time she's finally come?"

Conn shifted to the left and moaned.

"Easy for you to be so calm. Americans love dogs. Dogs and pirates."

Duncan slid out from under Conn and walked to the bed. He removed his boots and fell back across the bulging feather mattress.

He closed his eyes as the window panes rattled in the storm. The Lady's image appeared and then began to change, her youth disappearing before his mind's eye—and she laughed. Duncan sat up and rubbed his eyes. He turned toward the window, wondering if the phantom had penetrated the glass and made her way into his thoughts. He got up and walked back to the window, searching the shore in the distance, looking for his *leanan sidhe*, his fairy mistress. A melody he thought he had long forgotten drifted through his mind. Then words came—slowly, softly, sweetly. A lover's lullaby.

> Where Lagan stream sings lullaby
> There blooms a lily fair:
> The twilight-gleam is in her eye,
> The night is on her hair.
> And, like a love-sick leanan-sidhe,
> She hath my heart in thrall:
> Nor life I owe, nor liberty,
> For Love is lord of all.

Flora entered the Great Hall, carrying a tray with a tea set and shortbread biscuits. She set it on the large table made of rowan wood in the center of the sitting area. She glanced up at Kathryn, standing in the middle of the room staring at the portrait.

"Sit down, dear. Won't you?" Flora pointed to the leather couches that surrounded the rowan table. "The fire will take the damp chill out of the air. How do you take your tea?"

"Milk and sugar, please," Kathryn said.

"And you lads?" Flora asked.

"I'll take mine black," Ian said.

"Plenty of sugar for me, no milk. Thank you," Sean said.

Kathryn sat down near the fire; the boys followed. They

thanked Flora as she handed each of them a cup of tea and a biscuit. She then sat down across from them and smiled.

"First, I must apologize for the absence of my brother, Duncan. He left in the wee hours of this very morning to cross the Minch for the Western Isles."

"How long will he be away?" Ian asked.

"I think, only a week this time."

"So, what does he do?" Sean asked.

"Guys," Kathryn said, frowning. "I'm sorry, Flora. This is really none of our business."

"No, no, not to worry," Flora said, smiling and waving her hand. "Duncan is quite a successful painter. He often goes to the Isle of Harris and other parts of the Outer Hebrides for inspiration. I suppose you must be wondering about the portrait just there above the mantel."

The three looked at the Lady and nodded.

"Well, I have to say I was a bit surprised to see you standing there at my front door, but Duncan always said you'd come one day. We just thought it would have been much sooner. That, and I don't think we thought you'd look so much like the portrait. Strange isn't it?" Flora smiled and took a sip of her tea.

"I don't know that I understand," Kathryn said, still staring at the painting.

"Well, it all started when my brother was nine years old—"

Kathryn interrupted Flora. "Oh, I know the story about Mairi MacDonald and the Fairy Glen and all of that. I just don't understand why—why it is that painting looks so much like me?"

Ian leaned over. "Mom, it's what Angus said. The Lady brought you here. It's who you are."

"What do you mean it's who I am? I'm Kathryn Silverton."

"You'll have to excuse our mom, she's having a moment," said Sean. He turned to his mother. "It's a bit of a shock to find yourself part of a fairy tale, huh, Mom?"

Kathryn stood and walked over to the painting. "Don't tell me you believe this, too? It's crazy, don't you think?"

"She's your ancestor," Sean said. Then he pointed to the painting. "It's hard to argue with that."

Kathryn looked up at the portrait. Sean could be right. If Mairi was her ancestor and the Lady of the Glen, that would account for the resemblance. And then, there was the necklace. *Who could ever explain that?* Kathryn thought.

"You all must come back when Duncan returns. Leave me your number, and I'll call the moment he's home," Flora said.

"That would be fantastic," Kathryn said more loudly than she intended. "Lovely, I mean, that would be lovely. Thank you."

After polite conversation and a delicious cup of tea, Kathryn and her sons took their leave, jotting down a phone number and thanking Flora for her hospitality.

They made it back to *Sabhal Mor Ostaig,* the Gaelic college where Kathryn had been taking classes, just in time to hear Molly perform. Ian and Sean sat spellbound by the mystical Celtic sound and her enchanting voice as she sang *My Lagan Love,* about a fairy mistress, an enchantress. They spent the rest of the afternoon listening to pipers and fiddlers—and Molly. In between sets late in the afternoon, Ian and Sean picked up a couple of acoustic guitars and sat in on a jam session. Kathryn found a quiet spot outside and called Jane.

"Hello, Donald Center. Jane MacDonald speaking."

"Jane, it's Kathryn. I've got something crazy to tell you about. Do you have a minute to talk?"

"Yes, I do. It's been quite slow this afternoon. What is it?" Jane asked.

"The boys and I drove to the MacDonald Manor of Glen

Rowan today, near Uig. Do you know where I'm talking about?" Kathryn asked.

"Yes, I know the MacDonalds, we're not close mind you, but we are acquainted," Jane said.

"Have you been to the manor then?" Kathryn asked, walking back toward the music hall. She could hear a band beginning to play.

"No, I can't say I've been there," Jane said. "Did you see the portrait?"

"I did, Jane. And the resemblance is crazy. It looks a lot like me when I was younger. And then there's the whole necklace thing and my dream about the manor."

"Keep talking," Jane said.

Kathryn told Jane about the necklace Beth had given her, and that the woman in the portrait was wearing an identical looking one. She also told her about her recurring dream about the stone manor. Jane was fascinated by everything Kathryn told her. They agreed to meet first thing in the morning at the center and talk more. Kathryn joined the boys and Molly's parents in the music hall, but she found it hard to focus on anything except the portrait.

After the last performance of the evening, Kathryn invited Molly to the cottage for coffee and conversation. Molly told her parents she'd be in late, and the four were off to the cottage. When they arrived, Kathryn went into the kitchen to get a snack tray together and put on the coffee. Ian and Sean had decided to take a two-day trip to the mainland exploring and asked Molly to join them. She agreed to go. After shortbread and coffee, seasoned with plenty of conversation about the upcoming adventure, Ian offered to walk her back up the hill to her house. She accepted.

The air was crisp and cool. A perfect Skye night. No clouds, a sliver of a moon, and a brilliant display of stars.

"You know, you couldn't do this in Austin." Ian zipped up his jacket and put his hands in his pocket as they strolled up the rocky road.

"Do what?" Molly asked.

"Walk around in the middle of the night alone. Not exactly safe."

"That's too bad. I walk a lot at night. Alone." Molly pulled the hood of her jacket over her head as the sea breeze picked up. "I do most of my thinking on long walks at night." She stopped in the middle of the rock road. "Listen."

Ian stood next to her, motionless. The wind from the Sound of Sleat made the slightest rustling noise as it moved up the hillside through the heather. The night sky was unusually clear, and the stars glistened.

"Do you hear it?" Molly asked.

"Maybe."

"The sound of the Hebrides breathing. She takes in a deep breath from the Atlantic and exhales across Skye to the mainland." Molly closed her eyes and breathed in deeply.

Ian was transfixed.

Molly opened her eyes and touched his shoulder. Her touch warmed every inch of his body, radiating from his head to his toes. "Close your eyes, and let her breath embrace you, body and soul."

Ian shut his eyes and felt the gentle wind caress him. Molly moved close and traced an imaginary line across his forehead, down along his strong jaw, across his chin, and back up again. She slid her finger down the bridge of his nose and rested it on his slightly parted lips. Ian slowly opened his eyes and drew her in even closer until there was no room between them for the sea breeze to pass. He reached for her finger still pressed gently against his lips, took her hand in his, and gently kissed her palm. Suddenly, green and blue ribbons of light danced across the dusky sky. They both gasped and stumbled backward. Ian still held Molly's hand.

"Wow! Amazing." Ian said.

"It's the northern lights. Have you never seen them?"

"Never in person. Only in pictures."

"I've grown up with them, but they still take my breath away." Molly turned in a circle, face to the sky.

Ian wrapped his arm around her waist. "I thought I caused it."

"You caused it?" Molly repeated, her eyebrows raised.

"Yeah, this always happens when I kiss a beautiful girl's palm." Ian smiled.

"Hmm," Molly said and pretended to turn away.

Ian pulled her back and pointed to the light show. "In case you're wondering, this is how I feel right now. If you could see inside my head, this is what you'd see."

"So show me." Molly leaned in, eyes closed, lips falling slowly apart.

Ian kissed her.

"I see it. I see inside your head." Molly smiled.

Ian leaned in and they kissed again. Molly pulled away slowly and took a deep breath, smiling. "I hate to put an end to this beautiful light show, but I have to get home. My father will be waiting."

"Can't we just stay here together a little longer?"

"This won't be the last aurora borealis we spend together. I promise." She kissed him quickly and ran up her drive, turning once to wave.

The rainbow ribbons waved across the northern sky. Ian stood on the hillside amazed that his feelings for Molly were mirrored in the electric sky. When she was out of sight, he walked back to the cottage. Molly had lit a fire inside him that no cold sea breeze could cool down. He arrived at the cottage and walked in humming "My Lagan Love." This was going to be a great vacation.

21

Fact or Fiction

Jane was standing on a stool reaching for an old parish registry, when Kathryn entered the library. Across the room stood a table piled high with books, a mountain of words waiting to be scaled and conquered. Jane stepped off the stool and opened the registry.

"Look, Kathryn, I think this might contain what we've been looking for."

"I see you've been busy," Kathryn said, pointing to the stack of books on the table.

"Yes. After you called yesterday and told me about your time at the MacDonalds and about the portrait—well, your story has my interest piqued, and it's just about all I can think about." Jane sat down next to Kathryn and looked through the registry. "I went home last night and told my husband all about the stone manor, and your dream, and the portrait of the Lady, and—oh, listen to me now."

Kathryn smiled. "Take a breath, Jane."

"I must say, you seem quite calm."

Kathryn ran her fingers through her hair. "I think I might be in shock."

Jane released a high-pitched trill of a laugh. "Where are the boys off to today?"

"I dropped them off at the ferry to Mallaig. They've decided to do some exploring along the west coast of the mainland with Molly."

"Did you tell them about the archery tournament on the grounds here in two days?"

Kathryn looked up from the books. "Oh no, I totally forgot. But I know they'll both be really excited, especially Ian. He's quite the expert bowman back home. My dad used to bow hunt when I was growing up, and he passed on the love for archery to Ian."

"You know, I don't think I've ever even held a bow," Jane said.

"I haven't held one in a very long time, but I loved to shoot when I was younger. In fact, I was quite good. But enough about bows and arrows. Let's talk about what you've found," Kathryn said.

She and Jane spent much of the day digging through records in search of more clues to the past. The passenger lists for the ships to America and Canada weren't much help. Kathryn laughed as she commented on the lack of variety in the names.

"This is why it's so hard researching ancestors from Skye," Jane said. "There might be, say, thirty Donald MacDonalds from the Sleat area living in the early 1700s. It's really difficult. You'd be surprised how many requests we get from Americans looking for their relatives. They'll say his name was Donald MacDonald from the 1730s." Jane giggled quietly. "I tell them, well, every fourth male on the Isle of Skye had the first name Donald in the 1730s."

"I know, I had no idea," said Kathryn, shaking her head. "I'm sure you thought, 'Oh no, not another one,' when I first emailed you."

"Oh, it's okay, dear. This is my job, you know. I love it. That's why I do it. In fact, you're the reason I do it."

Kathryn looked puzzled. "What do you mean?"

"Well, here you are so far from home. You feel a tie to the Isle, but you don't know why. And suddenly, we find a name and a date and a place that fits your story. Of course, yours is a bit more interesting than most, I must say." Jane carefully placed a card between the pages, closed the registry, and leaned toward Kathryn. "A fairy and a portrait and a stone manor. Why that's what legends are made of, and here I am helping you in my own small way."

"Oh, Jane," Kathryn said, reaching over and taking her hand, "there is nothing small about what you've done. I'll be sure to put you in my book, too. Credit you and the center for the research."

"Your book?"

"Yes, I've decided to work on a novel. Historical fiction. Like you said, this story could become legendary." Kathryn laughed.

"That'll be good for the center, you know. Thank you, dear. The MacDonalds have been a wee bit jealous of the MacLeods since they hung the fairy flag in their castle at Dunvegan. If we ended up with a fairy portrait, we just might call it even."

Kathryn cleared her throat and tried to sound poised as she asked her next question. "So, Jane, what do you know about Duncan MacDonald of Glen Rowan?"

"If you're asking me if he's handsome, then my answer is aye. If you're asking what he's like, I'd have to say, I don't know. He's a bit of a loner. I know he travels some. We've sold some of his paintings here at the center at special exhibits from time to time. I've spoken to him on those occasions only, and then, it was all business."

"He never married?"

"No, though I know he was quite popular at university when he was younger, but nothing came of it. I do remember a rumor about the curator at a gallery in Edinburgh. She actually made several trips to the manor last year. Story goes she got tired of competing with the Lady and stormed off, so to speak, back to the mainland. This is all hearsay, you understand."

"You seem to know quite a lot about Duncan MacDonald, Jane," Kathryn said, smiling.

"It's a small island. What can I say?" Jane opened a file on her computer and began looking through photos of family histories from bibles. "Hmm. Well now, Mary and Joseph, I think I may have found something."

Kathryn leaned over the table straining to see. "What, what is it?"

"Right here, the christening of Ranald MacDonald, the 7th of April, 1718, born to William and Anne MacDonald of Uig."

Kathryn was now sitting next to Jane. They continued moving slowly through the file, one page at a time until they came to another entry. *William MacDonald. Born 1686. Robbed and murdered the 18th of February, 1774. Buried in Uig Cemetery, the 20th of February, 1774.* Kathryn grabbed her notebook and began copying dates.

"I'll make a copy of these pages for you before you go," Jane said. "See, a piece here, a piece there. It's a puzzle."

A puzzle, thought Kathryn. She wondered how many pieces were in her puzzle, and with no picture to guide her, how would she ever put it all together? What she did know was that her puzzle was being shaped by murderers and immigrants, by fairies and glens, by cottages and manors, and somewhere in all of this—a portrait and a promise.

Kathryn and Jane continued their search and their conversation for the remainder of the day, stopping only for a small lunch at noon and then afternoon tea.

At five o'clock, Kathryn finally closed the book she was reading. "I think it's time we put away the books. My head is too full. I need to offload some of this information."

"An excellent idea. Are you hungry?" Jane asked. "I'd love it if you'd join my husband, Robert, and me for supper. Your boys are gone and besides, Robert's anxious to meet the person who's stolen my attention from 'all other living beings,' as he put it."

Kathryn smiled. "I accept. I can use the break and the company." She'd come to appreciate Jane's friendship even more than her expertise at finding lost ancestors.

Jane put away the books in their proper places, turned off the lights, and locked up the center. "You can follow me to the house. It's only about ten minutes away."

Kathryn loved the drive from the center to Aird. They drove along the Sound through Ardvasar, past a number of crofts and cottages. At one point the road became steep and narrow as it wove its way through a wooded area. Small waterfalls cascaded down the hillside between the trees, and wildflowers blanketed the roadside like Joseph's coat of many colors.

Soon they arrived at the far west point of Sleat. Jane turned left into a rock driveway that led down to a lovely whitewashed home on the Sound. Kathryn parked alongside her and stepped out of the Rover, taking in a very deep breath of salty Skye air.

"It's beautiful, Jane," Kathryn said. "And just look at this view across the Sound to Knoydart and across the Minch to that lovely island. What's it called?"

"Rum," Jane said.

"Hmm. Interesting," Kathryn said, as they walked into the house.

"I'm going to check on the chicken and tatties. They've been in the slow cooker all day. Just have a seat on the back porch. It's a lovely view," Jane said.

"It smells wonderful. Can I help with something?" Kathryn offered.

"No, thank you. I prepared it all ahead of time this morning before I left for work. Robert will arrive soon and likes to eat early. Just relax and enjoy the view. I'll join you in a moment."

Kathryn sat on the porch and watched the boats make their way in and out of the Sound of Sleat. A pair of otters appeared on the bank just across the lawn and played chase like children along the shore. Jane appeared from the kitchen and sat next to Kathryn in the white wicker chairs. There was a light breeze and the smell of the sea. A perfect evening.

Jane's husband, Robert, arrived moments later. She introduced Kathryn, and they went back into the kitchen. Jane pulled the chicken from the oven, while Kathryn set the final glass on the table, and the dinner was served.

"So, are there lots of cowboys where you live?" Robert asked. He pointed a finger and thumb at her and pretended to shoot her with his imaginary pistol.

"Not so much in Houston, but in West Texas, sure."

"I hear everyone carries a gun."

"There are a lot of guns. But it's not like a Wild West movie." Kathryn smiled. "I don't have a gun."

Jane elbowed Robert. "You sound like we've never left the island."

"Sorry, this is just what I see on the news and read about. That's why I'm asking."

"It's okay," Kathryn said. "People ask me if we have an oil well, and do I have horses? I feel sure we think the same way about ya'll. I imagined every man here in a kilt, and all the women red-headed and freckled. I expected to see a sword strapped to your side. I loved *Braveheart*."

"Aye, now you see that was a case of Hollywood romanticizing a very troubled time. Not particularly accurate either, historically speaking."

"The weather," Jane said, offering Kathryn more potatoes. "Let's talk about the weather. Something a little less violent maybe."

"The weather it is then," Robert said with a muffled laugh. "Though that can be quite violent here, as well. I suppose the weather is a bit different in Texas than what we have here in Skye."

"Well, I'd say it's as wet in Houston as it is on Skye. The difference is it's also really warm there, which makes it really, really humid. I can safely say I have never needed a jacket in June in Houston. Unless, of course, I was eating in an air-conditioned restaurant."

Kathryn took a bite of the roast chicken and complimented Jane on her cooking. She was grateful for adult conversation and company. Only now when her life was so full of people did she realize how painfully alone she had been back home. If not for Beth and Mrs. P., she'd have been left to herself. Night after night of eating at her kitchen table watching a TV show she cared nothing about. It was all about the voices. People's voices. It filled the silence.

She realized her world had become very small and very quiet, and she had lost herself in it. Her life had been black and white, like a silent movie, and she was the cast. But that had all changed. Skye filled her life with color again. Color and sound. Sounds of people, people engaged in conversations with *her*. Sounds of the sea and the wind blowing through the hawthorn trees outside her cottage. Sounds of skylarks singing and Molly's lovely voice—Gaelic melodies bringing smiles to everyone listening. Music, lots of music. Fiddles, pipes, and flutes.

Robert's voice broke through her thoughts.

"You're smiling. What's on your mind?" he asked.

Jane scolded him for such a personal question. He ignored her.

"This brings me to more interesting conversation than the weather. Jane tells me she thinks you're kin are from the Uig area. MacDonalds," Robert said.

"Yes, it appears that's right," Kathryn said.

"And she told me about your dream and the manor at Glen Rowan. It sounds like a movie script."

Kathryn laughed. "Let's hope it's not a tragedy. I'd be okay with a comedic romance. So far, though, it's been nothing but drama."

"So you've met Duncan then," Robert said.

"No, not yet." Kathryn poured another glass of wine. "Are you saying he's drama?"

"It does seem to follow him when it comes to women. Don't you agree, Jane?"

"Let's not bring on bad luck by saying such things. More tatties, Kathryn?"

"No, thanks. They're delicious, but I don't think I could eat another bite." She leaned back in her chair and rubbed her stomach.

"Coffee? I've also a plate of fruit. I'm afraid there wasn't much time to make a dessert." Jane stood to clear the table.

Kathryn said yes to the coffee and pushed back her chair to help, but Jane insisted she remain at the table while she made the coffee.

"Back to Duncan and drama," Kathryn said. "What exactly does that mean?"

"Now, I'm not saying he's a problem or he's bad. It's just that he's never been with the same woman for very long. I don't really understand it. It all has to do with that bloody portrait. I think it's cursed in some way." Robert laughed.

"Are you making a joke, or are you serious?" Kathryn leaned forward on her elbows, a concerned look on her face.

"Jane says he's unsettled in his soul. I say he's a man who knows exactly what he wants in a woman, and he just hasn't found her yet."

Jane walked in with fruit and coffee on a silver tray. Robert steered the conversation away from Duncan, talking instead about family. Kathryn talked about Ian and Sean and what it was like raising two boys. Jane and Robert had one daughter attending university in Paris. She was studying French and economics.

After drinking her last sip of coffee, Kathryn said good night and thanked them for a wonderful evening. The drive back to the cottage was quiet and uneventful. The moon lit the Sound; Kathryn loved the way it shimmered like a field of diamonds.

She returned to her cozy cottage. The weather had been unusually warm and sunny since Kathryn and the boys returned from the MacDonald Manor. They had driven home from the manor in a huge storm, but it passed almost as quickly as it began.

The westerly wind had blown every cloud from the sky toward the mainland. The Isles were clear, uncluttered. The mist was gone from the moors and the hills, but not from Kathryn's mind. She tried to make sense of all that was happening. The portrait of the Lady of the Glen lingered in her thoughts like a dinner guest whose face looked familiar but whose name had been forgotten. She had promised Flora that she and the boys would return the following week to meet Duncan. She had a lot of questions, and it seemed he was the only one who could answer them.

Duncan set up on the beach determined to paint. Hours passed and still not one stroke had reached the canvas. *Focus your mind, Duncan.* But it was no use; she held his thoughts captive. He had to know if she had truly come or if she was another apparition. Maybe what he feared most was true. He, like other men before him, had fallen in love with a fairy mistress, only to be driven mad. What would this cost him? An ear perhaps?

Wait for your one true love. How could those tiny words shipwreck every relationship he'd ever attempted? True love. What did that mean anyway? Those were words used in fairy tales, along with ever after. What place did they have in reality? Shouldn't a man be happy with someone who could meet the few needs he had? *I've never asked for much*, Duncan thought. A beautiful woman, great sex, adequate conversation. So—why after finding such women had he not been satisfied? *What man asks these kinds of questions? It's true then, I'm a raving lunatic.*

"Good God, man," Duncan yelled, "take hold of yourself before it's too late." He called for Conn, who had charged down the beach after a flock of sea gulls. "I must get back to Skye."

22

Aim for the Heart

The last two days had been full of research and writing, but in the back of Kathryn's mind hung the portrait. She couldn't get the image out of her thoughts. Only once, and only for a moment had she allowed herself to dwell on it long enough to think through to what it might truly mean. *The Lady of the Glen spoke to me in a dream. How could that be?* It had been nine generations since Mairi MacDonald walked the Fairy Glen. She and her two brothers had immigrated to America between 1746 and 1747. And nine generations later, Kathryn was born—not in Scotland, but in Texas. Now, here she had come full circle.

She sat down at her laptop and opened her manuscript file. She tabbed down her original beginning paragraph in chapter one, typed a line across the top, then scrolled back to the top of the page. And she began to write.

The dream began when I was eighteen…

About midnight, Kathryn heard a truck drive up and doors slam. Moments later, Ian and Sean walked into the cottage laughing. They both strolled over to Kathryn, a slight stagger to their steps, and gave her a kiss on each cheek.

"Hey, Mom," Ian said. "Sorry we're so late. Hope you weren't worried."

Kathryn closed her laptop. "I knew you'd come back sometime soon. I saw how much money you had between you."

"It was awesome, Mom," Sean said, a little louder than was needed in the small cottage.

"I take it you three stopped off at Saucy Mary's on the way home?"

"Yep," they both said in unison.

"And Molly? Where is she?"

"Dropped her off first. Home safe and sound," Ian said, smiling.

"Yep," Sean said. "She and Ian have become—a thing." He smiled a crooked smile.

"So who was your designated driver?"

"Umm, his last name was MacDonald, so we figured it was okay since he was kin and all," said Sean.

"We had him drop Molly off first, and then, well, here we are," Ian said.

"Yeah, you've said that already." Kathryn walked to the door and locked it. "I do hope you two behaved yourselves. Let's make this the only time you need a designated driver while you're here, okay?"

"Okay," Ian said. He elbowed Sean, who was standing, but half asleep.

"What?" Sean asked, rubbing his eyes.

"I'll see to it, Mom," Ian said.

"How about you two go shower and get a good night's sleep? Jane, from Armadale Castle, told me there's an archery tournament tomorrow on the castle grounds. I think you both should enter. It'll be lots of fun."

"An archery tournament? Sweet," Ian said, as he walked toward the bedroom. He suddenly stopped short of the door. "But wait. I didn't bring my bows."

"Jane said they would have some you can rent."

The boys walked into their room mumbling something about green tights and closed the door. Kathryn turned out the lights and retired to her room. The moon shone through the window, casting pale blue shadows across the white comforter. She slipped into a pair of blue silk pajamas, on loan from Beth, who told her she should leave the flannel pajamas at home. She'd said flannel was for children and old married women. Kathryn smiled, as she climbed into bed. She closed her eyes and thought she heard a faint melody playing somewhere in the distance. A flute whistled through the night air, a harp plucked the stars from the sky, a fiddle strung notes along the glen, and a distant drum beat in rhythm with her heart.

When Kathryn and the boys arrived at Armadale Castle the next morning, they saw that the grounds were crowded with archers of every size and age. The targets had been set up some distance across the grass of the castle grounds, and competitors were beginning to line up. Ian and Sean had found the sign-up table and paid the small entry fee and rental for the equipment. Ian was an expert back home with the long bow. Sean pretended to be Robin Hood when he was seven.

Kathryn wandered over to the craft tables set up near the castle entrance. They were featuring work for sale from area artists: ceramics, textiles, jewelry, and paintings. A gentle breeze blew the delicious smell of sweet bread in Kathryn's direction, while a small band played traditional Celtic music nearby. After admiring the local art and buying some hot bread, Kathryn walked over to the area where the boys were waiting their turn to shoot.

"Mom," Ian said, "one of the guys in line said there's a women's competition. You should enter."

Kathryn laughed as she took a bite of her sweet bread. "Right. I haven't shot a bow since I was your age. No, even younger."

"Oh, come on, Mom. Where's your sense of adventure? You've got to step up for the sake of the ancestors," Sean said.

"And which ancestors are you speaking of?"

"You're kidding, right?" Sean smiled. "What about all that Chickasaw and Cherokee blood? Just go check it out. Look over the competition. They said you could go to a practice range they've set up by the trees over there."

Kathryn looked toward the tree-lined drive. Maybe she would give it a shot. She walked toward the south part of the lawn where several younger women were practicing. *Come on, Kathryn. Make your great-grandmother proud.*

With a longbow and quiver of arrows she procured from the rental table, she set up in front of a target near the tree line. Placing an arrow on the string and pulling it back with all her might, Kathryn took aim and released. *Whoosh.* It pierced the edge of the bull's eye. She nocked another arrow, drew back the bow, and released. *Whoosh, thud.* The arrow hit dead center. Kathryn picked up a third arrow from the quiver and placed it on the bow. Raising it up and pulling the string back to her cheek, she took aim. Startled by the sound of a twig breaking behind her, she swung around, bow still drawn.

"Shoot for the heart, if you aim to bring me down," he said, arms raised above his head.

Kathryn let down her bow and dropped it to her side. "I'm sorry. You startled me." She smiled and thought he was by far the handsomest man she had ever seen in a skirt.

"I've been watching you. You're quite good."

"Thank you," Kathryn said, shifting her weight from one foot to the other.

"Well, good luck in the tournament." He turned and walked away.

"Thank you," Kathryn said. That's it? That's all I said? Not hello, my name is Kathryn, what's yours? Could I just say your legs look great in that kilt?

Kathryn turned back to the target and raised her bow. She was having difficulty holding her aim because of her short rapid breathing. She lowered her bow a second time and turned. *The view is just as magnificent from this vantage point.*

Kathryn smiled, turned back to the target, and took a deep breath. Aim for the heart, she thought, and released the arrow. *Whoosh . . . thud.* The heart it is.

Duncan walked toward his truck, with Conn following close behind. His heart was pounding against his chest like the waves against his boat in a summer storm. It was her. She'd come. She had pierced his heart and had driven straight into his very soul, without ever releasing her arrow.

Duncan had wanted to take her in his arms, but not here, not now. He would wait. He had wanted to tell her who he was, but he decided his introduction back at the manor might be a more commanding one.

Kathryn came in third place after two local girls. She felt pretty good about it. She was sure her great-grandmother was smiling. Ian won a first place ribbon and a pewter Clan Donald pin to wear on his cap. Sean finished without injuring anyone at the tournament. While the boys bought some of the local crafts for gifts for friends and family back home, Kathryn kept looking at a painting of the Fairy Glen. Even though it was only paint on a canvas, the artist had captured the magic of the glen, and it spoke to her. The rays of sunlight pierced the clouds scattered across the sky above the glen and caused the stream to sparkle like a sea of glass. The vibrant colors of the painting reflected the emotions she had felt when standing in that very place. Unable to make out the signature, she picked it up and looked on the back at the tag with the artist's name. It read: *Duncan MacDonald, Fairy Glen, Isle of Skye*

She smiled and paid for the painting. She had learned to accept the path her destiny now led her down. The Isle spoke to her so loudly at times she could hardly bear it.

They drove back to the cottage and changed for dinner, fish and chips at Saucy Mary's. Kathryn removed the painting of the *Sound of Sleat* that hung over her bed and stored it in the closet. In its place she hung the painting of the Fairy Glen. *What dreams I'll have tonight,* Kathryn thought.

After an evening celebrating her archery prowess at Saucy Mary's with Ian and Sean, they arrived at the cottage. Kathryn told the boys she was going to turn in early and do some reading. She went to her room and put on her favorite flannel pajamas, Beth need never know, and crawled into bed with a book she borrowed from Jane about the MacDonald clan. It was a typical cool evening on Skye, and she slid low under the down duvet and began reading. An hour later, Kathryn realized she'd read the same sentence five times. It was time to sleep.

Just as she'd imagined, Kathryn dreamed of fairies, sweet melodies, and handsome princes until the morning sun broke across her face and the warmth drew her from her sleep. There was a knock on her bedroom door.

Ian stuck his head in. "You awake?"

"Yes. What's up?"

He opened the door wider and walked in with a cup of hot tea. Kathryn sat up and took it from him.

"Thanks. What's this all about?" Kathryn asked.

"Sean and I are making breakfast for you. We'll call you when it's ready." He closed the door quietly as he left the room.

She lay in bed thinking about the handsome stranger she had

met the day before at the tournament. She closed her eyes and pictured his bulging calves as he walked away from her in his plaid kilt. His dark wavy hair hung loose around his shoulders. The gray around his temples and his dark, rugged face signaled more than a few years spent out of doors. She wondered if she would see him again. Maybe Jane knew who he was. Maybe she would ask her next week when she returned to the library.

23

Female Conversation

The boys called Kathryn to breakfast. The three ate and talked about their plans for the next two days. While Kathryn put her research into words, the boys were heading to the mainland again, exploring. They had been told about a piping contest in Inverness and were determined to make it by nightfall. Molly had volunteered to drive them to Kyleakin to catch the train. From there it would be a two-hour train ride.

Kathryn reminded them only two more days and it would have been a week since their first visit to the manor. Flora had said she would call when her brother returned and invite them back to meet him. They heard a horn honk outside the cottage. It was Molly. Ian and Sean agreed to be back in two days. They grabbed their bags and headed out the door. Kathryn's thoughts wandered as she waved goodbye. In two days Duncan MacDonald would return to the stone manor, and they would finally meet. Or maybe—she would meet the kilted stranger from the tournament again. Both happy thoughts indeed.

Kathryn closed the door and walked to her room. She set her clothes out for the day and turned to walk into the bathroom to shower. Her cell phone rang. "Hello?"

"Kathryn, it's Beth. How are you?"

"Beth, it's so good to hear your voice. Where are you?"

"Tunisia. Let's Skype. I want to hear what's been happening. I've finished up here, and I'll be flying back to Houston tomorrow. Check on the store, unpack, do laundry, repack. I arrive in Inverness in six days. I'll send you my itinerary. So, let's Skype. This is an expensive call."

They both got on their computers and continued the conversation

Kathryn began to trace the polar bear pattern on her pajamas. "I'm so excited you're actually coming. So much has happened since we last talked." *Silence.* "Well, okay. I *have* met someone." Kathryn paused and cleared her throat, as if the words were caught and wouldn't come out. "Well, not really met him exactly."

"And . . .?" Beth asked.

"The boys and I went to an archery tournament yesterday on the Armadale Castle grounds, and I came in third place in the women's category."

"What do you mean you came in third place? You actually competed?"

"Yes," Kathryn said. "Anyway, there was this guy who came up behind me while I was practicing."

"And you shot him?"

Kathryn laughed. "No. But he was wearing a kilt, and I must say he was quite handsome."

"A quilt?"

"No, Beth. A kilt. You know, a plaid skirt. Like *Braveheart.*"

"I know. I know. Just kidding. Okay, so he was in a skirt. What do you mean by quite handsome? I could use some details here. So far my mental picture is not too impressive."

"He was very tall and had broad shoulders. He had great calves, and he had dark hair that was tucked behind his ears and hung down over his collar." Kathryn paused. "There. How was that?"

There was a long silence.

"Mmm. So I'm picturing Johnny Depp in a kilt. What happened?"

"Well, nothing really. He said I shot well, and maybe he said good luck in the tournament. I can't really remember. Then he left."

"He left? That's it?" Beth's voice cracked from excitement.

"Yes, that's it. But it's a small island. I'm hoping to see him again. Anyway, that's not all that's happened."

Kathryn spent the next hour telling Beth about the portrait in the stone manor and the Fairy Glen. And about Mairi and Alexander. And Duncan MacDonald. Beth seemed satisfied by the end of the conversation that enough romance and intrigue existed to warrant a change in her ticket to Skye.

"Okay, it's decided then. I'm coming to Skye earlier."

"What? How much earlier?" Kathryn asked.

"So, you don't want me to come sooner?" Beth asked.

"No. I mean, yes, I do. I do want you to come. Please come. And yes, the sooner the better."

"Okay, enough said. I'm about to call and change my flight. I'll let you know as soon as I have details. You know, I've never been to Skye. It'll be a great buying trip for the shop, too."

When Kathryn said goodbye, she realized just how much she'd missed Beth and their female conversations. It would be good to have her there. As she opened her dresser her phone rang again. It was Flora.

"Hello, Kathryn. It's Flora. How are you, dear?"

"Hello, Flora. I'm doing well, thanks. And, how are you?" Kathryn asked.

"Oh, lovely. Thank you. I called to tell you Duncan has returned early from his trip. We'd love for you to come today, if it's not too much trouble."

Kathryn could hardly breathe. She wanted to say yes, but the boys weren't back from the mainland. "Oh, Flora. I can't believe I'm saying this, but I'm afraid I'll have to wait for a couple of days. My sons are off sightseeing on the mainland and won't return for two more days. I really want them to come with me. Is that silly?" Kathryn asked.

Flora laughed. "No, no," she said. "Not silly at all. We'll expect you in three days. Is that right?"

"Three days, yes," Kathryn said. "I'm really looking forward to it. Send my regards to your brother." Kathryn shook her head. *Send my regards to your brother. Who am I? Jane Austen.*

"I will, Kathryn. Good-bye now."

"Good-bye, Flora."

Time passed slowly the next two days with Ian and Sean away on the mainland. Kathryn spent most of both days writing with a fire burning in the fireplace, and drinking endless cups of hot tea. The weather had turned to rain and cold. It was a good time to be writing. At the end of the second day, Victoria called Kathryn and invited her to dinner at Kinloch Lodge on Sleat. She'd made reservations for seven o'clock. Claire MacDonald, world famous for her fine cuisine, was the owner of the lodge. It was a must for anyone visiting Skye. Kathryn agreed, and Victoria said she'd be by at half past six.

On the short drive to the restaurant from the cottage, Kathryn asked Victoria about her classes, and how they were going. She held back the news of the stone manor and the portrait, trying to be polite. Victoria spoke of a new student from South Africa, a middle-aged woman whose husband was working for the Caledonian Ferry lines. All Kathryn heard was *blah, blah, blah.*

Unable to wait a moment longer, she blurted out her discovery. "Victoria, I found the stone manor. You remember, I told you about my dream and how I'd been looking for this stone manor all my adult life. Well, I found it!"

"Kathryn, that's fantastic. Where is it?" Victoria glanced over as she drove along the southern coastline of Sleat.

"Do you know the MacDonalds of Glen Rowan?" Kathryn asked.

"Are you speaking of Flora and Duncan MacDonald?"

"Yes, they would be the ones."

Victoria put on her blinker and turned right on the narrow road that led to Kinloch Lodge. "Flora and I are good friends."

"Really? So have you seen the portrait in the Great Hall?" Kathryn asked.

"The illusive Lady of Glen Rowan, you mean?"

"Yes. Did you notice anything unusual about her?"

"That's it, then!" Victoria yelled, skidding to a stop in her Mini. "I have been trying to think of who you remind me of ever since you walked on campus. It's the portrait. You look like the Lady." Victoria frowned. "But why?"

"I think she was my ancestor."

"Oh my God. Kathryn, that's incredible, isn't it?"

Victoria pulled forward through the gate and parked in front of the lodge. As they walked to the restaurant Kathryn explained how she'd found her ancestors with Jane's help. Then she met Angus, and he told her and her sons the story of the Lady of Glen Rowan. She told her how they'd been to the stone manor and the Fairy Glen.

Once they were seated at a table overlooking the inlet, the two women each ordered a glass of wine.

"And what did Duncan say about it?" Victoria asked.

"I've not met Duncan yet. He was off painting somewhere. He's back now, though, and the boys and I are going for the day tomorrow."

"I know this story. Are you saying you're the one he's been waiting for?"

"I don't know. It's all very confusing." She pulled her collar open a bit and showed Victoria the necklace. "I found this in a box my sister gave me. The box had Celtic designs carved on it. This looks exactly like the necklace the Lady's wearing in the portrait."

"It's destiny then," Victoria said. "Do you believe in destiny?"

"I never thought about it until now."

The waiter returned with the wine and asked if they were ready to order. They asked about the house special. It was roasted lamb with fresh vegetables steamed and topped with an herbal butter. They each ordered the special, and their conversation continued.

"Tell me about Duncan MacDonald," Kathryn said.

"I happen to know that Laird MacDonald—you know he's a laird—is an artist. A very accomplished artist, in fact." She leaned forward and talked quietly, like an informant in a spy movie. "I also know that he has only recently broken off a serious relationship with the curator of an exclusive art gallery in Edinburgh."

"And how do you know this?" Kathryn asked.

"Flora and I have lunch together on occasion. We meet in Portree."

Victoria took a sip of wine and continued. "It seems everything was going along just fine until this woman, let's call her, came to Skye to the manor in Glen Rowan. They'd only been together in Edinburgh and London until then. She saw the portrait you were talking about and began asking questions."

Victoria looked around the intimate dining room, as if people might be listening. She spoke just above a whisper. "Flora told her all about the Lady of the Glen and Duncan's encounters. This woman laughed it off, which offended my dear friend, and she told Duncan. Well, it seems they got into an argument, something about silly island superstitions, I think it was. And she told him if he believed in such nonsense, he'd gone off with the fairies. She pressed him for a more permanent commitment, and he told her he was not the marrying type. She then made an offhanded remark about inbreeding and stormed out of the manor never to be heard from again." Victoria picked up her wine glass and tilted it toward Kathryn. "Flora was quite pleased she left."

"Gone off with the fairies?"

"Yes, you know, crazy."

Kathryn couldn't help but smile as she thought of her mother. Such magical terms for dark thoughts. "So, do you think he's gone off with fairies, so to speak?"

"No. I believe there are things happening all around us you can't explain. Forces acting outside our human realm."

"Hmm." Kathryn was surprised to hear Victoria talk about such things, but then many people on the Isle felt comfortable living with both worlds. She found it fascinating and exciting. "You know Duncan then?"

"Yes, not nearly so well as I know Flora. But yes," Victoria said.

"Would you say he's handsome?" Kathryn asked.

"I'd say he's magnificent. And, this woman from Edinburgh was a fool for walking out on him. He's a bit moody, I think. Artist, and all. But I don't know of a single woman on Skye who'd not stand in line for an opportunity to be Lady of Glen Rowan."

"Lady of Glen Rowan," Kathryn said. "That's got a nice ring to it."

The two friends laughed, and the waiter arrived at the table with their food. As they ate dinner, Kathryn told Victoria that Beth was coming for a visit and they would have to meet. The remainder of their conversation centered around Victoria talking about what it was like to grow up on Skye. When they'd finished their meal, Victoria drove Kathryn back to the cottage. She made her promise to call after her meeting with Duncan and fill her in on all the juicy details. Kathryn agreed, said good night, and walked into the empty cottage.

She sat down at her laptop and tried to write, but her mind was occupied elsewhere. She imagined Duncan walking into the great hall, dressed in a kilt and a smile. Kathryn closed her laptop, built a fire, and lay on the couch fantasizing about what a woman could do with a kilt and a smile.

24

A Hidden Destiny

Kathryn was up early after a restless night's sleep. A week had passed since they had first seen the MacDonald Manor, and she couldn't still her thoughts. This was the day they were driving to the stone manor to meet Duncan. Ian had called the night before to tell her they were arriving on a morning train from Inverness. She'd already showered and dressed and was on her second cup of coffee when her cell phone rang. It was Ian. Their train would be arriving in half an hour. She quickly finished her coffee and drove to the station. On the drive back to the cottage, they told her all about their adventures on the mainland and the great music they'd heard. Kathryn found it hard to concentrate.

"I'm glad you guys had a good trip. I hope you're ready for our drive north to the manor." Kathryn pulled into the carpark at the cottage, and they all got out of the Rover.

"There's just time for a quick shower and change of clothes. Are you hungry?" Kathryn asked.

"No. We got something in Inverness and ate it on the train," Ian said. "We'll make it fast."

As Kathryn rinsed out the coffee pot, the phone rang. It was Flora, telling her everything was ready for their visit. *If only Beth were here*, she thought. *I think I might feel braver.*

"The boys have just arrived from the mainland," Kathryn said. "We should be leaving within the hour for your place." She looked at the clock on the wall in the kitchen, 9:55. "It might take two hours, so we'll arrive around one o'clock. Will that be all right?"

"Lovely," Flora said. "I'll have a light lunch ready. Nothing fancy, mind you. Just some sandwiches and fruit. Does that sound alright with you?"

"Yes, perfect," Kathryn said. "We'll see you soon."

They said good-bye, and Kathryn tried to busy herself in the kitchen. She absentmindedly wiped down the counter several times before the boys were finally ready to go.

The three quickly headed north. Sean and Ian were placing bets on what Duncan would look like and whether they would be having haggis for lunch. Kathryn smiled and tried to appear calm. Truth be told, she was unraveling with each passing mile.

"Welcome back," Flora said. " Please come in. How was your journey? Without problems, I hope."

"It was a beautiful drive. No problems," Kathryn said. "Thank you so much for having us. I've…we've…really been looking forward to it."

Ian and Sean let out a faint laugh as they followed Kathryn inside. She turned and raised an eyebrow. Ian put his hand to his mouth, but his eyes were still smiling. Sean cleared his throat and looked the other way. And for a moment, Kathryn thought she noticed the faintest smile on Flora's face, as well.

Flora pointed down the hallway. "Please follow me to the Great Hall. You can wait there. I'll tell Duncan you're here." Flora opened the door and motioned for them to enter. "You must be thirsty after the drive. What would you like, something hot or something cold? Tea, coffee, soda?"

"I'd love a cup of coffee. Thank you," Ian said.

"A Coke would be great. Thanks," Sean said.

"And you, Kathryn?"

"A cup of tea would be lovely. Thank you, Flora."

"Please sit down. I'll be back in a flash." And with that, Flora left the room, closing the large wooden door behind her.

The portrait of the Lady was just as captivating as the first time they saw her. They stood staring in silence. Kathryn found herself quite content as she looked at her kindred likeness hanging above the mantel.

The great door opened and as the three turned, Duncan MacDonald, Laird of the Manor, entered the room. A smile broke across Kathryn's face as he walked toward her. Duncan stopped beside her and looked up at the portrait. "Beautiful, isn't she? I heard she was quite good with a bow in her day. This is only hearsay, mind you." He turned and extended his hand. "Hello, my name is Duncan MacDonald."

Kathryn took his hand. "It was you at the archery tournament."

"Yes, it was. So you remember me then?"

Kathryn smiled. "Remember you—can I just say your legs look great in a skirt." *Finally.*

The room filled with laughter, and Kathryn continued. "Why didn't you say something at the tournament?"

"I don't know. It was a bit of a shock, I guess, to see you."

"A shock? A good shock or a bad shock?"

The corner of Duncan's mouth curved up slightly. "It was a good shock." He looked back at the portrait. "The resemblance is remarkable." He looked at Kathryn's hand resting in his and ran his thumb across the delicate surface. His gaze shifted, and he stared into Kathryn's eyes. She drew back her hand and looked toward the boys.

Flora walked in with a tray and broke the awkward silence. "Well, I see you've all met. Good then. Let's all of us have some refreshment, shall we?"

Duncan moved toward Sean and Ian, who were standing in front of the sofa. He extended his hand. “We’ve not all met yet. I’m Duncan. It’s a pleasure to meet you.”

Ian shook his hand immediately. “I’m Ian. Thanks for having us.”

Sean reached out his hand. “I’m Sean.”

“All right, now. Don’t be shy. Please have a seat,” Flora said, laying the tray on the large coffee table, next to a stack of plates, napkins, and silverware. “I’ll be back with our lunch. We can eat in here, if that’s all right with everyone.”

“Let me help you, Flora,” Kathryn said.

“No, no. Thank you, dear. Everything is ready and waiting on a tray. I’ll just bring it right in.”

They all sat down. Kathryn sat next to her sons on the sofa. Duncan sat in a leather chair across from them. Conn curled up next to Sean’s feet.

“Tell me where you’re from in America, and what brought you to Skye?” Duncan asked.

Before Kathryn could answer, Ian spoke. “We both in live in Austin, Texas.” He pointed to Sean. “I just graduated from the university there, and we’re on a backpacking trip through Europe. We decided to end the trip here, with Mom.”

“And what do you think of Skye?”

“It’s awesome. We’ve traveled back to the mainland a couple of different times and explored. Scotland’s amazing.” Ian pointed to Sean. “I didn’t mean to speak for both of us.”

“I agree. It’s been really cool,” Sean said.

Duncan looked at Kathryn. “And what brought *you* to Skye?”

Kathryn squirmed a bit and ran her finger back and forth across the seam on the arm of the sofa. “I came in search of ancestors. That, and a recent divorce.”

Flora entered the room with lunch and set the tray on the table. She sat down in the remaining leather chair next to Duncan.

"Ahh. So you're not married then?"

"No, I'm not," Kathryn said.

"Our dad lives in London," Sean said. His face was red.

"Oh, I see," Duncan said.

"Well, let's all have some lunch, shall we?" Flora smiled and quickly changed the conversation to the weather. The remainder of the afternoon Duncan entertained Kathryn and her sons with tales about the manor, the glen, and the Isle. As the fire faded in the hearth, he offered to give them a tour of the grounds, including the horse stables. They walked through the stables first. It housed three beautiful Arabians, one raven black, one white, and one chestnut. There were also five Eriskay ponies, a Scottish breed, descended from ancient horses.

"Do either of you ride?" Duncan asked, looking at Ian and Sean.

"Yes," Ian said quickly.

"We've ridden before, is what he means," Sean said. "We never had a horse ourselves."

"Well, you're welcome to come ride anytime you'd like while you're here. Our groundskeeper, Alan, will be happy to help you, if I'm not here. Kathryn, do you ride?" Duncan asked and turned to face her. She was rubbing the white Arabian between the eyes. "I think he likes you. He's quite particular; you should know that. Do you ride?"

"I know how to ride, yes. And I love it," Kathryn said. "I've always wanted a horse."

"I thought everyone in Texas had a horse." He smiled.

"You're teasing me now." Kathryn said and continued rubbing the horse's nose. "What's his name?"

"This is Ghajeera. It means 'gypsy'," Duncan said.

"Hello, Ghajeera," Kathryn said. She pointed toward the other two stalls. "And the other two?"

Duncan walked over to the chestnut mare. "This is Qismah. Her name means 'destiny'. And my black beauty is Layla, which means 'night'."

Sean and Ian stood in front of Layla's stall. Conn leaned against Sean's leg.

"She's beautiful," Sean said, running his hand along her thick mane.

"As I said, you're all welcome to come back and ride," Duncan said. He looked at his watch. "Is anyone hungry?"

Ian and Sean raised their hands. Duncan recommended they all drive to the Lady of the Glen Pub for dinner. Everyone agreed. They left the stables and walked toward the manor.

"We can tour the remainder of the grounds another time," Duncan said.

"I'll give my daughter a call and see if they'd like to meet us there," Flora said. "You all go on ahead, I'll follow shortly in Duncan's truck." Flora opened the front door and turned to Kathryn. "Did you leave anything inside?"

"No," Kathryn said. "Should I stay behind and ride with you?"

Flora smiled. "No, dear. You go on ahead with Duncan and your lads. I'll only be a minute or two behind you."

Sean opened the back of the Land Rover and called for Conn. He jumped up into the back. Kathryn climbed into the driver's seat.

"Duncan, you take shotgun," Ian said.

"Shotgun?" Duncan asked.

"Passenger's seat, I mean."

They all loaded into the Rover and were off to the pub. Conn leaned over the back seat and rested his hairy chin on Sean's shoulder. A friendship was being formed, and Sean seemed happy for it.

They arrived at the pub and hurried in just ahead of a rainstorm. Angus greeted them with a loud crow and beer all around.

Although cold rain fell outside the pub, nothing could dampen Kathryn's mood. The boys asked Angus for another story, and just as he was about to begin, Flora entered with her daughter, Julie. David, Julie's husband, followed them holding their son, Charles, and an umbrella.

They joined the table, and Angus promised a story the next time they came in. Kathryn and her boys and Duncan and his family spent the evening getting to know one another over dinner. It was during coffee at the end of the meal that Flora told how she'd lost her husband, Andrew, to the sea shortly after Julie's birth. She'd never remarried and thought that Duncan spent entirely too much time in his boat for her peace of mind. David cradled a sleeping Charles, and Conn snored at Sean's feet.

"I think you've made a friend for life, Sean," Duncan said.

"He's awesome." Sean leaned down and rubbed Conn's massive head.

"I hate to break up the party, but we should be getting Charles home." Julie stood and gathered her coat and bag.

Everyone said their good-byes. The rain had stopped. Duncan walked Kathryn to the Land Rover, while the others followed a few steps behind.

"Kathryn, would you like to have dinner with me tomorrow night? Just the two of us?"

Kathryn slid into the driver's seat as Duncan held open the door. "I'd love to."

"I'll pick you up about half past seven. There's a very nice restaurant in Portree near the water. I'll make the reservation." Duncan leaned against the open door.

"You'll need directions to our house."

"The boys said you're at Alastair MacDonald's. I know where that is."

Ian climbed into the passenger's seat, and Sean crawled into the back. Duncan said good night and shut the door. Kathryn closed her eyes and replayed Duncan's grand entrance over and over in her mind. The ride back to the cottage was quiet but not from the lack of something to say. Kathryn looked at her sons and knew they were waiting for her to speak. Something, anything. The problem was she didn't know what to say. She was still confused about all that was happening, and it was then that she realized, they must be, too.

"I'm thinking we need to talk about what just happened back there."

"It's okay, Mom, you don't have to talk about it. It's really none of our business. You're an adult," said Ian, trying to sound mature and unrattled by the events of the day.

"So how about you, Sean?" Kathryn asked.

"I'm not sure. It all seemed like a big joke at first. I mean—*the plan*. But now that I think I've seen *the plan*, I'm not sure I like it so much."

"What are you talking about?" Ian asked.

"Oh, come on. You saw them. Isn't it obvious? Big Highlander swoops down in his kilt and boots and sweeps Mom off her very unstable feet. Are you okay with that? What about Dad? He's not even cold yet."

"Okay, we need to talk,"Ian, Kathryn said and pulled the car off to side of the road.

The car came to a halt, and the three sat quietly surrounded by rocky hills and the heather-covered moor. The only signs of life were the sheep that grazed in the field alongside the road.

Kathryn was the first to speak. "I know this has all been very hard. We haven't really talked about it a lot. Mostly, because I don't know what to say. This is not the way I had planned for my life to turn out—our lives to turn out. I intended to die a very old woman, still married to your father. But he obviously changed his mind."

"Yeah, and why is that? What happened?" Sean asked.

"Well, I think we all know what happened," Kathryn said.

"No, I want to know *why* it happened. What did you do to make him go looking for someone else? I thought you two loved each other, I thought you were happy."

"Sean, shut up. You don't know what you're talking about," Ian said.

"Well, it seems none of us do," Sean said.

Kathryn cleared her throat and held back the tears that threatened to break through at any moment. "You're right, Sean. I have asked myself over and over what happened, what I did to cause your dad to find someone else to take my place. And you want to know what I came up with? Nothing. I did nothing to cause him to leave. He made this choice on his own."

Kathryn tried to keep her voice from trembling. "I'm sure there are things I could have done better—differently—because no one's perfect. But I can tell you, I always loved your father, I always will. When he left he took part of me with him." Kathryn brushed back a single tear. "I was really angry and hurt at first, but I'm going to be okay. I don't know what's going to happen with Duncan, but whatever it is, it will happen slowly and carefully."

"You know what? I don't see anything slow or careful about what's going on here. I know we're supposed to be grown up and all that, but this has been really har—hard." Sean's voice began to break up as he continued, "I was really mad at Dad at first, then I was mad at you 'cause I thought you must have done something to make him act this stupid." Sean looked at Kathryn. "Now, I guess I'm just mad. I don't know what to do about it." Sean put his face in his hands and wept like he was five again.

Ian leaned over the seat and put his hand on Sean's shoulder, tears escaping onto his cheeks one at a time, as though they hoped to go unnoticed. Kathryn's heart ached as she watched the full weight of the divorce come crashing down on her two sons. How fragile they looked. And she knew she was powerless to console them. This was not a path they chose to be walking down, but it was where they found themselves. Kathryn leaned toward Ian and placed one hand on his arm and reached across to the back, laying her other hand on Sean's head.

"I love you both, so much. We'll all get through this together. I promise," Kathryn said, thinking how anemic her words sounded.

Rain began to fall, and Kathryn and her sons sat in the Land Rover, in the heather-covered glen, all three wishing for what should have been.

A storm blew in the next morning, and heavy rain covered the island all day long. Kathryn decided to write while the boys slept late. Once they roused and dressed, the boys drove to Saucy Mary's for the afternoon and evening. They'd met a group of Australian backpackers staying at the hostel in town and had arranged to spend the evening listening to an Irish band at the pub. Nothing was said about what happened the night before.

The day passed quietly enough with the boys away, but Kathryn could not calm her thoughts. She found it impossible to write, so instead, she spent much of the afternoon trying to figure out how she would wear her hair. Just before seven-thirty, there was a knock on the door, and there stood Duncan in a dark green wool jacket and jeans. He smiled.

"You look beautiful, Kathryn. You'll be the envy of every woman on the Isle."

"Thank you," Kathryn said. She'd chosen to braid her hair down the back, weaving a piece of white lace through the braid and had picked out a black sweater dress and leggings to wear.

"Shall we go?" Duncan asked. "We've a reservation in Portree."

"Sounds wonderful." Kathryn grabbed her rain jacket and followed Duncan to his truck.

On the drive to Portree, Duncan told Kathryn about meeting the Lady when he was young. He described Mairi to her in detail, down to the sound of her voice. Kathryn talked about the first time she had the dream of the stone manor and her early adventures searching for it. They arrived at the restaurant just as she told Duncan how she and John met in Indonesia.

"Here we are," Duncan said. "Maybe we could save speaking about *him* for another time." He parked in front of the restaurant on the narrow street.

Kathryn reached for the door and turned to face Duncan. "I'll not talk about John again unless you ask. Will that work?"

"Aye," he said. "Nothing like talk of another man to spoil a perfectly pleasant evening."

Kathryn smiled and hopped out of the truck.

Once seated at the restaurant, Duncan ordered a bottle of wine and gently reached for Kathryn's hand, but confusion caused her to draw it back. His touch was electrifying, his gaze piercing, but her mind said no.

"What is it?"

Kathryn fumbled with the napkin in her lap. "I don't understand."

"Understand what?"

"This—all this."

Duncan looked around the dining room. "All what?"

Kathryn ran her fingers back and forth across the white linen tablecloth, as nervous as a young girl on her first date. "You, the manor, the Fairy Glen—the Lady. That's what. Then, there's the whole thing with John and the divorce." She shook her head and looked up at Duncan. "Oh, sorry I mentioned him. But, what am I supposed to do with all of this?"

"Why do you have to do anything with it? It's fate, Kathryn." Duncan picked up his glass of wine, stood, and walked to the large window with the view of the loch.

"Wait." Kathryn followed him.

"Wait?" Duncan half-smiled and turned to Kathryn. "I have waited—for over thirty years. You know, this is not quite what I had envisioned either." He paused for a moment, and then laughed.

"What?" Kathryn asked.

"I'm sorry. I just—"

"You just what?"

"I just expected you to be—"

"What? You expected me to be what?"

"I expected you to be a Highland lass. You know, a girl who loves haggis and speaks Gaelic—and dances to a Highland reel."

"Hey, I can hurl haggis as good as the next gal. I've got Highland blood running through my veins, you know." Kathryn held up her wrist. "It's a little watered down by this time, but I can feel it." Kathryn looked around the room. "So you're saying every woman in the room loves haggis, speaks Gaelic, and dances or whatever you said? It was quite a list. And just so you know, I *do* have a plaid skirt of my very own."

"No, you're right. I was just trying to make a point, and it takes more than clothes to be—one of us."

"I know that. And I'm telling you, all joking aside, I feel it. I can't explain it, but I feel at home here."

"Come let's not argue our first evening together. What say we order?"

After dinner, Duncan suggested they take a drive. Forty-five minutes later, they arrived at the Fairy Glen—the only place on Skye that the midges, tiny biting bugs, refused to inhabit. Duncan sat down in the thick grass and patted the ground. Kathryn dropped down next to him, and they sat silent. The wind blew briskly through the glen, and they watched as a herd of deer grazed below. Kathryn shivered. Duncan moved close and put his arm around her.

"You're cold?"

"Always."

"I promise to be only a wind block."

"Thanks," said Kathryn. She felt safe and very much at home leaning against him.

"What are we to do, you and I?" Duncan asked.

"I'm still trying to find myself," Kathryn said.

"So you're lost then?"

"You're laughing at me."

"No."

"No?"

"Okay, okay. Aye, I suppose I was laughing a wee bit, and I'm sorry. It's just that I don't know what that means really—trying to find yourself. I think maybe this is an American problem?" Duncan raised one eyebrow and smiled.

"You're saying Scots don't have this problem?" Kathryn shifted her weight away from Duncan and turned to face him.

"No, we don't have this problem. We know exactly who we are, and we're constantly trying to convince the rest of the world of it."

They both laughed as Kathryn leaned back against Duncan's shoulder.

"I gave myself heart and soul to one man already, and he—well, let's just say it didn't work out. I don't know, maybe I wasn't enough for him, maybe I changed. All I know is he went looking for someone else and found her. So, here I am in Scotland, trying to find my ancestors and at the same time find my way back to who I am—who I'm supposed to be. I'm afraid this may take me some time."

She felt Duncan's body sink ever so slightly and added, "Maybe you could help me find the Highland lass who lives deep inside my soul. She's in there. I know it. In fact, sometimes I hear her voice."

"Aye, it's her voice that calls to me, I think." Duncan rested his chin on Kathryn's shoulder. "So, you think my legs look good in a kilt?"

"Aye, I do."

As the mist began to roll in over the glen, Duncan and Kathryn sat quietly and listened to the wind carrying an ancient song that only they could hear. Their spirits were tied to that place, to an ancient past, and to a common future, one that had not yet fully revealed itself to Kathryn. But destiny is not often in a hurry when it is working its magic, leading a lost soul down the path chosen from before time began. And even though Kathryn's mind was troubled, her heart felt at peace. And Duncan continued to wait as destiny lay quietly resting in his arms.

25

An Unexpected Guest

Kathryn saw an unfamiliar car parked in front of their rented cottage as they pulled into the driveway.

"The boys must have invited someone over from Saucy Mary's. I should probably just say good night and go in," Kathryn said. "I had a lovely evening. Thank you."

"My pleasure, Kathryn. I'll call you tomorrow." He took her hand in his and gently kissed it.

Kathryn blushed and said good night.

As she opened the front door, she saw the figure of a man standing in the kitchen talking to Ian and Sean. He turned to face Kathryn.

"Mom, look it's Dad," Sean said.

Kathryn stood motionless in the doorway.

"Hey. Surprise?" John walked toward Kathryn, who had not moved any farther than the front door. "Uh, boys, could you give your mother and me a minute or two alone? The fridge seems to be empty of beer." He tossed Ian the keys. "Maybe you two could go pick us up some local flavor."

"How did you find us?" Kathryn asked.

"I still have a friend on the inside, don't I, Sean?" John turned to Sean and smiled.

"Sean?" Kathryn tried to rein in the anger that was quickly coming to a boil.

"He said he wanted to come back, Mom. Just talk to him."

Kathryn turned to John and stared, trying not to lose control in front of Ian and Sean.

Before John could answer, Kathryn said, "Ian, you and Sean take a drive while your dad and I sort this out." She moved away from the door. "It won't take long, trust me."

As the boys drove away, Kathryn walked into the kitchen and made herself a cup of tea. John stood in the living room waiting. Hot tea in hand, Kathryn sat on the couch, her heart beating as loudly as the clock on the mantel. John sat in the chair across from her.

"Kathryn, you look—wonderful," John said.

Kathryn looked through the steam into her tea, searching for her voice. Unable to retrieve it, she took a sip and pulled both feet up underneath her on the couch.

"I'm sure you're wondering what I'm doing here." John moved forward to the edge of the chair, his hands clasped together.

"*Braveheart*," Kathryn said. There it was. A word.

"*Braveheart*? What does that mean?" John looked confused.

"I'm thinking you're very brave to come all this way—unannounced. Are you alone?"

"Yes." John shook his head. "Kathryn, she's gone."

Kathryn looked up from her tea. "What do you mean she's gone?"

"I know you must hate me. I know I don't deserve a second chance. But that's why I'm here. I'm begging you for a second chance." John moved next to Kathryn on the couch and took her hand.

Kathryn set down her cup of tea and pulled her hand away as she stood. "A *second* chance?"

"Okay, let's not number them then. Another chance," John said.

"Where's Courtney? Are you deserting *her* now?"

"Whoa, whoa. No, Kathryn it's not like that. Look, I made a huge mistake. I wasn't thinking. I was—distracted. She lured me in with compliments and tight shirts."

"Oh my God, John. Stop it. Don't play the man card with me."

"What do you mean?"

"I mean blaming your lack of control on someone else. It's always someone else's fault with you." Kathryn crossed her arms. "No more excuses, John. This was your choice. You said she's gone. What happened?"

"I don't know. Once we moved in together in London, everything changed. She always had to be doing something, going somewhere. I just wanted to be home if we weren't traveling on business. We began to argue and—"

"Of course you argued. She's really young, John. You moved to London. What did you expect?" *Why am I defending her? This conversation is crazy.* "Where did she go?"

"She went back to Houston."

Kathryn interrupted. "Wait a minute. What if she hadn't left you? Would you be here right now, begging for me to take you back? Do I look that stupid—or desperate?"

John stood and moved toward Kathryn. "Come on, Kathryn, it's not like that. I love you. I never loved Courtney. It was just about the . . ." He stopped himself.

"The sex, John? It was just about the sex?"

"No, no. Kathryn you're putting words in my mouth. Why are you doing this?"

Kathryn moved to the door and opened it. "Where are you staying?"

"I thought I might stay—"

Kathryn raised her hand as John began to speak. "Please, just go."

John stood next to her in the doorway. "Please, Kathryn. What about the boys?"

"The boys? The boys are having a hell of a time, but they'll get through it just like I will. And, so help me God, if you ever use Sean like this again, I'll kick your ass." *I've always wanted to say that to someone. I'll kick your ass. Good Lord, did I really just say that?* Kathryn continued. "That whole 'having a friend on the inside' crap. What is that? Ian and Sean are your sons, and they love you. Don't you dare use their pain or confusion to try to get to me."

John just stood with his mouth open.

Kathryn turned to leave, then hesitated. "You know, John, had you come back before I came to Scotland, while I was still stupid and desperate, and asked for another chance, I might have given it to you."

Kathryn stepped out of the cottage. John walked out and stood beside her, still speechless.

"I found the manor, John."

"What manor?" He found his voice.

"The one in my dreams. It's amazing really. I belong here. I know that now."

"Crazy talk, Kathryn."

Suddenly the sky opened up, and the rain came down in sheets. They ran back into the cottage and closed the door.

"Kathryn, I'll go in the morning. I promise. Just let me stay tonight and spend a little time with the boys. What do you say?"

"No, you can't stay here tonight, and you don't deserve a minute of the boys' time, but I know they'll want to see you. So, you can wait until they get back and stay a bit longer." At this point, Kathryn slowed her speech and calmed her voice. She pointed first to John and then to the cottage door. "But, and hear me clearly John, I want you gone before the evening is over. I don't care where you go. It's a big enough island to find a bed somewhere for the night. And then I want you to go back to London where you belong."

John walked toward her. "Okay, I promise. Thanks, Kath—"

She closed the door to her room before he had time to finish her name. She fell back across the bed. He wanted her back. The boys wanted them to be together again, like it was before. *Like it was before.* That was the problem; it would never be like it was before. *What was he thinking coming here?* Kathryn thought. *Asking me to take him back.*

Kathryn closed her eyes and saw Ian and Sean crying in the car. She sat up quickly. *I can't fix this. Getting back with John won't fix this. It'll only happen again. And again.* She released a long and cleansing sigh. Kathryn knew that now, and for the first time, without regret or guilt, she was relieved to be free. She dressed for bed. Her thoughts drifted to the hillside of Glen Rowan, and she slid under the comforter. The steady rain and wind had become for Kathryn the sound of peace. The Skye storm took her little cottage and washed it clean. The westerly wind carried a lullaby from ancient times and rocked her gently to sleep.

26

Sink or Swim

Duncan sat at the kitchen table with Flora and watched as the sun broke through the east window. Flora poured another cup of coffee and observed her brother as she sipped in silence. Having a quiet breakfast with him was not particularly out of the ordinary, but she knew he had not slept, for his bed was made when she went in to wake him for breakfast—and he was not in the habit of making his own bed.

Unable to bear up under the silence or her curiosity, she spoke. "Duncan, tell me, how did you pass the time with Kathryn? You've not spoken of it since she and her boys returned to their cottage in Sleat."

Duncan took a sip of his coffee and gave Flora a half-smile. "Not what I'd imagined, I suppose. But it could've been worse. She could have refused me completely."

"Refused you? Mary and Joseph, Duncan. Whatever do you mean? You didn't ask her to marry you last night, did you?"

"No, no. I just meant she seems to be open to our seeing each other. She said she was confused. She said she had to find herself first."

"Find herself?"

"Yes, American and all. My only hope is she asked me to help her find herself."

"And you know where she is, I'm supposing? Seeing as she's lost and all." Flora smiled and began to clear the table as Duncan stood and stretched.

"Sounds a bit daft, doesn't it?" Duncan put his arm around Flora and kissed the top of her head. "So, will you help me then?"

"You know I'll do anything in the world for you. Just be yourself. Let her see Duncan, Laird of the Manor of Glen Rowan. How could she refuse?" Flora grabbed Duncan by the arms and moved him away from the table. She stepped back and looked at him, like an artist observing a subject about to be sketched.

"What's this about?" Duncan asked.

"You need to run upstairs and wash up a bit. Put on what you wore to the archery tournament. Didn't you say she seemed to take special note of you there first?"

"Aye, she did. But I'll not dress up in a kilt just for a morning visit, no matter how much she liked the look of my legs. You've been reading those romance novels again, haven't you?"

Flora placed the last dish in the sink and laughed. "You're right. So hurry up and get yourself dressed. You've no time to lose."

"Is that a comment on my age, Flora?" Duncan stood in the doorway.

"No, no." Flora laughed. "You want her to know you're interested."

"She knows."

"Aye, but she needs to know this is bigger than the both of you. It's her destiny. Just don't push her too hard. You can't drive her like sheep."

"I'm not to lose any time, but I'm not to push either? How will I know if I'm pushing?" Duncan reached down and patted Conn's head.

She pointed in their direction. "Be sure and take Conn—the lads really took to him. Hurry up now." And with that Flora blew Duncan a kiss and walked to the pantry. She paused at the door. "Oh, if she starts to bleat, you're pushing."

Two miles from Kathryn's cottage Duncan began to rehearse what he was going to say. *I've been awake all night thinking of you, Kathryn. I had to see you again this morning.* Just before the cottage a group of sheep blocked the roadway. Duncan slowed down and whistled out the window to hurry them along. They bleated. Maybe that was too much then.

There was a loud knock on the cottage door. John answered it dressed in a T-shirt and boxers, sipping a cup of steaming hot coffee. As he opened the door, he jumped back, spilling coffee down his T-shirt and onto the floor, for in the doorway, with the sunlight unable to pass, stood Duncan, with Conn at his side.

John pulled off his wet shirt and threw it on the couch. "Can I help you?"

Duncan apologized. "Sorry, I must have the wrong place. I was looking for Kathryn Silverton."

"Silverton? Huh. You've got the right place. Hang on a minute." John turned and yelled. "Kathryn, there's a very large man looking for you." He looked back at Duncan. "Oh, and he's brought his horse."

Kathryn walked out of the bedroom in her robe with her wet hair wrapped in a towel. "Duncan."

"Duncan?" John asked. He reached out his hand, "Hello, I'm John, Kathryn's husband."

"John!" Kathryn yelled.

"John?" Duncan asked and stood for a moment, his gaze and his feet glued to the floor. Then, he looked up at Kathryn as though he was just stepping out of a deep sleep.

"Duncan, it's not what you think."

"So, do you ride that thing sidesaddle?" John asked.

Duncan stepped forward and punched John's smile down his throat with a hard hit to the face. John fell back to the floor moaning and holding his nose, which was bleeding.

Duncan turned and walked quickly toward his truck. Conn stood in the doorway for a moment and then raced after him. Kathryn stepped over John without a word as if he was a pile of dirty laundry. When she reached the door, she called out, but it was too late. Duncan was already driving away from the cottage, gravel flying and tires spinning.

"What was that about?" John sat up, grabbed his T-shirt from the couch, and wiped his nose on the hem.

"No!" Kathryn turned to John and kicked him in the shin.

"Ouch!" John grabbed his leg. "What? What did I do?"

"I told you to leave. How could you have stayed? Now look what you've done."

Kathryn ran into her room and quickly dressed in jeans, T-shirt, and a hooded jacket. John stood holding out a cup of coffee to her as she emerged. She walked past him shoving her wet hair under a wool cap.

"Kathryn, wait. Here, have a cup of coffee, and let's talk about this."

Kathryn stopped in the doorway. "I want you gone when I get back." And with that she slammed the door.

The boy's bedroom door opened, and they walked into the living room.

"What just happened?" Ian asked.

"Sorry, boys. Didn't mean for you to hear that. Did you hear that?" John asked.

"Yeah, Dad," Sean said. "Small cottage, you know."

"Maybe you should take off. I don't think this was such a good idea," Ian said.

"I just wanted to fix it," John said.

"I guess some things just can't be fixed, Dad," Sean said. "We'll call you before we leave to go home."

And with that brief conversation, the Trent family was finally laid to rest. In the last ten months, there had been times of grief and times of anger, but now was the time for healing. And Skye's wild and barren landscape would be just the balm they needed.

Flora heard someone pounding on the door and hurried to answer it. Kathryn stood shivering and in tears.

"Is Duncan here?"

"Why no, Kathryn. He's not with you?"

"No."

"Do come inside. What's wrong?" Flora led Kathryn into the Great Hall to the warmth of the fire.

"Oh, Flora. There's been a mistake, a terrible mistake."

Flora helped Kathryn sit down on the couch. "Calm down now, Kathryn. What's happened?"

"My ex-husband, John, showed up last night. He said he wanted me back. I told him no." Kathryn shook her head. "I was so stupid. How could I be so careless?"

Flora listened quietly.

"He wanted to stay. I said no, but he begged to see the boys, so I told him he could stay long enough to talk to them, you know. But I told him to be gone before the evening was over, and I went to bed." Kathryn rocked back and forth, rubbing her hands back and forth on the tops of her legs.

"Deep breaths, dear."

"Duncan came over this morning."

"Oh no, I'm afraid that's my doing."

Words spilled out of Kathryn's mouth like water over a dam.

"John answered the door. I didn't know he was still there. I walked out in my robe with my hair in a towel—and you can imagine what Duncan must have thought." Kathryn pounded her fist on her forehead. "Just when I thought my life was making sense." She bent forward and rested her face on her knees.

Flora gently patted her back. "Kathryn, Kathryn, this will all be made right. You'll see. Why I bet Duncan is at Angus's pub right now."

Kathryn sat up. "Do you think so?"

"Aye, I'm sure of it. But you'd best hurry. He'll be out to sea next."

Kathryn rushed out the door. Flora stood waving as the Land Rover tires spun, throwing loose rocks into the air.

Kathryn opened the door to the pub and saw Conn sleeping soundly at the end of the bar.

"Conn." As soon as she spoke he jumped to his feet and trotted to her. Angus smiled. "Lass, it's mighty early for you to be visitin' a pub."

"I need to talk to Duncan. Where is he?"

"I'm afraid he's gone."

"Gone?" Kathryn looked around the room as she petted Conn to calm him. "But I thought—well, I saw Conn and…"

"He was here a wee bit ago but seemed to be in a big hurry. He said he'd be gone for a time, and he'd call Flora and have her come for Conn."

"Oh, I see. Do you have any idea where he'd go—if he were upset?"

"Just how upset might that be now?"

Kathryn told Angus what had happened, and no sooner had she finished her story than he grabbed her by the arm and led her out of the empty pub, then locked the door behind them.

"What about Conn?"

"I won't be long. We're just goin' to the pier. We must be quick about it. If he left Conn, he can only be headin' to one place, the Edge of the World. Jump on."

"What do you mean the Edge of the World?" Kathryn asked.

"St. Kilda, the island. No time to explain now."

Angus pointed to an old Indian motorcycle. On any other occasion, Kathryn might have paused for a moment to consider the safety of such a proposal, but she was too distracted and upset to think about it now. Angus cranked up the bike, and they were off to Uig Bay.

Minutes later as they approached the pier, Angus pointed toward Duncan's truck. They parked the motorcycle next to the pier and ran to the end where Duncan's sailboat was passing about fifty yards from the pier. Kathryn and Angus jumped and shouted, like schoolchildren, trying to get his attention. Duncan turned and saw them on the pier but didn't acknowledge their presence. Instead, he turned facing the mouth of the bay and continued sailing toward Harris and beyond.

Kathryn turned to Angus. "Angus, what do I do? I can't let him just sail away thinking the worst."

Angus thought for a moment. "Kathryn, just how well do you swim?"

"What?"

"Can you swim, lass?"

"Well, yes. But you can't be suggesting I jump in and swim after him. I'd never catch up to him. Besides, it looks really cold."

Angus looked over the edge of the pier and noticed a small skiff with oars. "Kathryn, you could borrow this wee boat."

"What? I can't possibly row fast enough to catch him." Kathryn stood on the end of the pier and watched as Duncan sailed out of Uig Bay toward the outer Isles.

"I'm sorry, Kathryn."

She turned to Angus and spoke just above the wind. "I've had it with men. What the hell was I thinking? I need Beth and a stout beer." She walked toward the motorcycle.

"Come on now, Kathryn. There's no need to give up men just like that." Angus hurried to catch up. "Who's Beth?"

27

The Edge of the World

Duncan sailed to Leverburgh, Harris, and stopped for supplies and a toothbrush on his way to St. Kilda. He phoned Flora from the shop and asked her to pick up Conn at the pub. She pleaded with him to come back and talk with Kathryn. He refused to hear what she had to say and cut the call short before Flora could pass on what Kathryn had told her.

After stowing his supplies, he set sail for St. Kilda. *The Edge of the World.*

Angus and Kathryn arrived back at the pub and decided even with all that had transpired it might be too early for a pint. Angus drew up two cups of strong coffee and sat down next to her at the bar. Kathryn told him her sister Beth would arrive in Skye the next day, and she'd know what to do. She told Angus she was tired of chasing down her dreams, and if destiny wanted her, he would have to come find her.

"So, St. Kilda. Exactly how far is that from Skye?" Kathryn tried to give the appearance this was a casual question, nothing more.

"It's about thirty-one miles off the island of Lewis. It's the ancestral home of his mother, Lady MacDonald. She was a MacQueen from St. Kilda, no relation. After the first war, they moved to Lewis, then to Skye." Angus took a drink of his coffee. "The island is a National Trust now, but Duncan is friends with the ranger there, and when he's had enough civilization, he sails away to St. Kilda. Oh, and no dogs are allowed on the island. So—no Conn."

Kathryn finished her coffee and offered to pay.

"Keep your money, lass." He picked up the cups and saucers and set them in the sink behind the bar.

Kathryn pulled her keys from her pocket and walked toward the door.

Angus called out, "He just needs a bit of time to sort this through, that's all. He's a bit proud, you know. In the best of ways, I mean."

"When he returns from the edge of the world, you can tell him I've taken control of the helm of my own ship. And if he wants to talk, he'll have to navigate through new waters, because he'll find—I'm off the map now."

Kathryn closed the door firmly behind her and drove back to the cottage. She chose to block out all thoughts of the last few days and allow the wildness of the moors to capture her heart and carry it higher than her problems to a place empty of voice or form, both ancient and present.

Duncan anchored near the jetty and lowered the skiff to row to the beach. The sun was out, and the winds had been light on the way to St. Kilda. It had not always been this way on his visits to see his friend, Ranger Will. Weather in the Atlantic was like an ill-tempered child. The least little event could set it off into a full-blown fury.

Here she is, Duncan thought. *Hirte, you're as barren as Abraham's wife, Sarah.* Hirte was the main island of the archipelago of St. Kilda. Not a tree or shrub stood on the isle. Village Bay had a small beach on which to land his skiff, and then it was a short walk up the hill to the old Factor's House, where his friend the warden lived. A young man approached Duncan as he jumped out of the skiff and pulled it up onto the rocky beach.

"Hello, can I help you with that?" he asked.

"No thanks, I've got it in hand," Duncan said. He looked around. "Where's Will?"

"He's gone to the mainland. Some special meeting in Glasgow. He'll be back in four or five days." Andrew reached out his hand. "My name is Andrew, I'm one of the archeologists for the summer."

"Well, it appears I'll not be staying long then. I'm a friend of Will's and just came to spend a few days—taking photographs and sketching." He had to think of some excuse for being there.

"So, you're a photographer then?"

"No, actually I'm a painter. But at the moment I'm a thirsty sailor. Is the Puff Inn bar open for business?"

The young man smiled. "I'm sure we can pour up a couple of pints. It's been a slow day for visitors, and my team is off recording a site up the hill. It's my turn to stay behind and take care of things around here. I could use the company."

Duncan followed Andrew up the hill to the inn, not in the mood for company, but thirsty just the same. After a couple of pints and a lecture on twelfth century Viking migratory patterns, it was time for Duncan to leave.

"Thanks for the hospitality. Please give my regards to Will. Tell him I'll look for him next time around," Duncan said. "I'll be staying on my boat tonight and leave for Skye, most likely in the morning."

"You're welcome to stay on as long as you like. If you change your mind, we're hosting a beach clean in the morning. A group of volunteers are coming to help out."

“A beach clean?” Duncan asked.

“Yes. I’m told last year they retrieved hundreds of plastic bottles from as far away as China and Dubai. It’ll be interesting, though sad, to see what littered the waters. I’ll be sure to pass along your regards to Will,” Andrew said.

Duncan walked back to the skiff and rowed out to the *Leanan Sidhe. Now what?* It was decided then, he would spend a couple of days here on the isle of Hirte, in spite of his friend’s absence, and then return to Skye to gather his equipment, pack a bag, and retrieve Conn. Then it was off to—somewhere far away. That was all that mattered now. As he sat on his boat looking toward the hills of Hirte, he thought a hike at dark up to the Gap would be good for both body and soul. He grabbed some bread and cheese from the larder and sat on the deck waiting for the sun to set. *There’s nothing like the view of Boreray and the Stacks to put my mind at ease, and the blinking lighthouses along the horizon are better than any Christmas lights.* He watched as the sky filled with puffins, kittiwakes, and the great skua. Their songs were not so beautiful as the skylarks back home, but they were comforting all the same.

As she pulled into the gravel drive of the cottage, Kathryn saw that John’s car was gone, but the boys were sitting on the stoop, like two pups put out of the house for some type of mischief. She stepped out of the Rover. *When can I get off this roller coaster?*

“Mom,” Sean said, as he jumped to his feet. “I’m sorry.”

Kathryn thought his face held the same guilty expression it had when he was eleven and blew up the fish tank with a giant firecracker. This was a bit more serious. Kathryn put her finger to her lips. “Shh. No apologies. None of this was your fault. I’m the one who’s sorry.” She sat down between them and patted the pavement.

Sean sat down, and the three stared out across the Sound toward the rugged hills of Knoydart. Ian picked up a handful of rocks and dropped them one at time to the ground.

Kathryn spoke first. "We should have talked about things—feelings—questions, sooner. I just was still trying to sort things out myself." She looked at both of the boys. "Not that that's an excuse, it's just…" She leaned back against the front door and pulled her knees to her chest.

Ian dropped the rocks and dusted his hands together. "Mom, it's okay. Sean and I have been talking."

"About what?" Kathryn leaned over and began flicking stones across the drive.

"About you and Dad. About what happened," Sean said.

"Hmm," Kathryn looked at Sean. "Your father has always been a man on the go. And at some point, I just got left behind."

"We all got left behind," Ian said.

Sean picked up a small rock and threw it across the driveway. "Maybe so."

Kathryn rested her chin on her knees. "You know, when you guys get back to Austin, I want you to call your dad and make sure he's okay. I think he might be feeling quite alone. And our last words were not stellar, so I'm guessing he might be wondering what horrible stories I'm filling your heads with." She held out both hands. "Deal?"

They each took a hand and squeezed hard. "Deal."

Sean grabbed a handful of rocks, stood, and began throwing them one at a time toward the Sound. "So, you threatened to kick his ass?"

Kathryn shook her head. "I see you did get a chance to talk before he left."

Sean dropped the rocks and offered Kathryn his arm. "Yes, we did. And I'd say before you're in any shape to do any major ass kickin', you need to hurl some haggis and pound down a pint or two. Lunch anyone?" He gave a broad smile. "Aunt Beth will be here tomorrow. And let me just go on record as saying, I'd love to see a match between the two of you."

Kathryn's heart somehow felt lighter. She took Sean's arm and walked to the Rover. Ian grabbed the keys, and they headed to the Ardvasar Hotel and a lunch that any Scot would be proud of.

Kathryn, Ian, and Sean waited for Beth at the baggage claim exit in the Inverness airport. As the doors opened, a crowd of tourists walked through, but only one was wearing a Balmoral bonnet, complete with long red fake hair, and a single braid hanging to one side. It was Beth.

The four yelled and hugged.

"So, what do you think? Do I look like a true Scot?" Beth asked.

"Where did you get it?" Ian asked.

"Airport in London."

"I'm not sure you're being very culturally sensitive. Seeing that we *are* in the Highlands." Kathryn was looking around at all the people coming and going in the airport terminal.

Beth took the hat off and ran her fingers through her hair. "Sorry, I thought it was funny."

"Hey," Sean said. "You better not upset Mom. She's in an ass-kickin' mood."

"Excuse me?" Beth asked.

"Sean," Kathryn said. "Can we just drop that? The one time in my life I say something like—let's just let it go. Okay?"

"I have obviously missed something. I knew I should have come sooner."

"John was here yesterday," Kathryn said.

"Holy crap! Well, that would explain everything." Beth grabbed Kathryn's arm

"How about we talk about it later." Kathryn quickly changed the subject by pointing out the Highland Gift Shop. "You're in Scotland. Are your nostrils flaring?"

"Do you see a handsome man in a kilt anywhere?" Beth asked, looking around the airport.

"No," Kathryn said.

"Then, they're not flaring yet." Beth smiled. "Hey, Kathryn you have color in your cheeks." She turned and looked at Ian and Sean. "Look boys, colo'."

Sean chimed in, "Look, she has colo'."

"What movie?" Beth asked.

"*While You Were Sleeping*," Sean said. "And if you tell anyone back home I knew that, I'll kick..."

"Whoa now," Kathryn said.

Kathryn gave Beth a kiss on the cheek as they walked to the Rover. "I'm so glad you're here. I've really missed you."

"And I've missed you. But don't think I've forgotten about John. When are we talking about that?" Beth asked.

"When the boys aren't around."

Ian and Sean loaded Beth's luggage into the back of the Rover, and they all piled in. The trip to Skye was interrupted with a long hard search for Nessie, the famous Loch Ness monster. The loch was beautiful, and Kathryn smiled as she watched Beth and the boys feign sightings of the monster. Sean handed her the camera, and she became the recorder of their latest Highland adventure. Beth blamed her silliness on jet lag, but everyone knew better. Her light heart and contagious smile infected all of them. *Everything will be okay now,* Kathryn thought. *Beth will know just what to do about Duncan, and John, and the boys. The only question remains, will I be able to do it?* Kathryn's throat began to tighten. Beth ran up from the loch and grabbed her by the arm.

"Hey, what a beautiful place. I do believe my nostrils are

flaring." Beth laughed like a child at recess and spun Kathryn around in circles. "Just look at the wildness of the mountains, and the loch—the loch is mystical. You can feel it. Can't you feel it, Kathryn?"

Kathryn pulled away and sat down on the hillside.

"What's wrong? Did I spin you too hard?" Beth stood with her hands resting on her hips. "Are you sure you're okay? You look pale all of a sudden."

"I'm fine, really," Kathryn said, rising to her feet. "I was just thinking about all that's happened the last few days and…" Kathryn looked out across the loch. "Well, you know, old habits."

Beth took her arm again and faced the loch. "You know what I think?"

"How could I ever know what you think?" Kathryn smiled.

"I think, you have been crazy brave, coming here alone and facing—life. But…" Beth paused.

"But, what?"

"But I think it's time you draw your sword, St. Stephen, and slay the dragon once and for all. And I will be at your side with my trusty axe chopping him down to size for you."

Kathryn turned to Beth. "And where is this dragon?"

"I don't know. You tell me. I just want you to know I came ready to stand with you and fight."

Kathryn laughed. "You've been reading way too much fantasy, I'd say. Whatever happened to Jane?"

"If you're talking about my dear friend, Ms. Austen, let's just say, the time for words has passed. We must lay down our pens and pick up our swords. We're in the Highlands, lass."

"Who has a sword?" Ian asked.

"Did we pack any food?" Sean asked.

The boys had climbed back up from Loch Ness in search of dinner. Kathryn walked to the Rover and pulled out a picnic basket.

They threw a blanket onto the grass and sat down to eat. The wind picked up, and the sky was turning darker.

Beth grabbed a piece of bread and placed a slice of cheddar cheese on it. She pointed it at Sean and Ian and said, "Gentlemen, we will be on a dragon hunt for the next several days. Keep your eyes open and look to the skies."

"Dragons," Sean said. "I love dragon hunting."

Ian made himself a cheese sandwich and took a bite. "There is no one I'd rather be with on a dragon hunt than you, Aunt Beth," Ian said, his words half muffled while chewing.

As they finished the last of the bread and cheese, the first drops of rain began to fall. Time to head on to Skye.

When they arrived back at the cottage, Beth settled into Kathryn's room, and even though she was exhausted from the flight, she refused to let Kathryn turn off the light until she had told her about John. For the next hour, the two sat in bed while Kathryn told Beth again about finding the stone manor and the portrait with the Lady of the Glen wearing the same necklace she'd discovered in the box Beth had given her. She told her about Duncan and their date and coming home to find John waiting for her and then the horrible ordeal the day before she arrived with Duncan and John.

"You've been busy," Beth said.

"Yes, it appears I have been." Kathryn turned off the lamp.

Beth snuggled into the feather pillow. "I vote we get up tomorrow around noon, of course, and drive to this stone manor. I want to see everything—the portrait, the Fairy Glen, and I really think I need to meet Angus. I have a feeling we could be very good friends, he and I. He sounds like a dragon slayer to me."

As quiet settled over the room, the sound of rain gently falling outside the cottage sang the two sisters a sweet lullaby; and they slept deeply, content to be in each other's company.

28

A Votive of Buttons for a Slain Dragon

Kathryn climbed up the winding sheep trail toward the portal to the Otherworld in the Fairy Glen. To the left, she noticed a large spiral pattern made of stones. As she looked around the top of the hillside, she saw piles of rocks scattered like stacks of blocks in a nursery. Personal items sat atop some of the mounds—jewelry, a pair of pink sunglasses, a piece of red fabric, tiny notes with names on them. *I wonder if the people who left these stones, piled one on the other here beneath the fairy castle, received what they wished for,* she thought. *And look at all the belongings left here. How many of the visitors believed in the magic of the glen? Do I believe?*

Kathryn took the last few steps up the steep slope to the opening at the top of the knoll. The locals said this was the portal to the Otherworld, where the fairies lived. How ridiculous that sounded. But so many ridiculous things had happened since she'd arrived on Skye. Why question this one? She reached into the small fabric bag hanging on her back and took out the tin box of buttons.

Beth yelled at Kathryn as she stood atop the fairy castle with Ian and Sean. "Kathryn, come join us. I see a minivan pulling up below."

A minivan on Skye? Kathryn thought.

Beth continued. "Could be a soccer mom and family coming to

invade our wee glen. Will you be joinin' us to defend her?" Beth stood with both arms firmly pressed to her hips. "Come on, Kathryn, get your brave heart over here."

Leave it to Beth to enter headlong into the fantasy of the glen. Kathryn waved and told them she'd be right up. She shoved the box of her mother's terrors deep into the opening of the knoll. "I'm leaving this votive of buttons for you, my fairy friends. Please accept these as an offering of all our ancestral demons. Take them deep into the knoll and bury them. I've heard your songs, and I've followed them here."

"Kathryn, get over here. We're about to be overtaken by a herd of preadolescent boys." Beth was jumping up and down waving.

Kathryn blew a good-bye kiss toward the box and turned to climb down the fairy knoll just in time to see a group of boys attempting to climb Castle Ewan. Their mother stood below, yelling something about being careful and broken necks. Beth threw her hands into the air and then reached down and helped the boys up.

"They've agreed to join the clan. It was our only course of action seeing that we were about to be overrun."

Beth, Ian, and Sean climbed down to where Kathryn stood next to the stone spiral.

"Oh, look," Beth said. "I read about this on the internet."

"The internet?" Kathryn asked.

"Yes. I looked up this place when you said we were coming here." Beth stepped into the outer spiral. "People say it's been here for centuries and it holds magical power. But, their stories differ as to just what that power might be."

Sean jumped into the spiral next to Beth. "I chose flying. My magic power, I mean."

Beth continued. "I also read the tour guides have been known to propagate a tale having to do with young ladies dancing naked in the spiral and all *their* wishes coming true. I'm just not sure which *their* the tour guides referred to. The young ladies or themselves." Beth found a small stone and added it to the spiral. She then held her breath and walked from the outside to the center and then back.

"What are you doing?" Kathryn asked.

"Maybe this works in stone spirals as well as going across bridges. Remember how we used to hold our breath and make a wish whenever Dad would drive across a bridge? Try it. Make a wish."

Kathryn picked up a stone, found a spot at the center of the spiral, and placed it there. Sean followed. And finally, Ian.

"So what did everyone wish for?" Beth asked. "I want to meet the real Mr. Darcy. What about you, Kathryn?"

"If you tell it won't come true," Kathryn said.

"Mom wants to be the next Lady of Glen Rowan," Ian said. "And I wished for a lifetime supply of Cuillin's best ale."

"Sean," Beth said. "What about you?"

"I wished for a dragon. I'm ready to fly."

"All this wishing has made me hungry. When are we gonna eat?" Ian asked.

"Anyone else hungry?" Kathryn asked.

Everyone raised their hands like a classroom of children. It was decided the time had arrived for Beth to meet the much-touted Angus MacQueen. The Lady of the Glen Pub it was then. Ian and Sean raced back to the Rover.

As Kathryn and Beth walked down the hillside, Beth asked, "What were you doing at the hole in the side of the knoll earlier? Oh listen, that rhymes. The hole in the side of the knoll. That should be a song."

"I left an offering for the fairy folk, that's all," Kathryn said.

"You have indeed been swept away by the magic of the glen just as Ian and Sean said." Beth locked arms with Kathryn. "This is the Kate I remember from my childhood. And, oh, how I've missed her."

They took their seats at a table near the front window and waited for Angus to appear from the back. He walked into the room with a handful of clean mugs and raised them high above his head when he saw Kathryn. After stacking them up behind the bar, he hurried over to their table.

"I was wonderin' when you'd be back for a pint. And here you are." He paused for a moment and smiled at Beth. "And, I see you've gathered another beautiful lass along the way." Angus reached out his hand. "*Fàilte.* I'm Angus MacQueen. Pleased to make your acquaintance."

Beth grabbed his hand and shook it hard. "Hi, I'm Beth Silverton. Kathryn's *younger* sister."

"So, your family has decided to overtake the Isle now, have you?"

"Yes," Beth said. "And we've decided your pub will be our first conquest. Bring us a pint all around."

"Yes, my lady," and Angus bowed. "I sheath my sword in surrender." He left for the bar.

"Don't say it, Sean." Ian laughed.

"Hey, I…"

Kathryn covered her ears, and Beth punched Ian's shoulder. "You guys are terrible. Funny, a bit sick, but terrible. Just terrible." She turned to Kathryn and pulled her hands away. "Are they always like this?"

Kathryn shook her head. "College boys."

Beth laughed. "Say no more."

"What?" both boys said in unison.

Angus returned with five pints and sat down for his traditional first beer with a new customer. Food followed, and they spent several hours listening to Beth tell stories about her many adventures while traveling the world. For the first time, Kathryn realized she felt nothing but pride as she listened to Beth share stories about the full life she'd led. No jealous thoughts. And how could there be? Beth had always offered to take her along, Kathryn had just never been brave enough to say yes. Until now. *Dragon slayers!*

After lunch, Kathryn called Flora and asked if it would be possible to drop by and introduce her to Beth, and of course, let her see the portrait. Flora told her the tea would be hot by the time they arrived.

Beth stood in front of the portrait, jaw dropped and dumbstruck. She just shook her head. Kathryn walked forward and took her arm.

"So—what do you think?"

"Kathryn."

"I know. Crazy, isn't it?"

Beth placed her hand on the mantel and turned toward Kathryn. "I can't believe it. It's true. It's all true. Your dream, the voice. All these years, I've made fun of you."

"You've made fun of me?"

They smiled.

"And the necklace. What are the chances?"

Kathryn reached for the necklace. "I don't think anything has been left to chance. It's all been orchestrated from the beginning. Across several centuries and an ocean."

"I want my own dream, Kathryn. I've never been jealous of you. Never—until now."

"You can be my lady in waiting."

"After that intimate conversation with Angus in the pub, I think lady in waiting might be a bit over the top," Ian said.

The room erupted with laughter as Flora walked in with the tea and shortbread.

"I feel I've missed something," Flora said.

"Just family secrets," Kathryn said. "Nothing that can be repeated." She shot an *enough said* look at Ian and Sean.

"What?" Sean protested. "I didn't even open my mouth. Did I open my mouth, Aunt Beth?"

"Tea anyone?" Flora asked with a smile.

Conn entered the room and ran first to Kathryn, then to Sean, where he lay at his feet obviously hoping for a back rub.

"Good Lord, it's a horse," Beth said.

"Aye, this is my brother's dog, Conn. He must have heard you talking. He's been quite mopey since Duncan left him here with me. I'm sure he's happy for the company."

Kathryn felt a twinge of pain in her stomach. She reached over and began to rub Conn behind his ears. *I do wish your master was here,* she thought. *Why did he leave us alone like this? What shall we do?*

Beth asked Flora about the history of the manor and the origin of the tapestries in the hallway and the porcelain vases in the entryway. Flora's response interrupted Kathryn's thoughts.

"Well, this place is quite old. The east wing of the manor was built in the early seventeenth century. It's the ancestral home of the MacDonalds of Glen Rowan. It was expanded into what you see now over the centuries. For a number of years, in the 1800s when times were very hard, the family moved to the mainland and used the manor as a hunting lodge. Several small croft cottages in the glen, now abandoned, belonged to tenants of our ancestors. In the early 1900s our grandfather, Donald, moved the family back to Skye from Edinburgh and renovated the manor. The stables were repaired to hold the Eriksay ponies and the Arabians my family has raised for generations. We are the only family still living in the glen." Flora took a quick sip of tea.

"Our father was educated at the university in Edinburgh. Duncan also studied art there. I went to Cambridge to study and lived with my aunt, our father's sister. It was a lovely change of scenery and society, but my soul longed for the Highlands, especially Skye. So I returned after finishing at the university, met my husband and settled down in the manor with my family. I'm sure you're wondering how we can keep up such a place as this, just Duncan and myself." She glanced around the Great Hall.

"You see, our grandfather bought property all over the Highlands, which he then leased out. We inherited all this real estate, and it is how we are able to maintain the manor and not have to turn it into a bed and breakfast, like so many of our Skye neighbors. As for the tapestries, our great-great grandfather, Alexander, loved the sea and spent years traveling the world. Much of the art you see are pieces he bought on his adventures."

Flora looked at Ian and Sean. "Oh, dear, it seems I've gone on and on. You should have told me when you'd had enough."

"I'm a history major," Sean said. "This is right up my alley."

"Right up your what?" Flora asked.

"My alley," Sean said. "Sorry, I just mean it's what I know and love."

"Well, that's enough lecturing for one day, I should think. More tea anyone?" Flora asked, as she held up the blue floral teapot, imported from China in the 1800s.

Kathryn and Beth took a second cup of tea, while Ian and Sean took Conn for a run through the glen. The women spent the next several hours talking about family and the decided differences between growing up in Texas and in Scotland.

At the end of the visit, Flora walked everyone to the front door. "You know, this manor is quite spacious. You're all very welcome to stay here if you should tire of the cottage in Sleat."

"Thank you for your gracious offer, Flora. We'll certainly consider it," Kathryn said. As she walked to the Rover she wondered what it might be like to sleep under the same roof with Duncan. First as a guest, then well, who knows what the future might hold.

29

Fiddle-Dee-Dee

Kathryn and Beth awoke early and shared a pot of very strong coffee before waking Ian and Sean. They talked about things back in Texas. Kathryn asked Beth how their father was, and if Mrs. Podhorzki was taking care of Mr. Nightly while she was away. Beth told her she'd left him in the store to guard the place in her absence, Mr. Nightly that is, not their father. Mrs. Podhorzki was minding the store as usual and would be sure he had plenty to eat and drink. The buzzer in the kitchen sounded, and it was time to rouse the boys.

Beth asked Kathryn to join her for a walk across the moor while the boys showered. The clouds were sitting low across the sound, covering the peaks of the hills of Knoydart. A light breeze drifted in from the sea. The birds were already busy singing their early morning chorus, and the sweet scent of the hawthorn blossoms filled the air. Beth was the first to speak as they walked through the damp heather.

"So, have you figured out where this dragon is we're needing to slay?"

Kathryn shook her head and picked a bluebell. "No, but I just keep thinking about John and our marriage. We were together for a really long time. When he showed up here a few days ago, it just sent me reeling. One minute I was considering a new future with Duncan, and the next minute—John reappeared."

"You're not thinking about going back to John, Kathryn? He's not ever going to change. How many times—" She put her hands in her pockets and stopped talking.

"No," Kathryn said. "You're right. You just can't imagine how worthless his affairs made me feel. I just questioned everything about who I was. You know, why I didn't measure up, as a wife—as a woman."

"Do you hear yourself, Kathryn? You're speaking in past tense. This is all good. I think we've found the dragon."

Kathryn narrowed her eyes. "John?"

"No, your failed marriage." Beth closed her eyes. "What was it the voice always said to you in your dream? Your happiness would be…"

"'Your true happiness awaits you here. Love once lost, forever found within these walls,'" Kathryn said.

"That's it!" Beth said. "'Love once lost, forever found within these walls.' Don't you see it?"

"See what?"

"Love once lost—John. Forever found within these walls—Duncan."

Beth clapped and yelled. The skylarks in the nearby rowan started and flew away. She held her fist up in the air as if holding a sword. "Raise your sword, Kate, the Dragon Slayer."

Kathryn slowly held her arm up and looked around to see if they were alone, while memories of Ian and Sean posing in the heather in their plaid boxers flashed through her mind. "What are we doing?" she asked.

"When you told John to go, and meant it, you slew the dragon. It's dead and gone. Now, all you have to do is go find your handsome prince and wake him from his thirty-something years of sleep."

"What if I can't wake him?" Kathryn asked, lowering her imaginary sword.

"You've already roused him once. Did you kiss him yet?"

"No," Kathryn said. "Oh."

Beth grabbed her hand and headed back toward the cottage. "I say we take a detour on our way to Portree today. Before we go to the Accordion and Fiddle Festival, let's stop at Angus's Pub and find out exactly where your sleeping prince is hiding out. I'm feeling very much like a sea adventure about now. How about you?"

"Aye," Kathryn said. It was all they could do to hold their pace to a quick walk and not let it turn into a full out run.

The boys were eating cereal and drinking coffee when Kathryn and Beth burst into the cottage. They were both dressed and had a backpack stuffed with snacks waiting at the door.

"Hurry and finish your breakfast, men," Beth said. "We're about to head out to sea."

Ian and Sean exchanged a confused look.

"Looking for lost treasure?" Sean asked.

"You could say that," Beth said. "We just need to ask Angus for the map. We'll make it to the festival in time for plenty of music, and dancing afterwards at the *Ceildh*. I promise."

"Mom, you're awful quiet," Sean said.

"Just working on *the plan*, that's all." Kathryn grabbed her bag and the tartan draped across the back of the sofa. She walked to the open door and turned.

"So, this has to do with—*the plan*," he said.

"Yes," Kathryn said. "Shall we go, gentlemen? Our ship is waiting to sail, and I, for one, do not intend to miss it this time."

"What have you two been smoking?" Sean asked.

"Yeah," Ian said. "You're going to have to spell it out a little more for us."

"We're going to ask Angus where St. Kilda island is, and then we're going on a little sea cruise of our own to find Duncan," Beth said.

"Is he the dragon?" Sean asked.

"Nope. Dragon's dead. Duncan's the treasure," Beth said. "Come on, guys. We're burnin' daylight."

"I would just like to go on record as saying, you're both crazy." Sean said.

"Duly noted," Beth said.

As Kathryn reached the Rover, Ian and Sean jumped in the back with their pack of snacks and Beth took shotgun. The clouds had disappeared from across the sound, and the Hills of Knoydart were standing in all their majestic splendor. An eagle circled overhead and screamed. *It's a sign*, Kathryn thought. The mist had lifted, and the wildness of the landscape was calling out her name.

They walked into the Lady of the Glen Pub and found it empty. Kathryn looked outside and saw Angus's motorcycle. *Good. He's here somewhere.* She yelled his name and immediately heard footsteps above the pub. A moment later, Angus appeared in the doorway leading to the kitchen.

"*Fàilte.* What brings you all here so early?"

Beth stepped forward and grabbed his arm. "Angus, do you know exactly where Duncan is?"

"Aye, I do."

"Can you tell us how to get there?" Kathryn asked.

"What's this?" Angus asked.

"We're on a treasure hunt," Ian said. "And, it seems you've got the map. Or, so say the womenfolk."

"Actually, it's more like a rescue," Beth said. She winked and released his arm.

"Aye, I love a good rescue."

The door to the pub flew open, and Flora rushed in. She ran straight to Kathryn. "I'm so glad I found you. Kathryn, you've got to get yourself to the pier. Duncan came back from St. Kilda to pack for a long trip to—he's not sure where. I tried to explain about John and the whole misunderstanding, but I don't think he believed me. He left not long ago for his boat. I tried to ring you, but when you didn't answer, I came here to get Angus. As luck would have it, here you are."

Flora pulled Kathryn's arm. "Come on now, let's go. I'll drive you to the pier."

"Now, wait a minute there. I'll take her on my Indian. It'll be faster," Angus said.

Kathryn pulled free of Flora's grasp and paced to the door and back to the bar. "You told him what happened, and he's still leaving?" She put her arms on top of her head. "I won't go begging."

Beth held her hand up in the air, fist clinched. "A toast."

Everyone looked confused, but they all followed suit and waited.

"Kathryn, here's to destiny."

Angus held up his imaginary pint and said, "Puts me to mind of a proverb my grandfather often told me. God rest his soul."

"Can we hurry this up a wee bit?" Flora asked.

Angus cleared his throat. "One meets his destiny often on the road he takes to avoid it. So, go after him, lass."

"Go on, Mom. Get outta here," Ian said.

Kathryn looked at Sean. He held his imaginary mug toward her and said, "The future belongs to those who believe in the beauty of their dreams—Eleanor Roosevelt."

"History dweeb." Ian laughed.

"It's your dream. Go after him, Mom," Sean said.

"I love you all, so much." And with that, Kathryn ran out of the pub, yelling for Angus to hurry.

They arrived at the pier just in time to see Duncan's boat sailing away. Angus whistled, and Conn ran to the stern and began to bark.

Duncan looked back for a moment, then turned to face toward the Outer Hebrides.

"Swim or row, Kathryn. What'll it be?" Angus asked.

"Again?"

Angus ran down the steps to the skiff, which was tied to the pier. "Come on, lass. You can do it."

Kathryn hesitated for a brief moment and then followed him down the concrete steps. She jumped into the skiff and grabbed both oars.

"Can I get arrested for stealing?"

"No, we're just borrowin' it really. Off with you now." And he pushed the boat away from the pier.

Kathryn placed the oars into the water and clumsily paddled her way underneath the pier. She glanced over her shoulder to avoid the concrete piles supporting it. Duncan's boat was still in sight, but it would take a miracle—or magic, maybe a bit of both to catch him. Angus stood atop the pier and whistled as loud as his windpipes could bear. Conn heard the familiar whistle again and began to bark. Duncan never looked back. Kathryn rowed, although the paddles felt awkward in her hands, and each time they hit the water and she pulled them toward her, it was as if the bay was filled with maple syrup.

When Conn saw Kathryn in her little boat, he barked even louder than before and jumped back and forth from the stern to the helm, where Duncan was steering out to sea. Kathryn began to yell in between strokes of the oars. Suddenly Conn quieted and with one giant leap, propelled himself into the bay and began to swim toward Kathryn, as if he knew she could never catch them on her own. Shocked, she froze, with both oars up in the air and called out to Conn. Duncan heard the great splash and turned in time to see Conn swimming like a hairy pike toward the skiff.

"Conn, what are you doing? Damn you, get back here," he

yelled but to no avail. Whipping the sail around and steering the rudder hard to the right, Duncan sailed toward Conn and Kathryn. As he approached the two of them he dropped sail and threw over a ladder. Kathryn rowed even harder than before. Her arms were on fire, but she couldn't stop. She had to reach Conn. Kathryn did reach him, just moments before Duncan. She threw the oars into the hull and reached over the side, grabbing Conn's front paws, and tried to pull him up to the edge of the boat. The skiff began to rock, and Duncan yelled.

"Stop. You'll capsize the boat. I'll come alongside and take you both onboard." Duncan drifted slowly next to Conn and leaned over, pulling him up the ladder and into the boat. Next, he took Kathryn's hand and helped her up the ladder. He then tied the skiff to the side of the sailboat and motored back to the pier in silence.

Once they reached the pier, he threw Angus the ropes, and they secured the boat. Kathryn stroked Conn's soggy coat as he licked her over and over. *At least someone's glad to see me,* she thought. On the edge of the pier, a lone fisherman sat cleaning his net, pretending not to listen.

Angus helped Kathryn onto the pier. Duncan glared at him, as he and Conn climbed out of the boat.

"Conn, you're a hero if ever I've seen one." Angus knelt down and began stroking Conn's wet coat, avoiding Duncan.

Kathryn reached for Duncan, who moved away. "Duncan, I can explain everything. It's not what you think."

Angus stood up. "What say we go back to my pub, and I'll serve us up somethin'? The both of you could talk this out while I see to Conn."

"You're crazy, you know that?" said Duncan. "Rowing out into the bay. What were you thinking?"

Kathryn stood shivering on the pier. "I was watching my destiny sail away, and I couldn't let that happen."

"No more talk about destiny. Angus, take her back to the pub." Duncan turned and walked back toward the boat. "Come, Conn."

"But, Duncan..." Angus said.

Duncan interrupted him. "Just leave me be."

Kathryn grabbed Duncan's arm. "Wait."

"No more waiting."

"Oh, yes, you will wait, and you'll listen to what I have to say."

Duncan and Angus stood, mouths open, shocked by Kathryn's newfound boldness.

Everyone stood silent for a moment.

"So, you've found yourself then?" Duncan asked.

"Yes. That's what I wanted to tell you." Kathryn took a deep breath and straightened her shoulders. "John came over uninvited and unannounced. He wanted to get back together."

"And?"

Kathryn looked out across Uig Bay. "I told him I belonged here." Her eyes turned back to Duncan. "That's when I knew what I wanted. That's when I decided to believe—in a dream and a fairy tale."

Duncan stepped toward the ropes that held his boat to the pier and checked to be sure they were secure. "I think you'll find in every fairy tale with a happy ending there's only room for one prince."

Kathryn wrapped her arms around her shoulders and shivered in the cool damp air. "Duncan, I didn't sleep with John. I thought he had left that night after visiting with the boys. I was as surprised as you were to see that he was still there."

Duncan moved to Kathryn and put his jacket around her shoulders. "But I thought—"

"I know what it looked like," Kathryn interrupted.

Duncan stood with both hands on his hips and looked first at Angus and then turned to Kathryn. "We're crazy, you and I. Do you see that?"

"Yes." Kathryn glanced down at the weathered wood under her feet and half smiled.

Angus patted Conn's head and mumbled, "Aye, you can safely say we've all been touched by the fairies."

Duncan and Kathryn both laughed, breaking the tension between them. Duncan took her hand, and they stood holding each other's gaze.

"Do it, man," Angus said in a hushed voice beneath the strong sea breeze.

Duncan took Kathryn in his arms and kissed her. Kathryn felt her body go warm as she melted into his arms. They stood in a long embrace unaware of anyone or anything outside themselves. Angus whispered a triumphant "*Cha Gheil*" to Conn.

Finally, Duncan kissed Kathryn on top of her head as he held her tight. "We must to go back to the manor and tell Flora. She's been waiting for you almost as long as I have."

Kathryn looked up. "Actually, she's at Angus's Pub, with Ian and Sean—and Beth."

"Beth. Who's Beth?"

"She's my sister and my dearest friend."

Angus interrupted. "What say we get these two inside where it's warm and dry?"

Duncan called for Conn. "We'll be right behind you."

They walked toward Duncan's truck. The sea was calm, and the sun was peeking through the clouds. Conn chased a flock of seagulls that were feasting on fish parts in a bucket near the end of the pier. Kathryn breathed in the salty air and put her head on Duncan's shoulder as they walked. *Could I ever feel more alive than right here, right now?* she wondered. *Oh, please don't anyone wake me from this dream, and it must be a dream. How could anyone be this happy?* She reached for the malachite charm that hung around her neck and ran her fingers over the endless knot. Duncan noticed the necklace between her fingers.

"So, I've been meaning to ask where you got that?"

"I found it in a secret compartment in a box Beth gave me."

"Did you now? You know where it came from?" He opened the door of the truck for her.

"I think I've seen it somewhere before, maybe in a painting in the great hall of a stone manor."

Duncan leaned in and kissed her fingers that held the necklace, then, moved slowly up her neck. Kathryn felt her cool skin warmed by his lips. He found his way to her mouth, and they kissed. Slow and soft and gentle. Conn grew tired of chasing the gulls and ran for the truck. He jumped into the back and barked.

"Okay, okay," Duncan said. "Thirsty for a pint, are you?"

Kathryn thought she saw Conn smile as she climbed into the cab of the truck.

On the short drive to the pub, Duncan and Kathryn talked about their future. They talked about how long it might take to get to know each other enough to set a wedding date. Duncan commented on the little there was to tell about himself and how long could it really take to know what destiny had known all along. Besides, there never seemed to be long engagements in fairy tales.

Beth smiled and waved as Kathryn and Duncan walked to the table. *She woke him.* Kathryn introduced Duncan to Beth, and just as Angus was about to pour up a round of beer, Sean pointed out the time and suggested they continue the conversation in Portree at the Fiddle and Accordion Festival. Everyone agreed, and Ian drove Sean, Beth, and Angus in the Rover, while Duncan took Kathryn and Flora in the truck.

The competition was taking place at the Well Plaid Restaurant of the Royal Hotel, the site of the famous McNabb's Inn, where Bonnie Prince Charlie and Flora MacDonald said their final good-byes.

When they arrived, the room was packed with locals and a few tourists. As they looked for a free table, a three-piece band from Aberdeen consisting of fiddle, accordion, and drums played "*Si Beag Si Mohr*—Little Fairy Hill, Big Fairy Hill."

With every table filled, they stood in the back by the bar with a large crowd. Molly arrived before the first band had finished the competition and joined Ian at the bar. After the third band had finished its set, Duncan suggested a local fish restaurant with a beautiful view of the harbor was in order.

They enjoyed a meal of the local catch: lobster, mussels, monkfish, and sole. Afterward, it was time to work off their dinner by attending the *Ceidhl* at the old city hall. The dance was held in a large room with a stage. A bar had been set up in a side room, offering beer and a fruit drink that Kathryn couldn't quite identify. Duncan took her hand and walked out on the floor stepping into the already moving circle of couples. The band was playing the "Westphalia Waltz".

Halfway through the waltz, Duncan stopped dancing. "Kathryn, will you join me outside for a walk? I need to talk to you about something—and it can't wait."

Outside, the air was cool, and the twilight revealed shadows across the bay. They stood at the rail overlooking the row of brightly colored buildings along the shore. Duncan's hands were firmly placed on the rail, and he took a deep breath as he pressed against it.

"What is it?" Kathryn asked.

"Well, we really know very little about each other, you and I."

"I realize that," Kathryn said. "Are there things you'd like to ask me?"

"No. That's not it."

"I don't mind, really. I mean think about it. You only know I've just been divorced from my husband of twenty-seven years. I have two sons and a sister. I've ancestors from Skye and..." Kathryn paused and looked out at the boats anchored in the harbor. "I can't row a skiff very well at all." She turned to Duncan. "Ask me anything."

"You don't understand. I didn't bring you out here to ask about your past—or your present for that matter." He took one hand from the railing and faced her. He needed the other to brace himself for what he was about to say. "I don't know if I mentioned it, but I attended university in Edinburgh when I was young. I received an art degree from there and, my second term I took a drawing class." Duncan couldn't hold her gaze and turned to face the sea again.

"And?" Kathryn asked.

"And I met a young woman, she was a model for that class. And…" He turned back to face her, opened his mouth, but the words were wedged in his throat like a foot caught between two rocks. He tried, but he couldn't break them loose.

"And?" Kathryn realized her heart was racing. What ghost in his past could have stolen his words?

"Her name was Lilli, she was from New Zealand and she was—beautiful. Tall, red-haired, with dark green eyes. We spent a lot of time together, outside of class. When summer came, she told me she was going back to New Zealand to visit her family—she never returned. I got a letter from her the following year with a picture of a baby boy. She'd named him Taine Duncan MacDonald, after his father."

Duncan leaned over the railing and cleared his throat. Kathryn leaned next to him and put her arm through his. They were both silent. Only the sound of gulls and gentle waves washing against the pier below broke the silence. A light breeze blew, and Duncan wiped the moisture from his eyes.

"I have a son. He is thirty-one years old, and I've never seen him, only that picture and one other. I've never spoken to him. The only heir of Glen Rowan. How's that for fate?" He turned and looked at Kathryn. "So, there it is, my darkest secret and deepest wound. Only Flora knows about him. And now you."

"Does he know about you?"

"Yes, Lilli told him when he was young. I think he must resent me or even hate me because I never stayed in touch with him. Even though I tried."

"You don't know that," Kathryn said.

"I sent Lilli a letter telling her I wanted to help them. I told her I wanted to be part of their lives. She said I could set aside money for his education. That's all she asked. That's all she wanted. I made the arrangements. I wrote her often for almost a year, but she never responded. Then, seven years ago, I received another letter. In it was a photograph of Taine in his graduation robe and holding his diploma. She was standing beside him. I hardly recognized her. She looked fragile, not quite right."

"I wrote back asking a lot of questions about Taine. Where had he gone to university? What was he doing now? Was he still in New Zealand?" Duncan paused. "Was she all right?"

"Where is he now?" Kathryn asked.

"I don't know. I've not heard back from her." Duncan stood and patted the railing. "There you have it."

"I'm sorry. I can't imagine how difficult it must be to have a son and not know him."

"You know, you're very lucky to have your two sons. You seem quite close." Duncan stepped back from the railing and held out both arms. "So, what do you think?"

"I think there is a young man somewhere in the world who has no idea what he's missed out on, not having you in his life. And someday he may figure that out and show up on your doorstep. And when he does, I hope to be there to welcome him." Kathryn took Duncan's hand and kissed it.

An old man opened the doors to the hall to let the cool breeze inside. Music filled the air, and Kathryn placed Duncan's hand on her waist and held up her free hand. "Shall we dance?"

Duncan took her in his arms and they danced, alone, in the twilight.

When the waltz ended, the band started up an Irish reel. Inside the hall, a long-time friend asked Flora to dance. Molly and Ian followed, as Angus took Beth's hand, and they all took to the floor. Three octogenarian women were sitting together talking and laughing. Two stood and joined the dance, the third looked at Sean and smiled.

"Really?" Sean whispered. "What the hell."

He walked over to the woman and offered his hand. As they began to dance around the circle he explained he had no idea how to dance to the reel. She told him not to worry, she'd lead.

At four in the morning, the band played its last waltz, and Duncan took Kathryn around the dance floor one last time. He asked her to bring everyone to the manor for the afternoon and evening, after they all had a good sleep. Angus and Flora climbed in his truck, and he walked Kathryn to the Rover. Beth was in the driver's seat, and the boys were laid out in the back.

"So, I'll see you this afternoon?" Duncan asked as he took Kathryn's hand and helped her up into her seat.

"Yes."

"You'll not be changing your mind now?"

Kathryn leaned forward and kissed him hard and long. "You'll not be sailing away then?"

"No. I promise."

As they pulled out of the carpark, Kathryn glanced back at Duncan, who stood in the moonlit shadows and mist, and recognized his faceless silhouette. She shuddered as a chill ran through her body. Could this man of her dreams love her? Would he be satisfied with only her or was that a fairy tale after all?

30

Peace Comes This Way

Kathryn, Beth, and the boys arrived at the manor just in time for a late lunch. A light rain was falling, and Sean and Ian found Conn curled up by the fire in the Great Hall. Kathryn and Beth joined Flora in the kitchen, and Duncan was still upstairs showering after a long morning ride through the glen.

Just as he returned to the Great Hall, the women entered with trays of hot potato soup and bread.

"I thought we'd all eat in front of the fire. It's a bone-chilling summer afternoon, and it seems a shame to waste a lovely fire," Flora said.

Conn had moved from the fire to Duncan's side. Everyone gathered around the rowan table and enjoyed the warmth from the soup, the fire, and the conversation. After lunch, Beth offered to help with the dishes, while Sean and Ian, still tired from the night of dancing, stretched out on the sofas in front of the fire. A sea breeze had moved the rain out of the glen, and Duncan asked Kathryn if she'd care to take a walk.

She took his hand, and they stepped out into Glen Rowan.

He pointed to the hillside where he'd first met the Lady. "Let's walk over there."

As they reached the top, a light mist rolled in from the sea, hiding the glen floor as though it was covered in a thin veil. Kathryn began to shiver as the salty wind and the damp air cut through her light jacket.

Duncan moved behind her and wrapped his arms around her. "You're shaking. Let me help."

"Thank you, kind sir," Kathryn said. She leaned back against his chest and closed her eyes.

Could this be a dream? she wondered. She opened her eyes and looked across the glen toward the stone manor. This was no dream. This was real life. Her life.

Thunder rumbled in the distance.

"We should hurry back to the manor before the rain returns for a second round," Duncan said.

Kathryn pulled away and began running down the slippery hillside. "I'll race you to the fireside," she yelled.

Halfway down the hill she discovered the folly of her dare when she lost her footing and slid the remainder of the way. Duncan had already passed her but turned just in time to see her fall. He ran back and caught her just before she reached the bottom of the hill.

"Are you all right?"

He helped her up, and she twisted around, trying to see if her jeans were grass-stained.

"Of course, I did that on purpose, you know."

"Of course."

"It just seemed to be the fastest way down."

"Hmm. I think it was a planned distraction to keep me from winning."

Kathryn bolted toward the manor and yelled over her shoulder, "Last one to the door is a Lowlander."

She made a valiant effort, managing to stay on her feet all the way to the manor. Nevertheless, Duncan was already standing inside the manor, holding the door open to the Great Hall as she reached the top of the hill.

"Lowlander," he whispered, as she passed through the doorway.

She gave him a quick punch to the ribs and hurried to the fire. Flora had just called the boys to the kitchen for some hot chocolate, so they found themselves alone in the room. Duncan sat on the couch nearest the hearth and patted on the soft leather next to him for Kathryn to sit down. She moved to the fireplace instead.

"Are we crazy?" Kathryn asked.

"What? Why does this question keep coming up?" Duncan asked.

"Are we crazy?" Kathryn asked again, looking up at the portrait.

"What do you mean?"

Kathryn stood staring at the portrait. Duncan leaned back on the couch, both arms spread across the top of the leather. Kathryn turned. "You seem very pleased with yourself, all smiles," she said.

"You're mistaken. It's you I'm pleased with."

Kathryn blushed. "And why is that?"

Duncan stood and walked to her. He brushed his hand across her face. "Because you still blush when a man stares at you. That pleases me."

Kathryn drew her hands to her face. "It's the fire. I'm standing too close."

"There's no need to make excuses, Kathryn. You're quite beautiful when your face glows." Duncan moved over to her and kissed her neck.

Kathryn ducked from under his embrace and moved away from the fire. "So, you never answered my question."

"What question is that?" Duncan asked, leaning one arm against the mantel and stirring the fire.

"Doesn't this all seem crazy to you?" Kathryn asked.

"Hmm." Duncan smiled. "Welcome to my world."

"I'm being serious here."

"So am I."

Kathryn looked up at the painting of the Lady. "You're in love with a portrait and a vision of a fairy mistress you saw when you were a boy. The fact that I happen to look very much like her could be—" she turned to Duncan "—*is* very likely a coincidence."

Duncan moved beside Kathryn and looked up at the portrait. "My fairy mistress, as you call her, was no vision. I was very much awake, and I was no boy. I was eighteen when she last visited me." He turned to Kathryn. "I have tried for many years to forget you."

"Her," Kathryn interrupted.

"You," Duncan said. "It's you she called, and it's you I was meant to be with." He took her hands in his. "I can't explain it to you, Kathryn. Not in a logical way. What I feel for you is something mysterious and magical. Do you not feel it yourself?"

"I want to believe this is destiny, that there's some magic force that's reached across time and space to bring us together. But…"

Duncan ran his fingers through her hair. "But, what?"

"How do I know what you feel now will last? What if it cools and you get tired of me? What if I can't live up to the power of the portrait?" She opened up both arms and spun around slowly. "Look closely, Duncan. I am no fairy mistress. I am a flesh and blood woman. I'm tired of feeling like I've somehow not been enough, not measured up. I am who I am, a woman falling in love with life again, with all its joy and heartache. I want to be Kathryn, every inch mortal."

"Kathryn, you standing here, close to me like this—you, flesh and blood, yield more power than any image on a canvas. You're a masterpiece. And I want to spend the rest of my life getting to know you." He slowly ran his finger along her cheek, then traced her lips gently. "I want to learn every brushstroke, every shadow…" He moved his finger down her neck and across her shoulder.

Kathryn stood still, unable to move beneath Duncan's touch.

"I want you..." Duncan said, "because, portrait or not, I think you're more beautiful than any *leannan sidhe*, and you consume my thoughts."

"Beauty fades," Kathryn said.

"As will my vision. So there's no problem really."

"I'm not joking."

"Well, maybe that's what's wrong here," Duncan said.

"What do you mean?"

"Where's your sense of adventure? Look at the portrait, Kathryn."

She turned to face her likeness.

"She's the exact image of you, down to the necklace—which you found in an antique box with a hidden drawer. You've dreamed of a stone manor, and mine is the one in your dream. And if that's not enough, I think you're a bit taken with my legs in a kilt, are you not?"

Kathryn laughed.

"See, fairy tale or no, this *is* our reality," Duncan said.

"You're right. We have to trust fate and hope she'll be kind to us," Kathryn said.

"She will. She's gone to too much trouble to get us together. It'll bring the Lady peace. That's what she told me."

Kathryn slid her arms around Duncan's neck. "To peace then."

"To peace."

As they kissed, Kathryn felt herself giving in to what fate had led her to—and she felt peace.

Epilogue

Four Months Later

A gentle wind blew from the direction of the Fairy Glen as Kathryn, in an ivory silk dress, and Duncan, in his formal kilt, stood hand in hand on the hillside where the Lady had first appeared. A whole clan's worth of MacDonalds surrounded the couple, among them a young stranger, tall, red-haired. Ian, Sean, and Beth had flown in from Texas and stood among their Skye friends, Angus and Jane, Molly and Donald, to name but a few. A lone piper played while Kathryn and Duncan exchanged vows.

"*Cò leis a tha thu*?" Duncan asked.

"I belong to you and no other," Kathryn said. The garland of heather crowning her head gave an otherworldly aura to her smiling face. "*Cò leis a tha thu*?"

"I belong to you and no other," Duncan said.

Snow began to fall like stardust from the winter sky. It veiled Kathryn's hair. Duncan gently kissed her. And in that moment, there was an exchange of souls and the fulfillment of a promise.

In the Fairy Glen, a woman dressed in white could be heard singing a love song—and in the sanctuary of a cave just beyond the Druid Wood, an ancient woman smiled.

As the sun set behind Ben Edra, a familiar song echoed from its gentle slopes across Glen Rowan, and Kathryn knew that she had found her destiny: true love—a love that was ever now and ever after.

ACKNOWLEDGMENTS

The inspiration for this story is two-fold. It all began with a dream I've had of a stone manor. I learned several years ago, to my great surprise, that my father and my eldest son also shared this same dream. Next I began researching my ancestors looking for clues as to where this stone manor might possibly exist, and I discovered the MacDonalds from the Isle of Skye. Unfortunately, these ancestors were my mother's—but, you know, I'm writing fiction so it all works.

After finishing the novel, my husband and I took a trip to the Isle of Skye to see whether my research was correct. It was my first trip to Skye. It will not be my last. My thanks go to Peter MacDonald and his lovely wife, Jane, for the fantastic tour of the Isle and the wonderful stay while we were there. Thanks also to Maggie Macdonald, who helped me with research at the Donald Center library and to Seamus Mackinnon for the mystical boat tour of Loch Corusk. And, thanks to the fairy folk of the Fairy Glen, forever enchanted.

The Stone Manor began as a short story assignment in my first *Creative Fiction Writing* class at Stephen F. Austin State University, in Nacogdoches, Texas. This is where I thank John A. McDermott, my first writing professor, and a good friend. The short story became the makings of a novel in my third writing class, *Fantasy and Magic Realism*, taught by John's wife, Christine Butterworth-McDermott, also a good friend. You both helped me find my voice. Joe Landsdale, writer-in-residence, taught me the publishing end of writing, among other things. You pushed me to be tenacious and never give up. Everyone in my writing group while at SFASU and beyond was such an encouragement...and still is to this day. Thank you all.

Thanks to Charles Frenzel, who helped early on with character development input. A special thanks to Danelle McCafferty, my main editor. You are the reason this book is in print today. Thanks for taking my first draft and seeing what it could be. Thanks to my son, Trevor, for performing the all-important final edit. Thanks to my son, Matt, for designing the fairy logo that appears throughout the book. Thanks to my daughter Rachel for the author photograph. And, thanks to my son, Sean, for allowing me to use his name for one of my favorite characters in the novel. I'm truly blessed to have such a talented family. Thanks to Kelli Ann Morgan for the beautiful cover design, and to Bob Houston for the lovely interior design.

To all my many friends on both sides of the pond who read my first drafts and gave me encouragement and editorial advice, thank you.

Last but by no means least, thank you to my family. For believing in me and in this story. For reading it in its many stages. Thanks to my parents for always encouraging and supporting my dreams. Thanks to my sisters who were the inspiration for the bond that exists between Kathryn and Beth. Thanks to my brother for encouragement and love throughout this process. Thanks to my kids, for letting me fictionalize them somewhat in my novel. And finally, thanks to my husband and dearest friend...you are my Duncan.

ABOUT THE AUTHOR

TERRI HALE was born in Arkansas and grew up in Texas. She and her husband Jim have lived in Germany for the last five years, working for Young Life Europe. They currently divide their time between Europe and Texas. They have four grown children and two grandchildren. When not traveling and training for Young Life, Terri likes to spend time with her family, write, read, travel for pleasure, and eat chocolate. Lots and lots of chocolate. This is her first novel.

www.terrihalebook.com

https://www.facebook.com/terrihalebooks

6002059R00169

Made in the USA
San Bernardino, CA
28 November 2013